Not As It Seams

NIKKI ROADMAN

LOCAL PRESS

Copyright © 2024 by Nikki Roadman

All rights reserved.

No part of this book may be reproduced in any form or by any electronic or mechanical means, including information storage and retrieval systems, without written permission from the author, except for the use of brief quotations in a book review.

The characters and events portrayed in this book are fictitious or are used fictitiously.

All brand names and product names used in this book are trademarks, registered trademarks, or trade names of their respective holders. Local Press and Nikki Roadman are not associated with any product, person or vendor in this book.

To my friends and family that continue to support and cheer me on...your encouragement has been unforgettable.

Part One

Chapter One

SELENA

I pulled my right arm out of the gown and stepped up to the massive metal shelf connected to the apparatus that accounted for nearly half the room. The technician was an older woman, I would guess somewhere in her mid-sixties. She had blonde, processed hair held together by copious amounts of hairspray and a banana clip. Her face was kind, but damn, her hands were cold.

"Can you take one step forward?" she asked, now cupping my right breast in her cold, gloved hand. I took a step forward and braced myself, knowing what was next. She began pooling together as much skin as she could grab atop the metal shelf, pulling from my armpits and neck in a way that shockingly didn't feel violating, like scraping one last ball of cookie dough out of the mixing bowl.

My right arm was above my head and my left hand gripped the side of the metal shelf for dear life. I had already begun holding my breath. *Breathe, you fool, or you're never going to make it.*

"You're going to feel a slight pinch," she said calmly while pushing a button that sent the top shelf down, smushing my breast in a way that first made me worry it might just explode right here on the table. But this was my third mammogram. I was practically a pro. I knew that breasts did not explode, nor did they get severed from the body during this agonizing process.

"Hold your breath until I say otherwise," said *cold hands*.

One. Two. Three...the counting wasn't helping. I was running out of air. I needed to breathe. What if I passed out right here? She sure wasn't going to catch me. There were so many sharp corners, I would probably hit my head and bleed out.

"And...breathe," she said, as if I was holding a pose in her vinyasa yoga class. I sighed, rocking my weight onto my back heels and tucked my body back into my gown.

"I will meet you in the hall," 'cold hands' instructed me, as if suddenly there were secrets between us about my body and she hadn't just pulled skin from every remaining part of my upper body to turn my smaller B cups into C's.

We met back up in the hallway, now ready to break bread and make small talk.

"We don't often see women as young as you here voluntarily. I assume you have a strong family history?" she asked, with a blend of sympathy, confusion and a dollop of judgment.

"Well, no. I just take my personal health very seriously."

"Oh, I see," she went on. "You know that younger women tend to have dense breast tissue, the mammograms don't pick up much."

Yes, I obviously knew that. I was fully prepared to get a phone call in two to three days relaying that my breast tissue was dense and I would need an ultrasound for further evaluation. But the way the US healthcare system works, I would only have to pay out of pocket for the mammogram. I really should be patting myself on the back for playing the system on this one.

"Yes, I'm aware," I said, grateful to arrive at the checkout desk.

At age twenty seven, the only women I knew also suffering through mammograms were my mother and Nonni. My twin sister, Sylvie thought I was a lunatic for paying out of pocket to be tested for something that could potentially be an undetected death sentence. I offered to buy her a mammogram for Christmas and she declined. *Suit yourself girl.*

After I made my appointment for next year I stepped outside hoping to be greeted by a late winter sun. It was February fifth and the Parker Miller School was only nine days away from Winter Break, which is the equivalent of two days before Christmas in the world of a teacher. I looked up at the cold gray sky, shaking my head as I folded my sunglasses back up and put them in the worn leather case I had been carrying with me for years.

The sidewalk was empty and the streets were likely the quietest they would be all day. Holly, Connecticut was a seaside town about forty minutes north of New York City. It was a wealthy and privileged suburb that boasted CEOs, film and television stars, news anchors and sports stars, and everyone in between. I have lived here my entire life and I wasn't even 'everyone in between.' My family's income bracket could be best described as 'everyone below.'

My parents were working class people. We lived paycheck to paycheck growing up and to be honest, it was a wonderful childhood. My mother worked at *La Sarta* alongside her mother, my Nonni, a seamstress shop that they owned together in town. My sister and I grew up in the shop surrounded by pins and needles and unbelievably expensive gowns and clothing. My sister loved it so much that she decided to forgo college and now works at the shop with my mom so that our Nonni was able to retire.

My dad has spent the last thirty-four years working long hours at a bottling plant on the other side of town. Needless to say, I left college with over one hundred thousand dollars in student debt. Good thing teachers make a lot of money...right?

It was only eleven and I had the entire day to myself. I left the substitute teacher a minute by minute lesson plan for the day that was sure to go sideways no matter how closely she followed it, but I would worry about cleaning up that mess tomorrow.

I decided to stop by *La Sarta,* to see if my mom or sister were free for lunch. I opened the door to the familiar ring and was immediately met with my sister sitting at her desk staring into space. She looked bored. Depressed even.

"Selena! What are you doing here? Why aren't you at school?" she asked, standing up to give me a hug.

"I took the day off for my annual boob squeeze. Thought I'd stop and see if you and mom wanted to grab lunch."

My sister immediately rolled her eyes. I looked around, noticing that my mom was missing.

"Selena? Is that you?" my mom yelled from the other side of the curtain adjacent to Sylvie's desk. I looked over and saw her familiar shoes and a pair of mens feet wrapped in socks. She pulled back the curtain and stepped outside, looking concerned.

"I'll meet you out here," she said to the man. She turned to me. "You paid out of pocket for another one?"

I probably should have used some discretion before announcing my mammogram appointment to the entire shop.

"Yes mom, it's an annual checkup, you should be relieved that I take such great care of myself."

It was an argument that neither of us had the energy for at the moment. She nodded, and then began shaking her head as she walked to the front of the store carrying a pair of high end trousers covered in pins. She placed them on the desk and leaned in for a hug. Before our bodies could meet, the curtains pushed back and if this was a dream, there would have been a fog machine, slow motion effects and an Al Green song playing overhead. But this was real life, so instead, out walked a man that looked like he had been ripped from a Calvin Klein runway. He had the most perfectly coiffed hair, tortoise framed circular lens glasses, a very well-fitting cashmere sweater and jeans that completed his look. I looked down at his ankle cut boots and immediately looked for his wedding ring because he could not have possibly put this look together himself. But alas, no sign of a ring.

"Connor, my daughter Sylvie will write you a slip; I'll make sure these are done by Tuesday, the latest."

I watched as my mom winked at him. What was she doing? He was now looking at me, and then back at Sylvie. This happened often. Although we were fraternal twins, our deep brown hair, similar heights and figures made our connection undeniable.

I raised my hand a bit, gesturing between myself and Sylvie.

"Twins," was all I could muster up.

Heat rose up from my neck.

He looked right at me. Like right into my eyes, cutting through me as if staring into the deepest trenches of my soul.

"I figured," he laughed.

Sylvie cut in and broke off the staring contest.

"Here is your slip Connor; we'll see you next week!"

She handed it over to him as he turned towards the door, giving a smiling nod to each of us as he walked out, though his eyes stayed an extra second on mine.

He wasn't even in his car before Sylvie eyed me suspiciously.

"What the hell was that Selena?" she asked, staring, waiting for my answer.

"What are you talking about?" I asked, innocently while making my way to the bottle of hand sanitizer on her desk.

"Umm, you were flirting with him."

"Was not!" I responded.

My mother just stood there, staring at the both of us, shaking her head. Sylvie and I have always had what I would often refer to as an 'honest relationship.' We call each other on our shit, and keep each other in check. Sometimes, too much.

"What? It just seemed like for a second there she forgot about Jack," Sylvie said to our mother.

"You're ridiculous, I did not."

My mom walked away, again, shaking her head. I'm still not sure what just happened. Sylvie was one hundred percent right. For about two minutes, I had completely forgotten about the existence of my nine month relationship with Jack Webber.

"Well? Does anyone want to grab lunch?" I asked, anxious to move on.

I hadn't even stood up yet from the chair I had collapsed into as I watched my sister power off her computer and my mom throwing the last of her scraps into the scrap bin. The lights were off and we were on the sidewalk locking up, all within what had to be the same minute I had suggested lunch.

Chapter Two

SYLVIE

I've spent the last nine years at *La Sarta Tailoring*, plugging away at the low-level hemming and tailoring projects that my mom thought I could handle. Mostly I had taken over the customer service, books and business end of things.

The town of Holly is not an affordable place to own a business and I didn't have it in me to share with my mom just how dire the books were looking. Everything had become more expensive and we weren't keeping up.

Unlike Selena, I did not have a ten year plan once graduating high school. There was no roadmap for my life, and I thought college would be a waste of my parents money and my future earnings. I opted out. I knew that Nonni was ready to retire and that the steady work would keep my mom and I busy. What I did not know was how monotonous, how grueling, how boring and mostly, how unexciting the 'family business' would feel.

I did my best to hide the unhappiness from my family, because, let's be honest, nobody made me stay at home and work at *La Sarta*.

(Although my mother would never admit it, she would have been devastated if both of her daughters had passed on the opportunity). I've quietly been plugging away at online night classes. When I started I checked the box as a business major, but I question my plan or lack of one, nearly everyday. How I have managed to hide this from Selena, has been an absolute miracle.

I honestly cannot believe that she hasn't questioned the "spin classes" that I've been taking two nights a week for the last fourteen months. Living only two floors and four doors apart, in the same apartment building, makes a secret life challenging.

It is bad enough that my guest parking spot is an automatic giveaway if I have an overnight guest and no secrets can be kept at my place of employment. But if Selena spent even a minute to think about the fact that I, Sylvie, her nonathletic twin that gets winded walking from the parking lot to the second floor was now taking spin classes - she would be on to me. But right now, I think Selena is so consumed with her own life, that she does not have any time to overanalyze mine.

Unfortunately for her, with the exception of work and school, my life currently lacks any form of excitement, so she is absolutely crazy if she thinks I didn't see the sparks going off in the shop today when she met Connor Steer. I could hardly blame her. It doesn't take a twin sister to see how completely wrong for her Jack Webber is. I get why she fell for him. On paper, he's perfect. Good looking...smart...successful... but that is where it stops for him.

Chapter Three

SELENA

By the following Thursday I had gotten the call for an ultrasound, made the appointment and suffered the dreaded cold wand that scrutinized every square inch of my boobs.

I was shocked when on the same day I received the amazing news that I was 'clear' of any signs of breast cancer. What an absolute relief. I had two days left until break which meant ten straight days of peace and quiet; life was feeling optimistic.

I have been an art teacher at The Parker Miller School since I graduated college, six years ago. Parker Miller is a private school for the grossly wealthy. The tuition was more than most colleges and it made me overthink every single lesson plan; attaching a dollar sign to it.

My first year was full of many challenges and lessons learned. I don't look a lot older than the high school kids that I was teaching (this is not so much a compliment to myself as it is an observation about teenage girls these days...wow). A lot of the boys felt it appropriate to comment on my appearance. Ala Mary Kay Letourneau, I was quick to abandon my usual wardrobe and avoid all eye contact with these hormone crazed, and slightly demonic boys. I now come to school dressed like a fashionable nun, and it works.

When I walked into my classroom I was greeted by two familiar faces; Tanya and Adam were taking the chairs down off the desks and both looked up at me with smiles.

"To what do I owe this honor?" I asked.

Tanya is the music teacher and Adam teaches AP Lit. We were three of the younger teachers here and had created a real friendship between us. Tanya and Adam had produced and directed the school musical for the last three years and last year they brought me in as an assistant to the costume designer. I was no fool, the next production was scheduled for mid-March and these people wanted something.

"You know how you were 'creatively stunted' last year when you helped Mrs. Frankens with the costume designs for *Hello, Dolly*?" Adam started, gesturing with air quotes.

"We know that the title 'assistant' was way below what you are capable of Selena," added Tanya.

They were buttering me up, but also they weren't lying. Working as Agatha Frankens' (the school's sixty-four year old guidance counselor) 'assistant' had been an absolute blow to my creative ego. I was essentially a glorified seamstress (no offense Sylvie, mom, Nonni). I was so glad to help Tanya and Adam, but the experience was far from enjoyable.

"Well we came here to offer you a major promotion," Adam said, smiling at me.

"We see those elevated dresses and skirts you're pulling off in your ode to Mother Theresa here Selena, and we know there is no store from Holly to Hoboken that carries those originals. How would you feel about being the Head Costume Designer for our production of *Into the Woods*?" she asked.

I laughed and rolled my eyes simultaneously. I had fun with my wardrobe each day and have almost made a game out of what I could create for myself with the scraps I find at *La Sarta*. My mom appreciated that nothing was going to waste and Sylvie mostly laughed at my creations. She never had an interest in creating fashion and seemed perfectly content altering other people's creations.

"And do I have a good budget?" I asked, doing my best to play hard to get.

Tanya and Adam looked back and forth between each other, smiling and simultaneously nodding their heads.

"Charlie Thibeault's mom made a huge donation at our last fundraiser. You don't just have a good budget Selena, you have an amazing one!" Adam was now jumping up and down and air clapping.

"How many costumes? And when do you need them done?"

I suddenly saw my Spring Break flash before my eyes, and I couldn't have been more excited.

"We would like your help in creating seven costumes, four of them are the showstoppers, the rest are quieter, ensemble pieces." Tanya said bracing for my reaction. "Oh, and we need them in three weeks."

"Three weeks! Are you guys out of your mind?!"

"You have complete creative control! We are announcing the cast tomorrow so you will be able to get inseams and stuff before they leave for break! The show is in a month," added Adam, hesitantly.

I loved a challenge. There was no doubt in my mind that I could pull this off. I mean, I planned to spend most of next week with my mom and Sylvie so this was actually perfect. My mom had a few dress forms that I could use, and a big budget would really make this fun. I had no reason to say no.

Except for Jack.

Jack appreciated the fact that I was an art teacher, but he often pointed out the fact that I was "just" an art teacher. Not an artist. Not a fashion designer. Not anything, "just" an art teacher.

This would definitely cut into our time together and I could already see him rolling his eyes as I stressed over the deadline. Before I had time to think more about it, I answered.

"I'm in."

They lunged towards me at the same time, embracing me in a dramatic group hug.

"You're going to kill this assignment, Designer Rossi!" Adam said and planted a kiss on my cheek.

"See you tomorrow for the measurements, we are meeting at three in the auditorium. Feel free to start researching and sketching! It's go time!" said Tanya.

Chapter Four

SYLVIE

Despite my very prominent status as the 'single' sister, I did not have a quiet social life. My social circle, although rooted in my hometown, had grown over the years to include friends in the city, the Hamptons and as far north as Fairhaven. With the mutually common theme of being single, there was always someone ready to meet for dinner, dancing or a fun night out. Some days were lonely, but I won't get bogged down by that today because it is Thursday - Ladies Night at Guiseppi's.

I was meeting friends at six for dinner at Lola's and as usual planned to be at our Thursday night staple by seven thirty to ensure we got a table. While Selena had spent her life bobbing from one long term relationship to the next, I was undoubtedly her opposite. I enjoyed my freedom and my independence. Don't get me wrong, I had men in my life...just none that I was interested in spending my Sundays with.

I closed up the shop right at five and headed home for a quick shower and to be sure that I had turned in all my school work for a group class project. Being remote made group work tricky, but I supposed this was how remote companies operated and maybe I should get used to it now? I still had no idea what I wanted to be when I grew up, business seemed like the safest major. I still felt unsettled; but my Bachelor's degree was a few years away, at this pace.

Like in life, I did not get to pick my group and instead was assigned by the professor to work with Simon, a cocky, buttoned up man close in age to me; and a gangly blond named Alexa that couldn't be older than nineteen. Our task was to review a company's sales process and then put together an improvement plan and presentation. I was naturally inclined to focus on their finances, but Simon and I appeared to be waging an epic battle of power to decide my role in the project as he thought I should be more focused on the marketing.

When I opened my computer I had seventeen combined emails that I had missed in our group chat. We all had very different schedules. Apparently Simon had nothing to do during the day, because he had essentially done the entire project himself and reached out to Alexa and I asking if we could take his work and turn it into a presentation.

Good Evening Simon - Very sorry for the delayed response to you and Alexa. I work during the day, which is why I take evening classes. I also do most of my work at night. However, I am unable to review your work until this weekend. With the project not due for another week, I am not concerned. Alexa, I prefer that we both give our opinions and make changes to this as we see fit, prior to the creation of any presentation.

Best -
Sylvie Rossi

I took advantage of my empty apartment (as I often do) and let out a very dramatic sigh that might be considered a harrumph and then went back to prepping my hair and makeup for our evening out. I wasn't sure what Simon's story was, but he seemed like a presumptuous ass.

I decided to fire up my espresso machine for one last hit of caffeine before I left. Thursday nights were getting harder and harder on my body. My mom knew exactly what I was up to, so I went out of my way to arrive at the shop on time on Fridays. While there I tried to dazzle her with an overwhelming amount of enthusiasm, but the efforts were taking a toll. It pretty much guaranteed a Friday night on my couch with my Bengal cat, Toffee.

When I arrived at Lola's the corner circular table that we always requested was nearly full with familiar faces. Chloe and Liv sat next to Sienna, Chris, Tanner and Lily were just taking a seat on the opposite side of Liv. I watched as Lily signaled for Marcel, which we all knew meant a round of shots were on their way. I was so lucky to have this group. We never knew where a Thursday night out might take us. Except, I kind of did. I would likely meet someone, or bump into someone I had met before, bring him home, awkwardly say goodbye and then deal with my raging headache in the morning.

Selena stopped asking me about my nights out. She strongly disapproved. She never said as much, but with Selena, her face told the entire story, words were not needed. I saw the flip side of my situation in Selena, and I had to say, it didn't pull me in. I did not think that Selena was any more happy than I was. But I knew she would say differently.

Sure enough, within two minutes Marcel lined up seven shot glasses and I shuddered as the vodka hit the back of my throat.

By the time we had finished our very hearty grilled chicken salads and made it over to Guiseppi's, I was three drinks in and feeling beautiful and flirtatious. My inhibitions checked at the door.

Ladies night at Guiseppi's was as much a draw for men as it was for women. While we enjoyed half priced martinis, men enjoyed either saving money on their date, or the extensive female crowd hitting the dance floor. On the weekends the dance floor filled up around eleven, but on Thursdays, it was like everyone knew they had to be home early. The dance floor was shoulder to shoulder when I looked at my phone and saw it was only nine. I was ahead of schedule. At this rate I could be home and tucked into my bed at eleven. I just needed to focus on that plan. I could not let this next vodka drink derail me...

Chapter Five

SELENA

The cast meeting oozed with excitement for the role announcements and it being the students' last commitment before break. I could barely get the kids to stand still for their measurements.

On my way out, Tanya handed me a credit card to use at the fabric store. I planned to visit Soho this weekend, and couldn't wait. A quiet squeal slipped out as I pocketed the goods; I couldn't wait to do some major fabric shopping.

Jack and I had dinner plans and Queso, my hyperactive Chihuahua, would be anxious for me to get home. My underwhelming one bedroom apartment was about a half mile from the school.

Jack lived and worked in the city. We met on a dating app, which I still found horribly embarrassing despite it being so common. When we first started dating I drove or took the train into the city to meet up with him. It's about a forty five minute ride door to door, depending on traffic, so we now try our best taking turns. He often likes spending quiet weekends in Holly, but if anyone was counting, (and let's be honest, I am...) I make the effort to go to him a lot more often than he comes to me.

Jack warned me that he only expected to stay tonight as he has a deadline next week that will require him to work tomorrow. Jack is an actuary. Which was code for *I don't actually know what he does*. Something about determining values and it somehow relates to insurance. According to Jack it requires extreme analytical skills and if I were to put all of his descriptions together, you have to be a genius to be good at it. And according to Jack, he was the best.

Jack's online dating profile described him as an outdoorsman; someone who spent his weekend looking for adventure, while finding side routes to breweries and wineries. His pictures left very little to the imagination, so I immediately knew I was attracted to him. On paper, he was everything I was looking for.

I had spent the last four years in and out of rather serious relationships, however never meeting anyone that I couldn't live without; at twenty seven I could feel my internal clock starting to tick. I was done wasting my time with men that I didn't see a future with. Jack was different. He was steady. He was mostly reliable and he was comfortable. Turns out he was not always open for an adventure...not the ones I suggested anyways. But we did find fun ways to stay busy on the weekends, when he wasn't working.

I heard the key in the door around six thirty. I had given Jack a key about two months ago, after he got locked out of my apartment while I was at the grocery store. When he stepped inside, his head was down, scowling at his phone.

"Hey sweetie, happy Friday," I said as I stepped towards him for a kiss.

"Hey babe, I'm so sorry, work is a total disaster," he said. I immediately noticed he was not carrying his weekend bag. "I want to take you to dinner, but I think I need to get back to the city tonight."

His eyes, still locked on his phone.

I could feel my face physically fall. This wasn't something he could have called and talked to me about? Like, hours ago? While staring at my feet I took a deep breath, brought my hand up to pull my hair back behind my shoulders and lifted my face. I tried to hide my disappointment, pushing my body towards him, pulling him in for a kiss.

He pulled away, now looking at me. If I didn't know him so well, I wouldn't have noticed his look of annoyance, frustration even. I looked at the phone in his hand and then back up at his face. He nodded, sliding it into his pocket.

"Well, I'm excited to try out this new restaurant," I added, camouflaging the hurt from my voice.

I grabbed my bag and coat and took one last look in the mirror. I wasn't Sylvie pretty, I didn't stop people in their tracks, but I knew I wasn't ugly. I was the cute one, the sweet one, the one that rarely said how I felt (around my boyfriend, anyway). The one that smiled and didn't mention that she felt last in line in the pecking order, behind her boyfriend's job. My deep red lipstick popped next to my olive skin and deep brown hair that ran down my back, hitting just below my bra line. I was wearing a classic black dress that I had created, with a pink crossbody bag and a nude wedge heel, because this is the way Jack liked me. I looked ...dull, boring even, but classy. I really did. I loved to play with fabrics and designs but Jack never seemed to appreciate the louder self-made ensembles.

If Sylvie was here she would be wearing an impossibly trendy outfit that asked the world to notice how strikingly beautiful she was. And she wouldn't just be 'wearing' it. She would be owning it. 'Slaying' it, as the Parker Miller kids would say. Her confidence was a ten out of ten.

I shook my head, willing the negative thoughts to stay behind as we made our way to the door.

"I think we should take two cars," said Jack.

"What? Really?"

I cannot believe he couldn't (wouldn't) take the extra ten minutes to drop me off at home before starting his trip back to the city.

"I'm sorry. Like I said, I just am under a lot of stress right now. Our deadline is Monday and I'm so behind. I'm screwed." he said, fidgeting with his tie. "I did drive all the way out here to see you at least, that's gotta count for something Selena?"

I had so much I wanted to say. I had questions. I had comments, but mostly I had feelings. I took a deep breath, pushing every thought, feeling, and question to the base of my stomach, where they would sit, swirl and linger for the rest of the night.

Chapter Six

SYLVIE

My alarm went off at six thirty. I rolled over to press the snooze button and was stopped by what felt like a concrete wall.

Shit, the wall was moving. I squinted, slowly opening my eyes.

As the world came into focus I saw a man. A man whose top half was naked, sprawled out beside me, his mouth wide open, drawing deep breaths in and out. I quickly reached down, feeling to see what I was wearing. As my hand met my unclothed chest I quietly whispered.

"Fuck."

I opened my eyes again, this time trying to examine the very well built man asleep at my side. His right arm, covered in tattoos, his left draped across his chest, rhythmically lifting up and down with each breath. A sheet was pulled up over his waist but based on my current attire, I didn't have to ask many questions.

I rolled over, closing my eyes, willing the previous night's events to come back to me. I remember dancing with Chloe and Lily. I remember Chris coming over and introducing us to some of his friends, who joined us on the dance floor. I remember one of them signaling over a cocktail waitress for a round of -

A wave of nausea came over me at the thought. I decided to skip that part and move to what happened next. I remember a group of us leaving, heading to Zoro's down the street for a slice of pizza. I remember making eye contact with…

Shit. Zoro's. I squinted again, now seeing the oven burn marks that lined the naked man's right arm. This was a new low, even for me. He was the sexy man running the pizza oven at Zoro's. I took home a guy that I met while drunkenly shoving my face full of pizza. At Zoro's.

I pulled the sheet up over my head. I could feel him begin to stir beside me. I had to get out of there. I did a very quiet roll into a tuck, throwing myself out of my bed. I grabbed the bathrobe that hung on the back of my door and ran into the bathroom.

Once the bathroom door was closed I leaned against the back of it, slumping as I exhaled, my hangover rushing to the surface. I had to get him out of here. I turned on the shower and continued to walk around in my robe, rehashing my situation. I'd be lying if I said this was my first time waking up to an unexpected and unwanted guest, but never had it been the sober kitchen staff.

Knock, knock.

What the actual…

"Got room for two in there?" said a deep voice playfully on the other side of the door.

I gripped both sides of my sink, staring at myself in the mirror. *Say something you idiot.*

"Oh, hey. I'm actually really sick. I think it's best if you leave. I'm so sorry. It was really great to meet you."

I waited, praying he picked up what I was putting down.

"Bummer."

"Yea, it is," I yelled back to him moving towards the shower as I now realized he might notice I wasn't actually in it.

"Can I get your number?"

Good lord this man wasn't giving up. If it was the difference between him staying and leaving, it was worth sharing it.

I gave him my number and waited quietly. The room was now

fogging up so I reached in and moved the handle to cold water. I could hear footsteps moving around my room and after a very long couple of minutes I could hear the closing of my apartment's heavy front door. I quickly ran out of the bathroom and locked the door behind him; grateful to have survived with as little drama as possible.

RIP Zorro's. Looks like I was going to have to find a new late night food stop.

Chapter Seven

SELENA

Last night I drove myself home from a date that felt more like a business dinner, not that I had ever been on a business dinner. But the coldness of arriving and leaving alone stayed with me throughout the meal and lingered as I returned to my apartment. Rather than overthinking it I decided to start my research and sketches for the play. I hadn't even bothered to tell Jack about it. He was so distracted by whatever was going on at work.

I had seven costumes to make. Cinderella, Little Red Riding Hood, the Witch and the Wolf were going to take most of my time and creativity. However, the Baker and Jack were going to require more technical work on my end as I didn't have a lot (ok, fine, any) experience designing for a man. I was up to almost two in the morning sketching, researching fabrics and drafting a few patterns.

It was nine in the morning and with the shop closed I knew that Sylvie would be sleeping in today, so I kept busy trying not to bug her, despite so badly wanting to. I decided to take Queso on a quick loop around the block and by the time I got back, I knew it would be an acceptable time to disturb Sylvie.

When we stepped outside, I was so grateful to feel a hint of heat coming off the sidewalk. Birds were chirping and the streets were busy with others enjoying the unexpectedly warm day. Things were looking up and it appeared to be a perfect day to go fabric shopping in the city. I just needed to convince Sylvie that she wanted to come with me!

It's not that I couldn't go into the city alone. I went in all the time to see Jack, but nothing beat the fun of taking the Metro into the city with Sylvie. Especially on a day, a weekend, actually, a week, when I had no plans. There was something so absolutely liberating about letting Sylvie lead the day. I couldn't give up that control every day, but she was the only one in the world that could convince me that we didn't need a plan.

Queso and I did two blocks. There was still a bite in the air despite the sun doing its best. When I got back to our building I took the stairs up with a spring in my step, convinced I was about to gift Sylvie with an exciting day that might change the whole trajectory of her weekend. We marched directly to Sylvie's door and knocked. I didn't do this often, but often enough that she would know it was me.

I waited, and then knocked two more times. Sylvie blew open the door and stood there. She scowled at me in an oversized t-shirt, bare footed, with an eye mask pushed up onto her forehead. Based on her makeup free face, I guessed that she had given it her all on Thursday and opted to stay in last night.

"Well, well, well," I said while sizing her up and down.

Queso was already inside her apartment and sniffing around for her cat, Toffee.

"Sleen, it's like seven in the morning."

"It's TEN AM!" I yelled while stepping inside and pulling her front door closed behind me.

"I have three weeks to make seven very intricate costumes for the school play and today I'm heading into Soho for some fabric inspiration. I thought it sounded like the perfect opportunity for a sister day!" I said, empathically while staring into her eyes pleadingly.

She shook her head and started walking towards her bedroom.

"You can make all the plans! We just have to go to the fabric shops!"

She stopped in the hall, and turned to look at me. A smile suddenly appeared on her face.

"I get to make the plans? Yea right Selena. You've let me do that twice and both ended in disaster!"

Clearly her memory serves her differently than mine.

"I'd hardly call a super quick visit to the ER a disaster! And the other time it was Jack's fault, and he's consumed with work all weekend, so I don't see bad oysters or jealous boyfriends in today's lineup! Cmon!"

I could tell she was now giving it serious consideration.

"Can I pick out your outfit?"

"What kind of stupid question is that? I am twenty seven years old. No. I will pick out my own outfit, thank you very much."

Sylvie turned and started walking to her room again, her hands up in the air as if she was 'out.'

"Fine! But it has to be practical, we will likely be doing a lot of walking! And you know it's always a bit cooler in the city!"

Did she just do a celebratory jump?

"Yay! Ok, I need like an hour to shower, hydrate and caffeinate. I'll be down to your place by eleven to pick out your outfit and then we can go! So be ready!"

I grabbed Queso's leash, feigning my best grumbling sigh as I walked out the door, trying my best to hide how happy I was to have her company.

Chapter Eight

SYLVIE

A day like this with Selena always sounded good in theory, but rarely did it end well. I left my apartment with low expectations, grateful for the small bit of patience I had gained after fourteen hours of sleep.

By the time she agreed on a black mini skirt with a gray cropped top (that I could tell she had laid her sewing machine into and transformed) and Converse, it was nearly noon when we arrived at the subway platform. Knowing she was incapable of relaxing without a plan, I suggested we go to the fabric stores first and then see where the day took us. She was thrilled.

Once we found seats and were settled on the train, Selena pulled a sketchpad out from her oversized bag. She flipped through the pages until she stopped about halfway through.

"Holy shit Selena, did you draw those?"

I couldn't believe how beautiful the sketches were. She had four costumes on the first page: Cinderella, a wolf, Little Red Riding Hood and a witch. The detail and design in each of the drawings was like something you would see in a designer's workshop.

She just smiled and nodded at me.

"I told you, I have to design and make seven costumes for a play at school."

"I know you're an art teacher and like to play around with sewing machines and forms, but I had no idea you could actually sketch and make patterns like this!" I added, my mouth dropping open while flipping through the pages.

"And, they gave me this!" she said, pulling an unfamiliar credit card out of her bag.

"How do you even know where to begin? There are so many different fabrics in these pictures!"

"I'm only shopping for Cinderella and the wolf today because I think they will be the most time consuming, and the biggest showstoppers!"

"Are they paying you?" I couldn't help but ask.

"Sylvie! It's a fancy private school, but they aren't crazy! No! I'm volunteering my time. But they are buying all the supplies."

"So you are going to give up your week off to work on these day and night?"

"I always spend most of my days off at the shop anyway, why not be doing something exciting like this while I'm there. I'm sure you're going to be excited to help when you can." she said, nudging me.

The truth was, I couldn't wait to watch Selena's process, and see these ideas come to life. However, I had absolutely no interest in helping her. With my classes on top of work, the extra time she's referring to, really didn't exist.

As it was, I had spent my Friday night reviewing Simon's (and the small bit that Alexa completed) work, making my own changes and sending it back to both of them around ten. I suggested that we meet on Sunday to finalize and work on our presentation.

After Selena left my apartment this morning I checked my email. We made a plan to have a Zoom chat at ten in the morning on Sunday, and Simon was sure to point out that he did not agree with all of my notes. I would have to set an early alarm tomorrow so that I would be prepared for whatever battle Simon had cooking.

By the time we got into the city and walked the four blocks into the

Garment District I was starving, hangry, really. We had loosely discussed making our way down to Soho after and catching the tail end of a brunch so I knew I had to fight the hunger pains and get through it.

"There are three different stores that I want to check out, I think the first one is right around this corner," she said, with an ear to ear grin.

I looked up and saw the oversized Starbucks positioned next door.

"I am decaffeinated Sleen, so I'm just going to do a few espresso shots and then I'll be right over!"

"No food or drinks in the shops, so hurry up and meet me in there. I'm going to want a second opinion!"

She nodded her head at me knowing that for her safety and happiness, it was best if I got some coffee. She started to pull her notebook back out as she walked into the first shop. She looked so excited, so happy.

When was the last time I looked like that? When was the last Saturday morning when I woke up excited to do something? Sure the trips out to the Vineyard were fun; the VIP nightclub visits were exciting and even spontaneous concert tickets...but they were all getting old. *When was the last time I truly felt excited?*

I shook my head looking down at my feet, waiting for my turn in line.

Today is Selena's day, don't make this about you.

After throwing back a double Americano and two biscottis (fine, I also had a package of chocolate covered almonds...for protein), I was ready to dazzle Selena with my interest and excitement in the fabric stores. I found her kneeling, in her black mini skirt with her back to me in the back of the store, spools of fabric surrounded her on the floor. She looked overwhelmed but at the same time, delighted.

"Whatcha doing, psycho?"

She jumped at the sound of my voice.

"Oh my god Sylv, who knew there were so many sparkly blue tulles to choose from."

"Deep breaths."

She looked up at me nodding. She was right, she needed me for this. I started picking up the spools and putting them back on their stands so that we could look at them stacked up against each other.

"This one screams Cinderella to me," I said, and she smiled, so clearly grateful that I was partaking in the decision-making process.

The next two hours went similarly, only my patience began to dip as my hunger levels once again rose. I could feel the window of brunch service closing with every delayed decision. Although late lunch was delicious and fun too, I would really miss those champagne specials. Even Selena looked tired and malnourished; I didn't think either of us had it in us to make one more fabric decision.

"Think it's time to call it quits, Selena. I'm starving and this is losing the excitement. Unless Tim Gunn and Heidi Klum pop out to give us an assignment, I feel the rest can wait."

She didn't even argue. Just nodded her head.

"Food. Must. Get. Food. You pick," she said.

Wow, I don't know if it was because she was so tired and hungry or trying to share the day with me, but so rarely did Selena put such a decision in my hands.

Chapter Nine

SELENA

It wasn't quite warm enough for outdoor dining, despite the portable heaters lining most patios, so I was relieved when Sylvie picked a trendy Soho spot for our late lunch that did not require dining al fresco. We arrived around three, and watched as they swapped out their brunch signage, starting to prep for dinner service. Sylvie did her best to hide her disappointment, but anyone who knows her, understands her soft spot for champagne spritzers and fruit filled glasses of Rose'.

Even at this odd time of day, the restaurant was buzzing. Young people who looked like they had been here for hours, enjoying the jazz brunch to its fullest, older people out to grab an early dinner and then a few groups like us that were just glad to be out on a rare warm, winter day in the city.

I was so grateful for Sylvie's company. Even if Jack wasn't working all weekend, there is no way he would have visited the garment district with me, despite only living a short distance away. Jack was intensely conditioned to seven pm dinners, rarely stopping for lunch. He would never have agreed to such a spontaneous meal.

"Jack is working all weekend," I blurted out, unexpectedly.

It was no secret that Sylvie wasn't a huge fan of Jack. And Jack did not hide that he wasn't a huge fan of Sylvie's. It was all awkward, and I had come to find it was best to spend time with them separately.

"Well that sounds miserable," she mumbled while looking through the menu. "Let's order our food when we order the drinks. I'm so hungry I might commit a felony if I don't get food in me soon."

As the waitress was finished taking our orders, Sylvie grabbed her arm, begging her to come back.

"I'm so sorry, but I'm overwhelmingly hungry, do you have bread? Or chips? Or something we could munch on before our food comes?"

I could tell she was embarrassed for herself as soon as the words came out of her mouth. With a knowing smile, our waitress smiled, shook her head yes and walked away to put our order in.

"What the hell Sylv? You're acting like a psychopath."

"Oh my God, I really am."

The waitress came back quickly with a bottle of white wine that Sylvie had assured me was fiscally more responsible than each ordering two drinks, as well as a basket with sliced pita bread and some hummus. After only a few bites, Sylvie looked like she was coming back...

"What was that?"

"Honestly, I don't know. I went out on Thursday, had a bit too much fun and felt so lousy all day yesterday that I don't really think I ate much."

Of course she did. We were having such a nice day that I broke character and did not roll my eyes.

By the time we finished our meals, our bottle of wine was empty and Sylvie was asking for a cocktail menu. I was hyper aware of the four hundred dollars worth of fabric and supplies in the recycled plastic bag draped over the back of my chair, constantly turning to assure myself it was still there. I could feel the wine hitting the system and didn't trust myself to get it all home safely.

"Can I surprise you with a drink that I think you will love?" she asked.

"No," I said quickly with a slight shake of my head.

"Lighten up Selena, you'll like it, I promise!"

"Fine."

I didn't even hear her drink order but decided to stay committed to the illusion of being easy going. As it was I had almost used an entire container of hand sanitizer. If I brought it out one more time I think Sylvie would rip it out of my hands.

"Want to share a dessert?" I asked her, waiting for her to point out the potential for germ sharing.

She looked shocked, but then she smiled.

"Wow, Sleen...that's my girl. Absolutely! You pick!"

When our french martinis arrived along with a ramekin of creme brulee, we clinked our glasses and dug in with two spoons. It was absolutely delicious, all of it.

I suddenly noticed Sylvie had a pained expression on her face and kept looking over my shoulder. She looked concerned, distracted mostly. I pretended not to notice, because if I was being honest, I was full on tipsy. I kept catching myself dancing in my seat to the music which at some point must have been turned up. It was truly the best day.

"What should we do next?"

When Sylvie didn't answer my question, I had had enough of whatever man she was likely checking out behind me.

"Earth to Sylvie...we're having a sister day, remember? Not pick up a hot man at Soho hotspot kinda day!"

"I think we should get out of here...don't you?"

She was acting so odd, this was not like her. Normally I would be dragging her out of a place like this.

"What is it? Old flame sitting back there or something?" I asked, as I started to turn my head.

Sylvie quickly grabbed my arm.

"No, nobody is back there."

I could see her scanning the restaurant for our waitress. What was her problem?

Chapter Ten

Sylvie

When I first saw him, I only registered him as a familiar face. He sat about six tables behind Selena, with only his profile visible, so I was grateful that he could not see me staring at him while I worked to identify him. I looked over to see who he was sitting with in case that would help tip me off. A beautiful blonde woman sat across from him. I was certain I had never seen her before. She was laughing flirtatiously and kept touching his hand...

Wait.

Holy shit.

I looked again and nearly jumped out of my seat.

Jack.

It was Jack fucking Webber. What an absolute scumbag.

I had to get Selena out of here.

She noticed that I kept looking behind her, I quickly grabbed her arm and suggested we leave. I knew I was acting like a raging lunatic. I was never one for leaving a good time early, so I had to come up with something quickly so that Selena wouldn't question me.

By the time I flagged down the waitress and we split the bill, anger was coursing through my body. I so badly wanted to walk over and smash a plate in Jack's face but that would be too much and too embarrassing for Selena; I had to get her out of here.

We started grabbing all of our belongings and she stood up, turning towards the door, which is when I realized that we were going to have to walk right past that douchebag on our way out. There was no avoiding it.

How was I going to get her out of this situation? I grabbed her hand, hoping that her eyes would focus on following me as I led her towards the exit. My eyes stayed straight ahead, hyperfocused on just getting out of there, which was dangerous because I could no longer see where she was looking.

I suddenly felt a tug and Selena let go of my hand. I turned, and the grief on her face told me everything. I grabbed her hand again.

"Let's get out of here Selena, fuck him."

Her free hand went up, covering her mouth. The heavy bag of fabrics that rested on her shoulder began to droop as tears filled her eyes and her face turned to stone. She stood there, watching Jack flirt across the table with this mystery blonde woman and then she began to walk in their direction.

I wanted to stop her. But also, I didn't.

Selena stopped at a table just before Jack's, grabbing a pitcher of ice water.

All I could hear her say was: *Working real hard this weekend Jack?* Which was followed by the entire pitcher of water pouring over his head.

The bustling restaurant stopped. The silence was deafening like it could be heard over the thumping music and every eye in the restaurant went to Jack and Selena. He sat there dumbfounded, as shock registered.

Selena marched towards me in her mini skirt, face red, no longer a tear in sight and I followed her as she continued straight for the exit to the street. She didn't say a word as we joined the crowds on the sidewalk.

We went about six blocks before she even looked at me. I hung by her side but said nothing. She stopped abruptly in front of a vacant storefront and stared into my eyes. I could see the hot tears now stinging her eyes, but I waited for her to speak first.

"I hate him Sylvie," she said as her head collapsed onto my shoulder.

Sobs breaking out, her whole upper body now wrapped around mine.

"I always hated him. You are so much better than him Selena."

She pulled away from my shoulder, now looking right at me.

"I hope that water was so cold that he pissed himself," Selena said with a little bit of a laugh.

She found an empty bench and we both sat down. I noticed that she sounded a bit out of breath, her hand was up to her chest.

"I think that I'm having a heart attack, Sylvie. I feel tightness in my chest, my heart is beating so fast, I think we need to go to a hospital."

Being her twin sister, I was prepared for this. Over the last twenty seven years I have talked Selena off more ledges than there were in Manhattan. If I had taken her to the hospital every time she wanted to go, she probably would be dropped by her insurance company.

"Look at me Selena. Deep breaths, in and out. You just witnessed something traumatic. It is very normal to feel everything you're feeling," I said, while exaggerating my breathing in hopes that she would follow.

When we were seven years old our seemingly healthy Papa dropped dead from a heart attack at a Sunday dinner in front of all of us. It rocked our entire family, Selena especially. Our family shared a duplex with them and as kids Selena and I would bounce back and forth from our unit to our grandparent's multiple times a day. Looking back they must have hated the lack of privacy, but if they did they never showed it.

Watching Nonni grieve the loss of her beloved Vincenzo was devastating, to say the least. We stopped going by as often, as we noticed it only upset our Nonni more. Our mom began working twelve, fourteen hour days to cover the work that Nonni wasn't getting to at the shop, the tension and stress were unbearable.

But things got better - eventually. After about a year, Nonni was bouncing back. Our mom was able to be our mom at night again and not be at work. Sure, they were sad, we all were, and deeply missed him, but Nonni, me, my mom, we were able to move forward. It was only then that we could all see the change in Selena.

She had become obsessed with everyone else's health, especially hers. She thought every runny nose, every cough was related to a terminal illness. Everyone coddled her and assumed it would pass; that this was her grief process. But here we are, twenty plus years later and I was convincing her not to run to the hospital for an EKG.

"Let's get you home Selena, I think we need to get another bottle of wine and get you snuggled up with Queso," I said, wrapping my arms around her.

How quickly we had both sobered up.

Chapter Eleven

SELENA

After two straight days on my couch with a box of tissues, my sadness had morphed into anger. Jack hadn't even bothered to call. He shot me a quick text on Saturday after the incident at the restaurant: *Selena, I never meant to hurt you. I wish you well.*

I immediately deleted it and then blocked his number. It read like a text that you might send to someone if you ran over their foot with a grocery cart. It was cold and rude, just like Jack.

On Saturday, Sylvie and I had come home from the city, showered and reconvened at my place in our pajamas. She brought two bottles of wine, chocolates and we had Chinese food delivered. She left just before midnight as she had some "mysterious plans" on Sunday.

Sunday morning I was at Urgent Care as soon as they opened asking for a full STD panel. Lord knows how many people Jack had been sleeping with during our time together. That thought alone made me want to vomit, and then shower, and then vomit again. And then cry. When the testing was complete I changed back into my pajamas, bouncing from my bed to my couch all day. I took Queso out the minimum amount of times necessary and was grateful for the rain that eventually pushed its way into town.

When I woke up this morning, I knew that with only a week left in my break, I needed to get to work on the costumes. It was actually the perfect distraction. I pulled out all the measurements and began cutting out patterns for the Cinderella and wolf costumes. The shop was closed on Mondays so I would have it all to myself. I could spread out with the tables and forms so that by Tuesday, my mess and presence would be unnoticeable.

I showered.

Turns out I really needed that. It was like a shot of medicine for my entire body and a valid start to removing any remnants of Jack on my person.

I was unlocking *La Sarta* by ten and spent the next few minutes unpacking my car full of materials, patterns, printouts, and even a cooler with leftover chinese food and seltzer waters to get me through. I was determined to get a lot done today.

I had locked the door behind me and kept the lights off at the front of the store and planned to work in the back corner of the shop, which was well hidden by Sylvie's desk. I connected to her bluetooth speaker and zoning out with my work to the sounds of Elton John's Greatest Hits. It wasn't until three in the afternoon that I began to fade. My hands were tired, my concentration was waning thin and thoughts of Jack rubbing hands with that blonde crept back into my mind.

Who was she anyways? I was so enraged and focused on Jack that I hadn't gotten a good look at her. Did they work together? Was she an ex? Did he meet her at a bar last night? How long has this been going on?

I had so many questions. As I overanalyzed and thought more and more about the past nine months, I wouldn't be shocked if he had been cheating on me for months. What a vile human.

I didn't even have tears left for him. Okay, that was a lie, as a new round of hot salty tears stung as they crawled down my face, passing over my raw nose.

My thoughts were broken by the sound of my phone ringing into the bluetooth speaker. I grabbed it and saw that it was my mom. Ugh,

Did Sylvie tell her? I turned off my bluetooth, took a deep breath, wiped my face, and then answered her call.

"Selena, honey?"

"Hey mom," I said solemnly.

"Hey, any chance you're at the shop? Sylvie thought you might be there today?"

"Yes, I hope that's ok. I'm working on a project for school. I had asked Syl-"

She cut me off.

"Of course that's ok. But honey, I have a client emergency. He has an unexpected event tomorrow and needs the suit I've been tailoring for him tonight. Is there any chance he can come down and get it from you while you're there? He can't get there until 5:30."

"Sure, how will I know what it is?"

My mom explained where to find it and reminded me to keep the doors locked and that she would tell him to knock on the front door when he arrived. This was good, it would force me to stay another few hours and get further along on these costumes. It would also force me to stop feeling bad for myself because I couldn't be opening the shop looking like I had forgotten my goggles at a swim meet.

Around five I turned the lights on in the front of the shop and turned down Alanis Morissette wailing 'You Oughta Know." We had just changed the clocks back, so although it was still very light out, I didn't want my mom's customer to question whether or not I was here. I stepped back and looked at the form that now held the bodice to the Cinderella gown. I was really happy with it, and so excited to see it through that I hadn't even started on the wolf costume. I did some cuts and prepped a bunch so that I could come back in the morning and get right to work.

Like clockwork, I heard a knock at the door at 5:30. I rounded the corner by Sylvie's desk and practically jumped when I saw the same handsome face that was here getting fitted when I visited last week. The same handsome face I have pretended not to think about at night while I lie awake begging the world for a hot dream that might make me forget about Jack Webber. What was his name again?

Connor.

I knew damn well his name was Connor Steer.

I pulled out my key and unlocked the door for him.

He smiled at me. A warmth trickled up from my toes to my ears, sure to leave my face red and glowing. I immediately began fixing my hair and wiping under my eyes for any melted makeup.

"I am so sorry to bother you. I couldn't believe my luck when your mom said that you would be here. You know, to get my suit," he quickly recovered.

"No problem, it's just over here," I said walking towards the rack next to the register.

"I should know better. My meeting was originally on Thursday, but they bumped it up to tomorrow morning."

"Isn't that always the way?" I asked, as if this was a frequent occurrence in my life as an art teacher.

"The meeting is actually with the suit designer's team so I couldn't just wear something in my closet," he said, now looking up at me. "I'm sorry, I don't know why I'm telling you all of this. I'm sure you would like to get on with your night."

I smiled.

"Why are you here, anyways? I thought your mom said you didn't work in the shop?"

I raised my right eyebrow and smiled.

"I come here a lot, your mom talks about you and your sister often."

Damn, I was hoping he had asked about me after we met last week.

"Yea, I don't. I'm working on a project for my school and it's just easier to do it here," I said, motioning to the form in the back corner behind Sylvie's desk.

"Oh, wow, so you're a designer?"

"Hardly, I'm just an art teacher, but I'm helping make the costumes for a school play."

His hands went up to his face, pulling down on his cheeks as if trying to wipe away a smile.

"Very cool. Looks like you're a lot more than just an art teacher," he said, beaming at me.

I paused and stared at him and let his words hold the space between us.

"Well, thanks for this," he said, breaking the silence. He grabbed the suit that was pressed and sealed in a garment bag. "Elsie said she hadn't written up an invoice yet so I'm going to stop back in later this week to pay for everything. You can call her if you want to be sure that's right?"

I smiled. "I believe you."

"Well, thank you again, Selena."

I've never wanted another human to say my name so badly.

"No problem," was all I could muster in return.

Before I had a chance to ask him anything else he was out the front door and unlocking his mid level BMW parked in front of the shop.

My phone was ringing, it was an unfamiliar number.

"Hello?"

"Ms. Rossi?"

"Yes."

It was the nurse from Urgent Care. We went through a series of questions to prove that I was in fact Selena Rossi, only to then find out that all of the tests came back negative. She did let me know that my D3 levels were a bit low, and suggested I get outside more. I used all of my self control to resist asking if she had spare money to send me to Aruba.

Chapter Twelve

SYLVIE

This breakup was really knocking Selena's world off kilter. For the last three years we met at Nonni's assisted living on Monday at four thirty to be her dinner guests. She had retired the year after I began working at the shop and quickly realized the stairs of her duplex and general housekeeping had become too much for her. After hearing so many nightmare stories about kids having to take their parent's keys away, and moving them into a facility against their will; my mom was so relieved that Nonni had come to this decision on her own.

Using the proceeds from the sale of her duplex along with my Papa's pension, Nonni was able to afford a beautiful studio apartment with harbor views about ten minutes from our apartment complex. Nonni had moved to New York from Italy when she was seventeen years old and like most Italian Americans, she did not enjoy anyone else's cooking. Upon moving to Connecticut, Nonni declared there wasn't a single restaurant in the state that brought her joy and the dining room at The Springs of Holly Valley was 'maybe the worst, most bland food' she had ever eaten in her life.

Selena and I tried to cheer her up by keeping her company on Monday nights, despite her assigned dining companions. My parents usually came by to have lunch with her on Sundays, but I think my mom found a reason to stop by every single day, though she would never admit it.

"Sylvie, where is Selena? This is not like her *nipotina*."

It was quarter to five and the waitstaff had already passed salads out to all of the tables. We occasionally got to use the private dining room, but not every Monday. Today they had added two extra chairs to the table Nonni shared with a very quiet woman named Jeannete, and a very not quiet woman named Shirley.

"Her and Jack broke up over the weekend, so she's been having a rough few days. I'll shoot her a text."

"Good, I didn't like him. What was he anyway, Irish?" my grandmother asked while gesturing with her hands as if to say *get out of here*.

"I don't know Nonni, but I agree, I didn't like him either."

My phone rang, it was Selena.

"Oh my gosh, I'm so sorry Sylv, please tell Nonni. I got so caught up in what I was doing here and then mom just called to ask me to open up so that a customer could pick something -"

"Don't worry about it," I cut her off as I had the attention of half the dining room.

I completely forgot to silence my phone.

"Will you tell her I'll come by sometime this week?"

"Yes," and we hung up.

"When are you going to meet a nice Italian man, Sylvie?"

My grandmother did not waste a second. My phone wasn't even in my pocket yet. This was part of our regular Monday afternoon banter, but usually Selena helped deflect the focus from me.

"Nonni, you will be the first person I tell when I do."

"You're a beautiful woman honey, but we don't stay beautiful forever," added Shirley while gesturing to her face.

Mind your goddamn business Shirley.

"Mind you business Shirley," whispered Nonni, loud enough to be sure Shirley could hear it.

I tried to stifle my laugh.

"Thank you ladies, yes, I'm aware of the fact that I'm getting older, but I refuse to settle, and so far, I have yet to meet anyone that hasn't felt like settling."

I was so grateful to see our regular waitress Cindy, walking over with a tray of shepherds pie. Nonni groaned as soon as she saw it.

While the trays were passed around I was distracted by thoughts of yesterday's Zoom call with Simon and Alexa. Turns out Simon was not the complete bulldog he had portrayed over email. Although he was gruff and a bit broody, and it was obvious he was looking to lead the group, he surprised me by not being a total dictator. He had reviewed all of our notes and created a Powerpoint explaining how he thought we could incorporate all of our ideas. I couldn't argue with him and Alexa couldn't either.

I tried to figure out what his story was. He was clearly speaking to us from an office of some kind and he was dressed in a crisp button down shirt with a sweater pulled over it. He did not look like your typical night school student.

Alexa suggested that when we meet to work on our presentation we do so in person. I thought it was a great idea as I hadn't actually physically met anyone from our UCONN campus in my fourteen months of classes. We were meeting on Wednesday night at a Starbucks off of Irving and Main, and I was oddly excited about finally meeting everyone in person..

By the time our Grape Nut pudding arrived for dessert I noticed how tired my grandmother looked. For years I had examined the different levels of aging at The Springs, including the 'active group' that enjoyed the walking club and the crabby group of women that sat in the patterned chairs lining the hallway all day long, waiting to secure their special seats for Bingo. Then there were those that nodded off in their dining chairs while waiting for the nursing assistants to wheel them back to their rooms. I wasn't really sure where Nonni fell anymore.

When she first arrived she was capable of joining the walking club, but it really wasn't for her; she was a bit too crabby for that happy-go-lucky crowd. She did enjoy going for rides in the van to reminisce and see some of the spots that her and Papa enjoyed together. Unfortunately she hadn't made many friends and I could tell she was lonely.

She started an Italian Immigrant Club last year, which boasts a 'robust,' pride-filled four members. They meet weekly in the Activities room and they occasionally bring old photographs to share, talk about, and reminisce; some weeks they have a special Italian treat delivered to share, or watch an old film. I sat in the group a few times at her request, and it reminded me so much of the stories her and my Papa once told.

"Nonni, why don't I get you back and settled in your room," I suggested, watching her begin to nod off.

We were sure to stop in her room during each visit to make sure that her laundry was being done, her bed made and that the staff was emptying her trash. After all, these were the services she was paying for and she deserves to be well-cared for.

I turned the brakes off on her walker and whirled it around to meet her at the side of her chair.

"You're such a good girl Sylvie, you will make such an amazing wife and mother."

"Thanks, Nonni."

"Time is ticking, you better hurry the hell up."

Chapter Thirteen

SELENA

Once I realized I missed dinner with Sylv and Nonni I decided to use the night to cleanse my apartment of any sign of Jack Webber.

I may have taken it to another level and actually transformed my apartment. I rearranged the living room and bedroom furniture and then flipped the direction of the dining table. By nine I was finished, having just brought the eighth and final bag of trash to the dumpster.

I feared the process might make me feel worse but I actually felt amazing and found it very therapeutic. I was going to make some serious changes, no more settling, no more panicking or rushing my decisions. I was going to take a page out of Sylvie's book for a while and play the field, and assume every man has ill intentions until they convince me otherwise. Our combined strengths made us a deadly combination, but I had to find a way to exhibit the confidence, conviction and dignity that Sylvie always had when it came to men.

AND I was going to wear more mini skirts. I came up with some patterns that I would try out on myself once the play costumes were all complete.

I had always been very conservative with my money. Maybe it was the way I was brought up, or maybe I would always be frugal, but I also decided that I was going to book myself a vacation. I never went away on spring break or any break for that matter. It was time that I got out of here, saw the sun, and leveled up on vitamin D. I've heard about house shares on the Connecticut shore as well as the Hamptons, so I was going to look into those if I couldn't find anyone to fly out of town with.

I was now halfway through my break and the Cinderella costume was nearly done. I had Sylvie squeeze into it twice now and it was absolutely stunning. A showstopper. The wolf costume made us all giggle, but I was wrapping that up as well. I had cut patterns for two more costumes and was happy with my progress.

The last two days I got a good glimpse of how my mom and Sylvie operated together throughout the day. Although I could tell she liked that I was there, Sylvie just looked disinterested. Was she like this every single day? I saw her watching the clock like I used to in my AP Lit class. For all the strength she had when it came to her personal and social life, seeing Sylvie like this made me worry. She appeared lost.

I still had a few hours of work left but it was five, and my mom and Sylvie were beginning to pack up.

"Don't stay too late, *bambina mia*," my mom said.

"I know, and I will lock the door the second you leave. And I will call you when I leave so that you know that I'm safe, Mom."

She smiled, approving the way I had just completely mocked her.

As she was grabbing her bag the bell over the front door rang and we all looked up.

It was Connor Steer.

I turned my back to him, focusing on the Little Red Riding cutouts spread out on my working table.

"Connor!" my mom yelled, putting down her bags.

What was she doing? She was walking up to him, arms open for a hug. She kissed both of his cheeks.

"I'm so sorry Elsie! I know you must be getting ready to close," he said to my mother while handing her yet another garment bag.

"No problem, *caro*."

Apparently my mom used her Italian sweet names on Connor too. I rolled my eyes, committed to keeping my back to him.

"Sylvie, I still need to pay for the suit I picked up on Sunday. Thank you again Selena!" he raised his voice as if to get my attention.

I had been holding my breath so that I could hear every goddamn word that came out of his beautiful mouth. I put down the cutout that I had been pretending to be so deeply concentrating on, and turned to smile at him.

He just stood there, smiling back at me, our eyes completely locked. I knew Sylvie saw it again. I quickly turned my back.

"How are the costumes coming?" he asked.

"Plugging along," I answered, still keeping my back to him.

"You should see her Cinderella gown. It is breathtaking," added my mom.

My mom did not appear shocked to hear that Jack and I broke up when I got to the shop on Tuesday morning. I had no doubt that Sylvie had completely filled her in, but I wasn't about to get into it and find out. She let me know that she never liked him and neither did Nonni, which did not make me feel better. All this time, all the people I loved knew he was a loser. What did this say about me? How could I have been so stupid?!

"Oh, can I see it?" he asked while paying Sylvie at the register.

I turned to look in their direction. Sylvie stared at me, her eyes bugging out of her head sending me sister vibes that I knew meant: *SHOW HIM!*

Sylvie handed him his receipt.

"Well I don't mean to be rude, but I really need to get going. Mom, you ready? Sleen, you good to lock up after you show Connor the dress?" she asked.

Since when was she in such a rush? Where was she even going? She was so embarrassingly obvious. I pretended that I didn't notice – that this was very normal and the type of relationship that we had with all of our customers.

"Of course."

My mom stood outside on the sidewalk looking into the windows raising her eyebrows at me as I turned to walk Connor over to the form that was tucked in one of the dressing rooms.

"This is it," I said, pointing to the dress.

He took a step back and walked around the sides of it.

"You did this?"

"Yup."

"Selena, this is unbelievable. I've never seen anything like it. Where did you get the pattern?"

"I drew it."

His mouth dropped, he brought one hand across his chest and the other up to cover his mouth. He was the neatest, most pressed, most together-looking man that I think I had ever spoken to. Many of the dads at Parker Miller looked like him, but rarely did I see them leave their cars at the pick-up line; let alone speak with them. I'm sure the credit for his suit's perfect fit should go to my mother, but his taste was exquisite. Was his sweater cashmere?

"What?" he asked, noticing me checking out his attire.

"I don't know, you're just so together. What do you do for work?"

The words were out before I could think better of it.

We were now walking towards the front of the store.

"Oh, well, it's a lot less exciting than it sounds. But I am an entertainment attorney. Which is basically a fancy way of saying *a man that reviews contracts.*"

"Oh, well I'm sure you do a lot more than that."

"Unfortunately, lately I do. I am working with a few clients that are now insisting I attend their negotiation meetings which is why I've recently been a panicked client of your mom's. I've had to majorly step up my wardrobe to avoid embarrassing my clients and my firm!"

He was smiling. I smiled back.

"Ahh, well that all makes sense."

"What do you mean?"

"You just seem like you know a lot, about a lot."

"Well then I fooled you!" he smirked. "Two of my big clients are fashion designers. So I feel like I'm moonlighting in the fashion world. I see and hear about how hard it is. How perfectly these pieces need to fit their models. What you created back there looks like something I would see in one of the fashion houses I visit."

"Wow, your job sounds really cool! I mean, you don't get to work with clay and watercolors all day, like I do, but it still sounds great," I laughed.

"Selena, are you in a relationship?"

He looked down at his feet in embarrassment.

"Sorry, that was very forward."

The question took the wind out of me.

"Yes, ugh, I mean, no," I could feel the blood rushing to my face.

"Uhh, which is it Selena?"

"I'm so sorry," I said, a little quiver in my voice, and tears welling. "We just broke up over the weekend, I'm still not used to saying it."

"Oh geez, I'm so sorry that I brought it up," he said, while searching his pockets.

He pulled out a pocket square. An old school pocket square like my Papa used to carry.

"I swear it's clean," he said, handing it to me.

"I'm so sorry, I have no idea why I'm crying. He was a complete asshole, I'm really not even sad."

Well, then why are you crying Selena?!

"Sylvie and I caught him with another woman on Saturday. I guess it's all a bit raw still," I added.

"I am so sorry, I had no idea. Well that is very shitty. Hey, when you're ready, I'd love to take you out sometime."

I was shocked. Especially after this dramatic performance.

"Yes, I'd really like that. Give me a few weeks to get all these emotions out," I said pointing to my eyes.

"Will do, have a good night Selena," he said, making his way towards the door, still staring directly into my eyes.

Maybe even my soul?!?

I followed him to the door and then locked up. I wanted to put my hands on my head and scream, but I knew he could still see me through the front windows so I had to remain calm. *Why the hell did I just cry in front of that delicious drink of a man?*

Something told me that my time thinking about Jack Webber was about to be a thing of the past...

Chapter Fourteen

SYLVIE

I raced home in time to grab a bite and print all my materials for our six thirty Starbucks meeting. We were scheduled to present the following Tuesday. Our professor had broken down his grading requirements and our presentation was going to weigh heavily on our overall course grade. We had to kill this.

    I reheated some of last night's dinner and then washed my face and redid my makeup. There was something so exciting about meeting Simon and Alexa in person. I remember Selena talking so much about her group projects when she lived and studied at UCONN. I always did so much to hide my jealousy of her life. I barely asked questions and pretended to have little interest in her college stories, as if I was living the same life back home in Holly. Like going home to my childhood bedroom at the end of every night the first few years was equally as exciting as her dorm life. Meanwhile, I was nineteen years old and working forty hour weeks with mom and Nonni.

    I pulled up to the Starbucks about fifteen minutes early and tried to grab the quietest table in the shop. I felt guilty taking up space without buying anything, so I went up and ordered a decaffeinated latte. Having never seen Simon or Alexa in person I stared at every face that came through the door.

I knew it was Alexa immediately. She was young, with a tiny frame, long straight hair and glasses with a light pink matching sweatsuit. I must have been easy to spot too as she immediately gave me a wave.

I got up to shake her hand and we organized all of our materials and waited for Simon. Maybe he was the pompous ass that I had originally imagined as he was now ten minutes late. What a jerk! Alexa and I decided to go through our revisions together, without him.

Just as we were beginning to look at powerpoint templates an absolute tornado walked through the main entrance. He was about six feet tall, broad shouldered, and thank God for that as he had multiple bags on both arms. He wore black trousers with a blue and white patterned button up shirt. The top two buttons were undone, suggesting to the world: *I've had a day*. On his feet were an expensive pair of black leather loafers. His black hair was loosely parted and combed to the side. He was a walking J. Crew billboard.

He was textbook handsome. Nonni would probably stop him in the street and first confirm that he was not Sicilian, and then inquire if he was single.

"Hi, I'm late. Sorry," he said like a robotic caveman. "We had a problem at the restaurant, and-" he stopped himself. "Nevermind. Anyways, I have everything we need," he said, pulling printouts of our notes from one of his bags.

Wow, can you say megalomaniac five times fast? Micromanaging control freak.

"Oh, of course, you guys already printed these," he said, noticing that Alexa and I were both already holding copies that we had made for ourselves. Like the grownups that we also were.

He was taking a seat, laying his bags on the floor. One a computer bag, another had the loose papers printed for the project, and the third bag was a complete mystery. He looked around and then reached down for the third bag which was a handled brown paper bag.

"Not sure if they will be thrilled by this," he gestured towards the baristas. "But I always work better with a full stomach so, I had the kitchen make these calzones just before I left," he said emotionless, pulling out paper plates and unrolling the foil from three of the most delicious smelling pies.

"Wow, you know the way to my heart, Simon," I said, noticing a coat of his armor had now been removed.

Maybe he wasn't a complete ass.

"These smell amazing, thank you," added Alexa.

"My family owns a restaurant and club across town, Guiseppi's. Everything is from scratch."

I could feel my face burning with embarrassment. I was at Guiseppi's at least two nights a month for the last two years. How had I never seen this guy before? But more importantly, I prayed that he had never seen me.

"Do you work there?" I asked.

"Worked there my whole life. Last few years I've been transitioning from front of house management to running the backend of the business. We're in the process of expanding, and I just think it's easier for people to take a college grad more seriously. I'm plugging away at a Business degree. What about you guys?"

And another wall had been removed. Dare I say his voice had even lightened?

"Oh, well I'm not really sure what my plan is. I'm a full time student, but this is the only Marketing class that I could get into this semester. I don't usually take night classes," offered Alexa.

"Similar situation for me," I said, speaking directly to Simon. "Only, I'm not sure that the family business is for me, just trying to pursue something that interests me, I guess."

I sounded like an idiot. But it was true, I did not know what I was expecting by taking these classes. The only thing I knew for certain was that taking them gave me hope and made me excited about the future. I just wasn't sure what that future looked like, but something had to change. I had to find my true path because what I was doing now was not sustainable. I couldn't carry on sitting behind a desk or cutting table in Holly for much longer.

We sat there for another two hours, until the baristas began closing up. Time flew, but we had a rough draft pieced together on our presentation and we all left with specific slides to work on over the next few days. Simon invited Alexa and I to the restaurant anytime; I just nodded and smiled pretending I had never heard of such a place.

Chapter Fifteen

SELENA

The weekend was uneventful, boring actually. Sylvie was MIA and I was too embarrassed to reach out to my friends to confess out loud what a disaster my current life was. I had a terrible habit of losing touch with friends when I was in a relationship and always feared that this might be the final time that they would welcome me back. Like how many strikes could I possibly have before I was completely out?

What I did know was that I could not handle any more rejection at the moment, so instead, I decided to use the last few days of my break to power through and get the base for all seven costumes complete.

I was sad for the week to end, but the distraction of returning to school today was exactly what I needed. Last night my mom called after her visit with Nonni. She was a bit of a wreck, which was out of character for my zipped up, straight shooting mother. Apparently Nonni was really not herself during their visit. When my mom showed up Nonni was still in her pajamas, her hair wasn't curled and she wasn't even sure what day it was. This was very unlike her; she was always such a proud, put together woman. I assured my mom that Sylvie and I would be there tonight and would call her as soon as we left.

I had taken multiple pictures of each costume on the forms so that Adam and Tanya could see my progress. I knew they were going to freak out over the Cinderella and wolf costumes, and they did not disappoint.

"I do not understand. You did this, all of this?! By yourself?!" Adam said.

"Well, Jack and I broke up at the start of the break, and let's just say, I had a lot of time on my hands!" I admitted.

I was surprised by how good it felt to get that out and off my chest. My voice remained completely steady, without any signs of emotion.

"I'm sorry, what?! Why didn't you call me?" Tanya asked.

We had really become close friends these last few years. We often got drinks after work, and would occasionally connect on the weekends. We even got tickets to a few concerts together.

"Sorry, I just had to deal with it alone, come to terms with it. But the good news is, I now see what a true asshole he is, so I do not even miss him!"

And I meant it. I hadn't thought about him in days.

I wanted to tell her about Connor Steer, but I realized how ridiculous that would be. Afterall, I was committed to giving Sylvie's approach a try. I refused to continue my pattern of relationship hopping. I was going to have fun, and play the field. Maybe even have my first one night stand. I always wondered what that was like. That's a lie, I always judged people for having them...

The day flew by and before I knew it I was waiting in the parking lot for Sylvie at The Springs of Holly Valley.

When she arrived she let me know that she spent the greater part of the day hearing mom stress about Nonni's decline. Sylvie insisted that she was here only a week ago, and that although she did notice that she seemed more tired, it was not as dramatic as our mother's account.

When we walked in, the entryway to the building was abuzz. Despite dinner service not starting until four thirty, everyone was usually in their assigned seats by four. I think they all arrived early for the socializing and people watching, and maybe for fear of food running out. We usually met Nonni in the private dining room or at her table. We checked both, she was not there.

We looked at each other and without saying a word took an elevator up to her floor. We knocked on her door. No one answered. My heart began pounding in my chest.

Selena grabbed my arm as she went to knock again. Tears rushed to her eyes.

"Oh my god Sleen, what if-"

"Nope, not happening. Not today Sylvie. She's fine, just off her routine."

I grabbed the door handle and was shocked when it opened.

We stepped inside and were hit by the heat that she had cranking inside. My eyes darted around the studio apartment, heart beating out of my chest, looking for her. There she was. Sitting in her reclining chair, staring at the television. She was dressed, but like my mom had mentioned, her hair was not done. I had never seen my Nonni without her hair curled.

"Oh, hi girls," she said flatly, as if we were from housekeeping.

"Nonni, you're going to be late for dinner," Sylvie said, pulling the walker out in front of her chair.

She had a huge stain on the front of her shirt. Did she not know it was there? I didn't want to embarrass her, but I also didn't want her to be surprised by it later.

"Can I get you a different shirt before we go down Nonni?"

She looked at me, annoyed.

"Now why would I want a different shirt?" she said coldly.

"Oh, you just have a little stain on yours," I said pointing to her chest, but quickly decided it was best to let it go.

Eventually we got her downstairs and settled at her table. She missed the salad service but they brought it out for us with the main course, Monte Cristo sandwiches.

I never enjoyed the meals here, but I loved the company. Nonni's tablemates could have their own television show. They were hysterical.

I watched as she looked down at her plate with a look of confusion.

"These sandwiches are actually something you really like," I said encouragingly.

I looked at Sylvie and under my breath whispered: "I'll be right back."

Luckily, I did not just stress over mine and Sylvie's health, I also read up on all the health concerns for women my mom's age as well as Nonni's. I went to the front desk and asked if she would page the on-call nurse so that I could speak with her about my grandmother.

"Is she ok? Who is it?"

"Mary Stefanos, room 319, it is not an emergency."

I waited on a couch in the lobby for about ten minutes. A surly looking woman with a short, gray haircut emerged from the elevator. She had a walkie talkie attached to her hip and a clipboard in one of her hands.

"Can I help you? Is Mary okay?"

"She's in the dining room with my sister. She is very off today. My mom noticed it yesterday too. She's a really proud woman, she never normally comes down to dinner without her hair done and definitely wouldn't leave her room with a stain on her shirt. I would like her checked for a UTI or a tooth infection," I responded matter of factly. Like I was Meredith Grey speaking to her interns.

The nurse raised her eyebrows.

"Ok, well you will need to make an appointment with her doctor and dentist, those are not tests that I am able to run here. But I agree, that does not sound like Mary."

"Ok, I'll have my mom call for appointments first thing tomorrow, until then, can you guys check on her a bit more than usual?"

"Of course," she responded while jotting down a note.

By the time I got back to the table, most of the dining room had emptied out. I found Sylvie following Nonni as she made her way to the elevator.

We got her settled back into her reclining chair, adjusted her thermostat and kissed her goodbye. We weren't even out of the building before I called my mom with instructions. For once she didn't question me and my health advice. I could tell she was going to listen and reach out to her medical team first thing.

Sylvie and I pulled back up to our building around six and despite being exhausted, I knew I had to get to work on the two costumes I had strewn across my kitchen table. I had eleven days until the dress rehearsal, and had scheduled final fittings in nine. I needed to make a final trip to the fabric store for detail work, but for the most part I could get a lot done at home. I was really happy with my progress up to this point.

I was so busy that I didn't have time to worry about when I would see Connor Steer again. I'd basically erased him from my memory. He was removed from my subconscious. I barely even remembered his name, or his eye color...or his inseam...

Chapter Sixteen

SYLVIE

Regardless of wishing it was in a classroom, I thought our online presentation went off without a hitch. Our professor seemed pleased and I was shocked that when turning in my own paper I rated both Simon and Alexa as great partners and collaborators. I would have never guessed such a turn of events!

On Thursday I sat at my desk at *La Sarta* and looked through my email. I had just received one from our class professor marked *Presentation Grade*. In the group he included a lengthy note about our team's chemistry, fluidity and overall top performance. I was so proud! I wanted to call my mom over to see it, but she still knew nothing about my classes. I was too nervous about how my family might react, so I decided it was best to keep it to myself until I knew what my plan was.

Secrets are so lonely. I didn't want to put Selena in the middle, but I especially hate keeping things from her. I had never wanted to tell her about my 'spin classes' more.

I didn't mean to keep so much hidden, but I felt shame and disappointment for not loving my work at the shop. I loved the time with my mom, and originally with my mom and Nonni, but I was not a good seamstress and I was never going to be a good seamstress. Also, and most importantly, I did not *WANT* to be a good seamstress.

Selena on the other hand was a natural with the sewing machine, and better yet, she loved it. I respected that she wanted to go to college, and she respected that I did not, but sometimes I wish we could pull a Freaky Friday and switch places.

I had no idea how to even broach this with my family, which is why I hadn't, and I had no intentions to. I was not one to cause ripples in the family. In fact, I was the easy kid that got good grades and kept my bad decisions to the weekends (and Thursday nights). I was the kid that chose the path of least resistance and interruption. I wasn't sure how this would be received by my family or what it would all mean for my mom but the weight was becoming heavy.

My phone buzzed. I looked down to see it was a group text from Simon to Alexa and I. I bet he just saw our grade too.

Amazing grade! We made a good team! Dinner tonight at Guiseppi's to celebrate? My treat!

Before I had time to overthink it, I wrote back. So this guy went from being a total ass, to now inviting us to break bread with him at his restaurant? I was so confused.

Let us know what time! I'll be there!

Oh my God.

It's Thursday. It's ladies night. I needed an out. How could I backpedal?

I have an early morning tomorrow, any chance we can grab dinner early?

I had to make sure I was out of there before seven.

No problem! Let's aim for five?

Perfect! See you there!

Sweet relief.

Hey guys! Celebrate without me! Can't make it! Thanks for the invite anyway, chimed in Alexa.

I hadn't even noticed that she hadn't responded. I wonder if Simon had.

Will do! Fun working with you! wrote Simon.

Ok, so we were really going to do this, and it was just going to be Simon and me. I couldn't believe that I didn't think this through. I looked over at my mom, there were so many things I wished I could tell her. She was sitting at her sewing table working on alterations to a prom gown. With her miniature television on the corner of her table playing one of the day time soaps that she watched in heavy rotation.

She looked so relaxed and happy to be transforming this dress to perfectly fit the young woman on her special day. She was doing what makes her happy. Today I was in charge of pressing all the clothes, bagging and then creating invoices. I was essentially putting the final touches on my mom's hard work but I certainly wasn't doing what filled my cup.

I had to make a change. I just wasn't sure how. My mom couldn't do this alone, but I felt confident that she could easily replace me. But how do I even broach this topic? And what would I be leaving to go do? I still wasn't sure of that.

"It's Thursday *figlia*, are you and Courtney going to Giuseppi's?"

She had stopped her machine and was looking up at me for a response. If only she knew...

"Kind of. I'm just headed there for an earlier dinner," I said, relieved that I chose to tell the truth.

"Oh, look at you growing up and making good choices," she responded with a smirk.

"Something like that mom."

I looked over at the clock on my computer, three more hours of work. What was I going to wear tonight? Was it going to be awkward just the two of us? I wondered if he regretted the invite now that Alexa wasn't able to attend.

I had to put some thought into how I was going to react when I arrived at his family restaurant. Should I feign a surprised reaction when I arrive? React like I had never seen the insides of the restaurant I had spent the last four years closing down? I had never actually been there when the sun was still out, or when the rooms were arranged for dinner service, so it truly would look much different to me. Come to think of it, I had never walked into the restaurant sober. We always had a few drinks somewhere else prior to our arrival. So really, it would be an honest reaction. I practically had never actually been there before.

"Would you mind if I left a little early tonight? Are you comfortable locking up?"

I rarely asked my mom for these types of favors, to a fault.

"Of course honey, go whenever you want," she said without looking up from her machine.

It was a little after four when I got home. I thought about what I should wear the entire ride home and came up with a very simple black dress. It actually looked like something I would have stolen from Selena's wardrobe. I turned on my hair straightener, washed my face and redid my makeup. I touched up my hair and decided on a pair of casual Nike sneakers so that it was clear that I knew that this was a casual dinner, not a date.

When I arrived, Simon was at the hostess stand speaking with two of the waiters. My eyes darted around the room searching for anyone that may seem familiar to me and with me... nothing yet. He looked up and smiled when he saw me.

"I saved us the best table in the restaurant," he said as he walked towards me.

I followed him to our seat, noting how nice the restaurant looked with all the tables out and dressed. I looked at the plates of food we passed and was amazed. Everything looked and smelled so good. Why didn't we ever eat here?!

I took a seat as he handed me a menu.

"I hope this isn't weird," he started. "I am so relieved that this semester is almost over, the stress of juggling classes and the restaurant has nearly killed me, and to finish with such a high grade on a project; I was so happy."

"I felt the exact same way! I have had some group projects go sideways! It was such a relief once we were all together and worked on the presentation."

"You thought I was an ass, huh? You thought I was being a control freak, and overbearing, right?"

I stopped myself as I began to laugh.

"Well, no...I mean, yes, kind of. But only at first. Once we worked together in person it was all good."

"I'm sorry, I'm getting better at reigning it in. I'm just so used to making all the decisions here, and stressing over the timing and stuff. To be honest, I'm only seven classes into my degree and I have not had a lot of good group work partners!"

"Yea, I hear you on that. I think my partner in my accounting class was about fifteen years old and his mom helped him with his part of the assignment. I've never felt older in my life."

"My days here are so quick and decisions are made on the fly, not to mention the tempers in the kitchen. I need to get better at how I-"

"You were fine," I said assuredly. "Honestly, don't overthink it."

The poor guy clearly needed a get out of jail free card. I didn't usually pass those out, but tonight, it just felt like the right thing to do.

He smiled as a waiter came over to the table to greet us. After some back and forth with Simon, a well-rehearsed and very detailed recitation of the night's specials and his personal suggestions, we agreed to share a bottle of Cabernet. I let Simon pick.

I had to make sure I was out of here by six forty, I could not risk bumping into my friends. They would out me immediately.

I was fine with letting Simon choose the wine, but I turned down his offer to suggest what I should eat for dinner. Nobody tells Baby what she should eat.

Ok, fine, it wasn't like that...but I still felt like I needed to maintain control.

When the waiter returned I ordered the chicken marsala and Simon ordered the braised short ribs special. Conversation was light and easy, and for most of the meal I was convinced that I was getting away with my secret.

The waiter had just removed our plates and brought over a dessert menu when he said:

"Your friends should be here soon."

"What?"

Shit. Shit. Shit. I felt a cold sweat cover my temples and wrists. My heart, beating like a drum.

"Your friends. You guys usually get here just as these tables are all cleaned up. Have you ever even seen it set up for dinner service?" he asked, basking in my discomfort.

"You knew? This whole time, you knew?"

"I knew the second I saw your face on our Zoom call last week. I just wasn't sure why you didn't tell me that you are familiar with our fine establishment?" he asked as I squirmed.

My elbows were on the table and my face dropped into my hands.

"This is humiliating."

"No, no, I'm not trying to humiliate you, I promise! I am just teasing you!" he said, wrapping his hand around one of my arms so that he could move it to see my face.

I looked down at the table.

"Look, I'm not ashamed that I come here on Ladies Night and have a good time. Ok, fine, like a really good time, sometimes three Thursdays a month..."

He was smiling.

"I guess I'm just trying to grow up a bit. I was really enjoying the idea of who I could be through these night classes," I said, honestly. "I'm trying to get my shit together."

"Sylvie, Sylvie, I am not judging you. In fact, I rarely stay past nine on Thursdays, so yes, I recognize you as a familiar face here, but that is it. No judgments. In fact, I think I should be thanking you for your patronage. I started the Ladies Nights five years ago when I was moved to a management position. It took off and it's a big reason why my family trusts me to expand into the city."

"Wow, really? That's amazing! We love Ladies Night! We have been coming on and off for the last five years!"

"Thank you," he said again, seriously.

I was beginning to relax and breathed a sigh of relief.

"So you don't need to keep checking the time. If we see your friends, it will be ok..."

"Oh my God, is it that obvious? I'm such a jerk!"

We were both laughing. It actually felt so good to have someone besides my family call me on my shit. The waiter came back with a cannoli that Simon insisted I try as well as two decaf cappuccinos. It was actually a perfect date. Ok, not a date. A perfect dinner.

I offered to split the bill, and when he wouldn't let me I left a cash tip on the table for our waiter. I got up to leave, and he stood up quickly.

"This was fun Sylvie."

"It was," I agreed.

"Could I take you out sometime? Like maybe to a restaurant that my family doesn't own? Like a real date?"

I couldn't hide my smile.

"I'd really like that."

He walked me to my car and I reached out to give him a quick hug before taking off. All of it felt foreign to me, but at the same time completely natural.

Chapter Seventeen

SELENA

I did my best to keep all my medical appointments before or after school to avoid using up a lot of my personal time, so I was thrilled when Dr. Kushir had an opening at seven on Monday morning. It seemed like a really good idea when I booked the appointment.

When my alarm went off at five thirty I groaned. I spent yet another weekend bouncing between my makeshift work station in my apartment and my family's shop. The seven costumes were just about complete but it was really hard to tell if the men's pants were going to fit. I had made plenty of women's trousers and had helped my mom alter enough men's pants that this shouldn't be stressful, but it was.

The first round of fittings were after school on Thursday and I was so excited to see how everything came together. My mom offered to come down and help me with pinning and all the tailoring that she excelled at. She was as excited for all of it as I was.

I arrived at the dermatology office about fifteen minutes early, hoping to be her first appointment of the day.

"Selena. What brings you in today?" she asked. "It doesn't look like you're due for your annual exam for another six months."

"Well I have been watching both that mole and sunspot and I just wanted to confirm that they hadn't changed since the last time you saw me. This one on my stomach seems to have grown a bit," I said, starting to open up my cloth gown.

She was scrolling through her computer and turned it towards me.

"Ok, here is a photo of the moles from the last four times you have visited. In those four visits it has shown no change. Let's take a look and match it to these pictures," she said, clearly placating me.

From my angle, it was hard to really see it, I usually took photos with my phone.

Dr. Kushir took a step back.

"It looks exactly the same, Selena. I will take a photo now if that's ok?"

I nodded, accompanied by a sigh of relief.

"Oh, phew. What about this sun spot on my cheek? Is it concerning to you?"

"Selena, you have beautiful, olive, Italian skin. Your chances of coming in here with anything concerning is about ninety percent lower than the rest of my patients. I highly recommend the annual exam, but outside of that, I really hate to see you waste your time and money."

"The way I see it, better to be safe than sorry!"

She smiled and made her way out to the hall so that I could get dressed.

I knew she thought I was over the top, just like I knew that my primary care doctor groaned and laughed with her peers with every email that I sent through the portal. But honestly, I did not care. Not one bit. I was not going to roll the dice with my health.

I was a few minutes early to school and decided to give my mom a call before she opened the shop. She had visited Nonni last night and I wanted to know what to expect at our dinner with her tonight. She did in fact end up having a urinary tract infection (see, my research had its benefits) and was treated for it last Tuesday.

"Morning *figlia*," she answered on the first ring.

"Morning mom, how was Nonni yesterday?"

"Oh, she was a bit better, but still not herself honey. Her hair wasn't done, so I made an appointment for her in the salon today. She just seemed tired and a bit out of it. I have a meeting with the nurses on Wednesday to talk about it. I think she needs some extra help."

My mom sounded so worried and sad. I hated it.

"We will be with her tonight, I'll check in with you when I get home. Love you."

It was becoming clear that life really did not ever let off the gas. My mom should be at a point where she could sit back and celebrate a job well done. Both of her kids were living on their own, supporting themselves...she should be toying with the idea of retirement. My mom always said that she would not work for as many years as my Nonni. In fact, at sixty three, her time to retire was soon. I know that my dad had one year left at the factory and then he would have his full pension and I hoped they would retire together.

The school day flew by and before I knew it I was in the lobby of The Springs of Holly Valley. I saw Sylvie's car in the lot and knew she was already here. I stepped towards the dining room and only saw Jeannette and Shirley, no sign of Nonni. I scanned the lobby and the chair lined halls and didn't see her there either.

"Selena!" my sister yelled from the other side of the room, panic had a hold of her voice.

"Where's Nonni?" I asked.

Sylvie's shoulders and arms went up.

"I don't know, should we go up to her room?"

I could feel a shallow pit forming at the base of my stomach as we boarded the elevator.

"Mom said she barely recognized her and dad during their visit yesterday. Even asked her who she was? She's beside herself, Sleen."

"Maybe it takes a couple of weeks for the meds to totally clear her of the infection," I said, trying to sound positive.

I knocked on her door and noticed that it was not closed all the way. I pushed it open and took a step inside. The television was on, cranked to what had to be the highest volume option. I scanned the room.

"She's not here Selena! Where is she?" Sylvie asked, trying not to cry.

We ran towards the stairs, forgoing the elevator as dinner always made it a busy time.

We popped out onto the second floor knowing that is where the nurses station was located. There was a familiar nursing assistant at the desk, working on charts.

"Our Nonni is missing!" I yelled, breathing loudly.

She stood up.

"Mary? Are you sure? What do you mean, missing?"

"I mean, she's not in the dining room, and she's not in her room. Nonni does not do activities or sit around and socialize anywhere except in the dining room or at the Italian Club meetings. Where is she?" Sylvie demanded.

The young CNA, her name tag said Emily, grabbed the pager off her waist.

"Has anyone seen 319? Repeat, need an attendance check on 319."

"On it," answered someone back into the small device.

"On it," said two more voices.

"Why don't you two go back down to the dining room as I'm sure she will be there any minute, and we will touch base with you. I have an aid on each floor doing an attendance check. We will get to the bottom of this within minutes," she assured us.

Just as we arrived downstairs, I saw a man wearing a custodial shirt run into the lobby.

"My cart is gone!"

Sylvie and I stopped to see what was happening.

"What do you mean it's gone?" Emily asked.

One of the administrators stepped out of her office, overhearing the commotion.

"What's going on guys?" she asked, looking at both the man and Emily.

"I took the golf cart to bring trash from the Alzheimer's unit over to the dumpster and then I left it parked on the side of the building while I took my break," the man, who was likely in his late forties, sporting weathered skin and hardened hands said quickly, breathlesly.

The administrator took out her walkie talkie.

"All, has anyone seen the groundskeeper's golf cart?"

You heard *no* repeated over and over again on their walkie talkies.

"Excuse me, I'm sorry to interrupt, but can we make sure everyone is still looking for our grandmother?" I asked, becoming even more agitated.

"Can I have an update on 319?" Emily voiced into her pager.

"Stay calm," said the administrative woman, now looking at the fright in our eyes. "I'm sure she's just using a bathroom or something outside of what you assume is her normal routine."

Suddenly the pagers began to go off again, and an aid from every floor confirmed that they had not yet been able to find 319.

My heart was beating out of my chest. Where could she possibly be?

"Hang tight girls, I know this is scary. We have a protocol for this, I am calling the police department and then I will be right back," the unnamed administrator said very matter of factly.

She was back within minutes.

"My name is Evelyn, I am the Executive Director," she started calmly. "I have alerted our entire staff of our situation and everyone is currently looking for Mary. If we have not found her in the next ten minutes, the police will get involved. It might be something very simple, such as Mary took a walk."

"She would never take a walk at dinner time. It's so cold out," added Sylvie, wrapping her arms around herself.

The lead nurse, Olga was now in the lobby. She smiled at us sympathetically and then asked to speak with Evelyn privately.

Sylvie and I took a seat, both now in tears, wondering if we should call our mom, or wait. Before I had time to give it additional thought, Evelyn was back.

"Ladies, Olga just informed me that there are multiple notes in Mary's chart stating that she's been a bit agitated and confused over the last two weeks, but we were hopeful that the treatment of her recent UTI was going to alleviate that. Have you seen her in the last few days? Do you know if she is improving?"

"Our mom was here yesterday, and said that she was still not herself," I started.

Before I could finish, Evelyn had her cell phone to her ear and stepped away.

Olga tried to offer us some words of comfort, but I couldn't hear what she was saying. The pulsing in my ears was so loud and I felt like it was taking everything in me to just breathe.

Suddenly Emily and Evelyn were both back in front of us.

"Umm..." started Emily. "So if Mary is missing, and so is the golf cart, do you think she could be -?"

"Oh my God!" Sylvie grabbed my arm and pulled me to the exit.

"We will go look for her!" I yelled.

Before anyone had a chance to say anything we were out the door and hopping into Sylvie's small SUV.

"You think she is out riding around on a golf cart Sylvie? That's crazy! It's such a cold afternoon!"

At the same time both our phones made a loud buzzing sound, like an emergency alert. I pulled my phone out:

Silver Alert: Female 83 year old Mary Stefano, last seen at Holly Springs, possibly driving a golf cart.

Now my phone was ringing.

Mom.

I answered on the first ring.

"Selena!!!"

She was hysterical.

"Evelyn just called me! Are you there? Oh my God Selena, I cannot believe this, I'm on my way."

"Mom, we will find her, Sylvie and I are leaving now to drive around. Please drive safely, we will call you the second we know anything."

I hung up.

"Where would she go Selena?" Sylvie asked.

"What do you mean?"

"She's confused, and has the means to escape, where would she go?"

In a rare twins moment, we looked at each other and in unison said: "Church!"

Sylvie took a right out of the complex and drove towards Sacred Heart. It was only about two miles away, so we were there in no time. We rounded the corner and turned into the parking lot, where we pulled up beside a white and gray golf cart, the back filled with buckets, rakes and a few trash bags.

The car was barely in park and we were both running towards the church entrance. We burst through the door running into the church and down the aisles. Our eyes darted from side to side scanning every square inch. When we got towards the lectern we stopped, both seeing her at the same time. She was kneeling in front of a row of candles, one she had clearly lit. Her head was bowed in prayer.

Sylvie stopped me by pulling at my arm as I went to approach her.

"Let her finish," she whispered, tears streaming down her face. "I'm going to call mom and

Evelyn. I'll be outside, just wait here for her."

I nodded, looking at my grandmother in awe, as if she were a painting that had just been completed. She was here for Papa. Sylvie was right. I had to let her have this so I quietly took a seat in a nearby pew, bracing for the circus that was sure to follow.

Chapter Eighteen

SYLVIE

I waited in the parking lot for my mom. The police and Evelyn both arrived, and my mom showed up only a few minutes later. I let them know that Selena was inside with her and asked if we could just give her the time to finish her prayer. I expected push back but was shocked by the compassion on every single face. We sat outside and talked about what would happen next.

Evelyn suggested we have Nonni evaluated for dementia and Alzheimers. My mom nodded in agreement; she looked prepared for this.

"If it is decided that she is at risk of wandering, which, I think after today we can all agree that she is, we can talk about moving her down the hall to a spot in the Memory Care Unit," Evelyn said gently.

My mom just nodded, tears rolling down her face.

Suddenly the door popped open and Selena walked out, arm in arm with Nonni, Selena's jacket draped around our grandmother's shoulders.

Nonni looked from me to my mom to Evelyn and finally to the cops.

"What the hell!" she yelled, waving her hands towards everyone. "Are you going to arrest me for going to church?"

We all looked at each other and laughed, yup, that was Nonni.

My mom brought Nonni back to her assisted living and got her settled in her room. They had pizza delivered and my mom spent the night with her as they were able to get an appointment for Nonni first thing in the morning. I told her that I had things handled at the shop and not to worry.

We both knew that was not entirely true. I could do a lot, but I had limits, I was not the talented seamstress that she was. I could hem, iron, press and bag better than most, but the reconstructions and dress bodice alterations were where I drew the line. Hopefully she would only need a day to get Nonni settled. The weight and the stress of mom's work coupled with my guilt felt heavy for me. I knew I should be helping more, but I literally was at my limit.

On Tuesday when I was alone in the shop I checked my email and saw one from Simon.

Hi Sylvie -

Wondering if I could make good on that offer to take you out to dinner? Maybe tomorrow? Let me know if there's a better day or whatever!

Talk Soon!

Simon

I sat at my desk, smiling to myself. I was surprised by how excited I was to hear from him. I didn't even want to play games, so I wrote him back immediately.

Hi Simon -

That sounds amazing. I think you forgot that we have class tomorrow night? I could go out after? Or I suppose I could skip Ladies Night on Thursday and go out then? Happy to go anywhere!

Best -

Sylvie

Ps - if it's easier, you can text me. Let me know if you need me to resend you my #!

I had just stepped away from my computer, making my way back to my sewing machine when I heard the incoming email ding. I dashed over to check one final time.

Sylvie -

I like emailing you, is that weird? I definitely forgot about class. I do that often, do you? Ok, unfortunately it's hard for me to leave the restaurant on Thursday nights, but I do treat myself to Friday nights off? How about Friday night? We could try the Oyster House?

Let me know! Also, if you would rather text, that is fine, I'm just teasing!

Sincerely,

Simon

PS - 'Sincerely' is a bit formal, (but isn't emailing someone about a date?)

He was funny.

Dear Simon -

Friday sounds perfect, let me know what time to meet you.

Deep Regards,

Sylvie

I was so busy that the rest of the day flew by. My mom called as I was locking up the shop.

"Hi Sylvie," she sounded exhausted. "Can you conference Selena in, I don't know how and don't want to have to go through all of this twice."

"Of course mom, one second."

I dialed Selena and then merged our calls.

My mom admitted she was exhausted. She had brought Nonni to her primary care doctor, the lab, and then her neurologist. Her medical team had called to confirm their joint diagnosis - dementia. They recommended we transfer her to the Memory Care Unit.

"How can we help mom? Can we come and help move her things?" I offered.

"Not today, honey. I need to get a good night of sleep. They assigned her an overnight personal care attendant and then the custodial team offered to move all her belongings for us. She will move tomorrow. She will have a private room which is good."

I could hear the quiver in her voice.

"I can take a personal day tomorrow and help you set up her room," offered Selena.

"That's okay *figlia*, Dad is going to take the day and help, it shouldn't be too much. The staff is doing most of the work. Sylvie, will you be okay at the shop alone again tomorrow?"

"Of course mom."

"I know I sound down and exhausted, but we did have some laughs today. Just imagining your grandmother driving a golf cart to church -"

Laughter erupted on the call.

"I just wish we got to see that. What must people have thought when they saw her cruising through town? And listen, this disease is going to be hardest on us, but we need to remember that Nonni is not in any pain, and the doctor said that dementia patients often travel back to their happiest days. Our job is to join her there. We aren't going to correct her, we are not going to make her feel sad or ashamed. She needs us girls, it's going to be tough, but we got this."

Tears filled my eyes.

"Love you mom, you're so strong. We got this, I sure hope I get to meet twenty year old Nonni, cause I bet she was a badass," I smiled through the tears.

"Yes! Oh my God, I hope she lets me make her some new clothes!" Selena added and we all just laughed.

Chapter Nineteen

SELENA

After the whirlwind week we were all experiencing, especially my mom, I was prepared to handle the costume fittings after school by myself. I was walking to the auditorium from my classroom wheeling a cart of costumes and passed by Principal DiMatino, when he stopped me.

"Selena, your mom is waiting for you in the lobby, I told her I would track you down!"

"Oh wow, thank you so much! She's helping me with the fitting for the musical!"

He smiled and gave me a thumbs up and continued walking down the hall towards the library, which was now converted into detention headquarters.

My mom stood up smiling when she saw me. I hadn't seen her since I left the church Monday night. She gave me the biggest hug and I was so relieved to see the smile still on her face when we pulled away.

"How are you mom?"

"I'm good, I promise, Nonni is safe, that is what's most important."

I grabbed her arm and wheeled my cart with the other. When we got into the theater we were greeted by pockets of activity with each step. The band was setting up off to the side of the stage, the set designers were on stage building and different groups of actors sat together practicing their lines.

Tanya smiled when she saw us.

"This must be the famous Mama Rossi," she said as she greeted my mom with a hug.

"The one and only! Where would you like us to set up? I figure we could use a bit of privacy."

"Yes, the seven actors are waiting for you backstage. You can set up in the lounge and they can get changed in the dressing rooms."

"Perfect!"

The fittings went as well as I could have hoped. Mom took the lead on the boys trousers as she was comfortable with the pinning and let me know she planned to get all their alterations completed by the end of the day tomorrow. I didn't even have to ask her. She was literally the best.

The actress wearing the Cinderella costume was a stunning junior that stepped into it like it was her glass slipper. She twirled, admiring herself in the mirror.

"This is the most beautiful thing I've ever worn. Oh my God, this would be the most show stopping prom dress!" she added.

I couldn't wipe the smile off my face if I tried. I had to take it in a bit at the bust and adjust the length but all in all, it could not have fit her better.

I could tell that the senior that was cast as the wolf took his role very seriously. His relief when he saw that most of his face would still be exposed to the audience was palpable.

"I was so worried you were going to cover my whole face! So much of a performance comes out in facial expressions," he added.

I just nodded and smiled at his dramatic reaction. His costume needed nothing, it was ready for showtime.

By the time we got out of there it was nearly five and I could see that my mom was exhausted.

"Can I take you to dinner or anything mom?"

"Not tonight honey, but thank you. I have to get home, Dad must be starving."

I tried to hide my disappointment. This was how their relationship worked and they were both very happy so I saw no point in acknowledging that my father was very capable of cooking or at the very least, ordering a pizza.

I caught up with Tanya and Adam in the parking lot after I said goodbye to my mom. They were visibly relieved when I told them I would have all the costumes finished and in their hands on Monday. They offered to take me out for drinks to celebrate, and since my mom wasn't around, I was grateful for the offer.

We walked two blocks from the school to a dive bar that the staff loved to visit, mostly knowing that the school's hoity toity parents wouldn't be caught dead inside. We were safe from the martini-slogging moms and scotch sipping dads. We could speak in peace.

"Well, you saw the costumes, how is the show? How's it going?" I asked.

"It's as good as it's gonna get," offered Adam, with a quizzical expression.

"We have a few singers that will hopefully carry the show and help the audience forget about the kids that are not great singers," said Tanya, making a crooked smile as she spoke.

"Little Red Riding Hood and the Baker's Wife should both get a Tony. Cinderella is beautiful, and I'll stop there. Rapunzel has moments of greatness and the rest of the cast make for a good ensemble," said Adam.

"I can't wait to see it! Remind me of the schedule?"

"Dress rehearsal is Tuesday, opening night is Thursday. We have shows Friday, Saturday and Sunday and then we get our lives back!" said Tanya, wiping fake sweat from her forehead.

"Enough about our play, how are you?" she asked.

"Honestly, I'm good. The costumes were a great distraction, but I know I'm better off without him."

"Have you started swiping right? Go have some wild nights out with Sylvie?" she pried.

"Oh geez, I don't know. I mean, probably. I am committed to not being committed if that makes sense? I'm going to take a page out of

Sylvie's book for a while and actually date. I don't want to jump into anything."

"Oh Selena, there is nothing wrong with being a serial dater. Just promise me you won't be someone that you're not," Adam said, genuinely.

"Haha, yea, we'll see."

I had enough of talking about me and signaled our waitress for another pitcher of beer. I don't know if it was the warmer air and smell of summer around the corner, but I couldn't remember the last time beer tasted this good.

Chapter Twenty

SYLVIE

Simon and I agreed to meet at The Oyster House at six thirty, he made reservations for seven. Despite his offer to pick me up, I stuck to my guns and met him there. I knew that the drive home would keep me to two drinks and force the night to end appropriately.

I didn't usually aspire for an appropriate ending to a night, something in me had definitely shifted. I don't know if it was the pizza guy, night school or Simon, but I barely recognized myself. I looked so pulled together in my white prairie skirt and black fitted tank. I wore a jean jacket, wedge heels and a chunky turquoise necklace. I had spent an embarrassing amount of time pulling the outfit together and gently curling each strand of hair.

I arrived at the restaurant a few minutes late and scanned the bar looking for Simon. When my eyes reached the far end there was a handsome man staring back at me. His well kept black hair perfectly swept to the side. Simon was now standing and waving in my direction. He was dressed casually, khaki pants a black golf shirt and a pair of Van sneakers.

Simon greeted me with a hug and I found myself inhaling deeply, taking in his smell of spice and sandalwood. *I sure hope he didn't hear that.*

I ordered a Prosecco spritzer reminding myself that this was a marathon. Conversation was easy, and relaxed. He was funny, which I wasn't expecting. I could feel the heat rise to my face at every mention of Giuseppi's, but he went out of his way not to mention our last conversation.

By the time we were seated and had ordered our meals my nerves were gone and I was completely relaxed. We talked a lot about school and the future and I realized how rarely (never) I got to speak of my true future plans out loud. I had let my unhappiness become such a secret and had locked myself into such a dark closet. It felt so freeing to talk about it all openly.

"So you don't love what you're doing, and there really isn't an opportunity for a different role there?" he asked.

"It's a really small tailor shop, I really do all the positions at the moment. I definitely prefer the business tasks and working with customers over the actual seamstress work. But no, I just can't see myself doing this forever. I'm miserable, and it's not fair to my mom," I offered.

"So what do you want to do?"

"Honestly, I really don't know yet. I'm hoping that going through all these classes will help me figure out my passion. I really liked the Management class that I took last semester. What about you? You seem like you have a great job, why the classes?"

"I want a degree. We are divesting the family's real estate portfolio in order to afford the new restaurant in the city. I want to do right by my family and make sure that my decisions are all educated ones, if that makes sense? Although I am quickly learning that the business world rides a lot on instinct and connections," he said, smiling at me.

"I've never really left Holly. I think I'm ready to. I just have to figure out my exit strategy, but the city is where I think I'd like to be too."

I was amazed by how much I was thinking out loud. Some of the things I was saying were thoughts that I didn't even realize I had.

The waiter came back after we had finished our meals and we both ordered a cappuccino. I didn't want the night to end. I could talk to Simon for hours.

"So Miss Sylvie? Why is a woman as beautiful as you single?" he asked, a giant smile growing across his face.

"I could ask the same of you Mr. Simon. I've never been a big relationship person. My sister used to lay around and dream of her wedding day. My dreams were more of traveling and seeing the world."

"Are you a big traveler?" he asked.

"Well, turns out travel requires both money and time. So I'm leaving that in the category of 'one day,'" I sighed.

"I had a lot of fun tonight, I'd really like to see you again."

"I did too," I sounded genuinely surprised.

"Wow, you don't have to sound so shocked Sylvie. Are you working this weekend?"

"No, no weekend shifts for me," I answered.

"Well I hope this isn't too soon, but ...what are you doing tomorrow?" he asked, looking directly into my eyes.

I could feel myself blush. Should I really admit to this man that I didn't have a single plan the entire weekend?

"I don't have any plans that I can think of."

"Great. I looked and it's supposed to be a gorgeous spring-like day. Would you want to go for a hike? Mount Maple is my favorite spot, it's only a forty minute drive, have you been?"

A hike? This was literally a worst case scenario. The most outdoorsy thing I did was hit outdoor flea markets and festivals. I wasn't even sure I owned a proper pair of sneakers.

"No, I've never been there, but that sounds great."

What had I just signed up for?

We made plans for him to pick me up in the morning at nine. He promised he would arrive bearing coffee and breakfast treats for the ride. He looked so excited. I didn't have the heart to forewarn him of my physical condition or athletic inabilities.

I would have to call Selena the second I got home and raid her closet. This was going to be a disaster.

Chapter Twenty-One

SELENA

I put my pride aside and reached out to Kara and Marley to let them know I was single and ready to mingle. The tricky thing about being a twin living in a small town is that Sylvie and I share most of our friends. Leaving for college gave me a chance to pull away and carve my own group. Although I kept in touch with my college friends, I was excited to start my adult life back in Holly and was so grateful for those childhood friends. And Sylvie.

I wasn't surprised that Kara and Marley's reaction felt very rehearsed. They acted as if they had no idea and were completely shocked by my news; however they asked next to no questions and couldn't even pretend to be sad for me. Turns out they hated Jack too. *What the actual...*

We met for dinner after work on Friday and had an absolute blast. They were occasionally part of Sylvie's Thursday night crew and knew where to go locally to have a good time.

I got a panicked text from Sylvie around nine. When we had just started a game of darts.

911! Long story, but I need to borrow hiking clothes! I need them tonight! Can I come over?

I laughed and looked up at Kara and Marley.

"You will never believe this. Sylvie just asked if she could borrow hiking clothes!"

Maybe it was the cocktails, but it was like I had never said anything funnier. Marley had tears in her eyes.

Are you home?

Wow, she was persistent.

Wow, you're gonna have to tell me more. I'll be home in twenty, meet you there.

Wait, you're not home? You're out?! What are you doing?

Her reaction stung a bit.

I responded with an eye roll emoji.

When I got home a half hour later, Sylvie was sitting in the hall leaning against my door. She looked beautiful in a long white prairie skirt.

"Sylvie! Where are you coming from? You look so pretty! And also, why didn't you just use my extra key?"

"I didn't want to be invasive. And I was on a date, and no I don't want to talk about it."

"Oooh, I assume that is who you will be hiking with?"

"Yup, tomorrow."

"Wow, so mysterious," I mumbled.

"Are you drunk?" she asked, laughing at me. "Where were you tonight?"

"I got dinner and drinks with Kara and Marley. Kara said she had asked if you were around tonight and you said you had plans -"

"Yup, I had plans."

"Ok, clearly you don't want to talk about it, so let's get you some hiking gear. What do you want?"

It's not like I was some crazy hiker myself, but I definitely was the more athletic of the two of us. Although Queso limited me to shorter walks, I did like to go on long ones too.

"I don't even know, Selena. I literally don't know what people wear on hikes."

"What time are you going? Tomorrow, in the morning?"
She nodded her head.
"Ok, so you should wear layers so that you can remove them as the day goes on."
"The day?!" she asked, terrified.
"Well, I don't know how long of a hike you're going on..."
"Oh my God, I'll just die if it's longer than an hour or two."

I couldn't help but giggle. Sylvie was the beautiful girl in high school that offered her cheers and to keep score at games. She was the unofficial team manager of most sports teams and everyone (including me) resented the lack of work needed to maintain her beautiful figure. Although I would hand it to her, no one could navigate the streets of New York in heels as well as she could.

"You have leggings, right? Do you need leggings?"
"Yes! Look at me, I'm practically an advanced hiker!"
"Ok, do you own a sports bra?" I asked, raising my eyebrows.
She was thinking.
"Yes! Check!"
"Ok, so you'll want a performance t-shirt or tank-"
She immediately put her hand up and interrupted me.
"That's where I draw the line. I definitely don't have one of those."
I opened up a drawer and signaled for her to take her pick.
"Ok, this is perfect, thank you, I have a sweatshirt I can wear over this, that works, right?"
"Yes, you should bring a lightweight coat or vest, it will be cold in the morning," I said while handing her a vest, knowing she wouldn't have one.
"Perfect, what about my feet?"
I couldn't help but roll my eyes.
"You must have sneakers, Sylvie!"
"None of them are very comfortable, they are all super cute though. Would Converse work?"
"Nope, you're lucky we are the same size," I said, handing her my only pair of comfortable sneakers.
"Thank you so so much! You're the best sister ever! I promise I'll take good care of it all and return it asap!"

She was walking towards the door.

"You're going to want to bring some kind of backpack so that you can carry some water, and some snacks."

"Selena, we are not hiking Kilimanjaro, I'll be fine."

Before I could argue the door closed behind her. I giggled at the thought of her on a hiking trail tomorrow. I couldn't wait to hear the stories. But also, I couldn't believe Sylvie was going on this adventure with a man. She was like a vampire, she really only had any interactions with men at night...

Chapter Twenty-Two

SYLVIE

I asked Simon to text me when he was leaving so that I could meet him in the parking lot outside of our apartment building. He pulled up exactly on time in a black Jeep Wrangler. I was grateful that he had left the top on. When I opened the door I was smacked in the face with the delicious smells of fresh brewed coffee and cinnamon baked goods.

"Mmmm... It smells so good in here," I said as I took a seat and buckled up.

I was wearing the outfit that Selena and I had put together last night. I even grabbed a stylish leather fanny pack that I bought off the street in Soho last year and had yet to find the proper use for; I had thrown my ID, credit card and chapstick inside, a roll of mints and a mini compact.

He was smiling at me. I wasn't used to this. I don't know if I had ever spent a Saturday morning doing anything other than finding an awkward way to say goodbye to a man.

"I got three of my favorite types of muffins, take your pick. There is sugar and creamer for your coffee in the bag too. It couldn't be a better day out for a hike," he said as we pulled out onto the road.

"Yes, it's a perfect day for a hike."

I wondered if he could hear the fear in my voice.

The ride there was easy and comfortable. Aside from getting crumbs all over his front seat and doing my best to clean them up one by one, it went as well as I could have hoped. Conversation was so easy with him.

We pulled off the highway and onto a road marked *National State Park*. That sounded fancy and advanced. I had lived here my entire life and did not even know we had National Parks so close by. I thought they were all in Utah and Wyoming or something?

"You said you've been here before, right?"

"Umm, no, I actually haven't."

"I can show you the trail map when we get out, they have all different levels of hikes, we can do whatever one you are most comfortable with."

I nodded. How would I know from a map what type of trail we should do?

When we got out he grabbed a backpack and pulled out sunscreen and bug spray. He held them up offering them to me, but I didn't want to be sticky or smell bad, so I passed.

We walked over towards a large wooden sign that was covered with dashed, dotted and bolded lines that almost all met at a point at the top.

"So there is beginner, intermediate and advanced," he said, pointing to the map key.

I nodded, my palms were beginning to sweat. It was clear that we were at the base of a mountain, but like, where the hell were the trails? All I saw were trees.

"Which do you prefer?"

"Oh, well, you're more familiar with it here, you can pick."

"Well, Wesley's Walk is my favorite trail. The views are unreal. About three quarters up you can see the city's skyline all the way up to the summit."

"That sounds great."

Summit? Why did that word rhyme with plummet? Was this going to be dangerous? Should I have brought ropes, and like a carabiner or something? I wanted to call Selena and run this all by her. Although our friends would tell you I was the more adventurous of the two of us, I think they would also say that Selena was the more athletic twin.

Also, what if Simon was a serial killer? Was he planning to hide my dead body in the woods?

"Ok, the trail starts over here," he said, pointing to a small break in the woods.

About twenty steps in I began to notice that the trees were marked with red dots.

"So are we following the red dots?"

Simon looked at me and smiled.

"Yes, exactly. Are you doing ok?"

I smiled and as he turned to lead the way I began to look closer at his backpack. It was awfully big, and full. It looked heavy. What could he possibly be carrying in there? Was it big enough to hold a shovel? Maybe a collapsible one? I wonder if he would just hit me over the head with a rock, or if he was carrying a weapon in there.

My heavy breathing interrupted my thoughts. Shit, this was embarrassing.

"Doing ok back there Sylvie? We can take breaks whenever you need one!"

"All good!"

I looked up at the path ahead. All I saw were rocks.

"Oh, wow, was there like an avalanche or something? Should we turn around?"

Simon stopped and smiled at me.

"This is part of the trail, they are pretty easy to climb."

Climb? Was he out of his mind?

"Why don't you go first so that I can spot you?" he asked.

"That seems like a really bold way of asking if you could stare at my ass."

He was laughing now.

"Just take your time, you'll see that there are rocks that you can use as stairs and easy places to grab with your hands."

I got to the top with a moderate level of ease and looked back down, stunned that I had just scaled such death defying terrain. I took my phone out to take a picture. Selena wouldn't believe me unless she saw it for herself.

"Want a drink?" Simon asked when he joined me at the top.

I was looking around.

"I thought you said there were views of the city up here?"

"Oh, yea, that's up further, somewhere near the halfway mark."

I think he could see the surprise on my face.

"Did you think this was the top Sylvie? I mean, we can still see my car from here!"

"Oh, no, no, of course not."

He opened up his backpack and I quietly looked over his shoulder to see inside. No sign of a shovel or weapon. He handed me a water bottle.

Thank God. Water had never tasted so good.

We continued on and I could feel the sweat now dripping down my back. I removed my vest and started to take off my sweatshirt. Simon saw me and offered to throw them into his backpack. I was so grateful. We were fairly quiet at this point; I think the hike was taking its toll on Simon as well. We had passed a few fellow hikers but for the most part we were alone with the sounds of nature.

We reached a point where an active stream angrily ran in front of us. Simon pointed out the logs and rocks that we had to jump to in order to pass over it. He made it look so easy. Like a child playing hopscotch at recess.

It was my turn to follow and I was confused on whether to focus on the current rocks or the ones I had ahead of me. My mind was spinning with a list of internal questions. As I went to jump to the final rock my foot just barely missed the landing place and slid into the water. Simon jumped out to the rock and grabbed my arm, pulling me up to him in an embrace.

"Are you ok?" he asked, still holding me tight against him.

Our three feet were balanced together on the rock while I dangled my wet foot out to the side. I couldn't help but inhale him in.

"Yup, I'm good. Only thing hurt is my ego."

He laughed and held my hand as we both jumped to the other side of the water. I looked down at Selena's wet and dirty shoe. Looks like I would be replacing these.

"Do you want to stop? We're about thirty minutes away from where I planned to stop for lunch, but I totally understand if you're done," he said, concerned.

Lunch? He had lunch in that backpack? When did he have time to pull together a lunch? I didn't want to miss whatever he had planned.

"Nope, I'm good. Let's go," I said, pretending to have a spring in my step.

I could see how this leg of the hike would take thirty minutes with just Simon out here, but I was definitely slowing him down. About forty five minutes later there was a clearing in the trail and the views took my breath away. You could see Long Island Sound and views of the New York skyline. It was unbelievable. I couldn't believe how high up we were.

I looked to say something to Simon and when I turned he was spreading a blanket out on the clearing and pulling more things out of his backpack.

"Why don't you take your shoe off so that the sun can hit it a bit? I actually have a backup pair of socks that you can use!" he said, handing them to me.

"Are you like an Eagle Scout or something?"

"Nope, just a guy that has seen his fair share of accidents on the trails."

He got out the two water bottles and then pulled out a brown paper bag that said Giuseppis on the side.

"I stopped at the restaurant on my way home and put together two grinders for us. I hope that's ok."

"I can't believe how hungry I am, that sounds delicious."

We were sitting there, eating, relaxing, laughing and sharing stories when Simon turned to me and said.

"Sylvie, have you ever gone on a hike before?"

A giant smile lit up his handsome face.

I immediately started laughing, and so did he.

Needless to say, the climb back down was a little slower, and a lot more honest. When we got in the car I looked at my phone. I had two missed calls and three missed texts from Selena. All were basically well-being checks. I forgot I had sent her the rock climbing picture. Thank God we took a green trail, Annie's Annex, back down to the car. Turns out I'm more of a beginner hiker.

Yes, I'm good. All good. I texted back to her.

I couldn't believe the dash in Simon's Jeep said that it was nearly three. Every part of my body hurt. My thighs felt like they had their own pulse. I could provide the table salt for a fifty person dinner with the amount of dry sweat caked to my face. I had never felt less attractive.

Simon looked over at me, staring into my face. I suddenly felt so self conscious.

"That was really hard. I'm so sorry if that was too much. You're such a sport Sylvie, really."

"Ha, what makes you say that? Do I look like I need an EMT?"

"You look beautiful."

His face was so serious. The silence in the car was deafening.

His body now turned towards me, and he was bending down towards my face. When was the last time I kissed a man without a sip of alcohol in me? How pathetic was it that I had to ask that?

His hands reached out, holding both sides of my face and he gently brought his lips to mine. It was so gentle, so sweet, to the point that it felt like a tease. He sucked at my bottom lip before he pulled away, still holding my face in his hands.

"I had a great time," he said, now relaxing back into his seat.

I was speechless. I had no idea what to do in this situation.

"Me too," was all I could mumble out.

Chapter Twenty-Three

SELENA

Despite a fun night out on Friday I spent most of the weekend tying up loose ends and helping out my mom. After all, she helped me so much. I couldn't believe how quickly she had made all the alterations to the boys costumes for the play. We met at the shop on Saturday to finish the rest of the costumes together and I was relieved to tuck all seven into their respective garment bags.

I knew from my own experiences that I preferred to share information about my life with my mom when I was ready. And in the mood. Sylvie and I both tried to keep each other's business to ourselves and not overshare with mom, so it really killed me to spend the day with her and not mention the fact that Sylvie Cecile Rossi was currently on a hike. With a man.

When the photo came in as well as Sylvie's replies to my well-being checks, I had to turn my back to my mom so that she wouldn't see the smile on my face. I knew mom would ask questions and lying was not my specialty.

I didn't get the full scoop from Sylvie until Sunday and even then I could tell that she was trying to downplay her date. Despite needing me to run to the store for muscle relief cream and some band aids for her blisters, Sylvie was glowing when I stopped by with the delivery. She informed me that the mountain 'ate my sneaker,' and that she had already ordered a replacement pair.

It wasn't that Sylvie was incapable of a relationship, it was more that she never seemed interested in one. We had been polar opposites in that regard. I could count on one hand the men I had slept with, while Sylvie likely lost track years ago. I did find myself slut shaming her a bit when I first got home from college. I couldn't believe how much she didn't care. But after a few lectures and deeper thought I came to accept it, and now I think I even respected it.

She had never brought a man home to our family. She had never stopped by questioning what to wear for a date. If she did go on dates, which I knew she did, she never talked about it. She was basically a dude. Except an exceptionally beautiful one. I envied her in so many ways.

When I asked her when she would see this mystery man again (she had yet to provide a name) she completely backed out of the conversation and switched topics.

Typical Sylvie.

I decided to leave her be, and not push; so today I suggested that my mom and I meet after Sunday Mass was over and take Nonni to church, when it would be quiet. It sounded like she was agitated and very confused all week. I hoped that a field trip like this might help her get her bearings.

We met in the lobby at two, knowing that we had to have her home for dinner by four. When we used the code to get into the Memory Care Unit we were greeted by an older man that whistled at us as we walked in. My mom turned to look at me and smiled. This was my first time here and I would be lying if I didn't admit I was a bit nervous.

"Walter, I want you to meet my daughter, Selena," she said loudly.

I waved at him.

"Hubba Hubba," he yelled from across the room while raising his eyebrows.

"Just go with it," my mom whispered under her breath as we continued to walk down the hallway.

She stopped before we turned into Nonni's room.

"I met with the head nurse here and she shared with me that the key to decrease agitation and confusion, is to just go along with whatever they think is happening," whispered my mom.

"For example, Walter thinks he is a twenty nine year old minor league baseball player that steals the hearts of women everywhere. I guess the family did some digging and despite never knowing it, Walter really did play in the minors when he was younger."

"No way! So is Nonni that confused?"

"No, no. But one day we could show up and she could be. Just don't correct her, let her be whatever and whoever she wants, 'k?"

I nodded and squeezed her shoulder.

When we stepped inside we saw Nonni sitting in her reclining chair, the TV was on and she was staring off to the side of it. I looked down and saw the rosary beads that filled her hands. She had a framed photo of Papa on the tray table beside her, as if she had moved it to sit beside her.

When she saw us she looked up and her eyes smiled up at us.

"Hi mom. Selena and I were wondering if we could take you to church for a little while today?

She simply nodded and slowly got up. Mom and I helped her and without incident, we were in the car on our way. I sat in the backseat and observed Nonni as she looked out the window with a smile spilling across her beautifully aged face.

Mom and I sat together in the back of the church while Nonni went up to light a candle and pray for Papa. We were there for a good forty minutes before she returned, shuffling behind her metal walker, golf balls covering two of its legs to ease her gait. She made her way back to us and announced that she would like to stop at the shop.

On the way to church I had told Nonni about the costumes I had put together for the musical, but because she didn't respond, I didn't think she'd fully understood what I was telling her.

"Show me, *nipotina*."

My mom smiled so big at me that I swear I saw tears fill her eyes.

We arrived at the shop and walked into the shop together as we had countless times over the years. When we got inside Nonni stopped and looked around, admiring the shop.

I pulled the garment cart to the front, next to her walker, and began unzipping the bags.

When I got to the last bag, Nonni took a step back and put her hands up over her mouth.

"Cinderella?"

I nodded, smiling with pride.

"I always want to make a dress like this *nipotina*. You very good."

My mom had told me that the nursing staff mentioned that my grandmother was speaking a lot of Italian all week. She was struggling with her English more than usual.

Rather than say anything, I buried my face in her shoulder and hugged her for as long as she would let me.

It was the validation that I never knew I needed.

Chapter Twenty-Four

SYLVIE

When Simon dropped me off after our hike, every bone in my body wanted to invite him in for a drink. And a shower. But I resisted. Something about him made me want to do things differently. I gave him one last melting kiss in the parking lot and suggested that I plan the next date. He agreed, knowing payback for the hike was imminent.

We only had a few weeks left in the semester but between the classes and homework, it really made weeknights a challenge. We decided to get together again on Friday. I was sad to wait, but I was excited that we only had a week left of classes.

I racked my brain to come up with a plan that might take Simon out of his comfort zone but was coming up empty. I don't know if I had ever planned a date before. This was truly Selena's department. When I shot her a text asking for her suggestions I was grilled with a litany of questions about my 'mystery date.' All of which I refused to answer.

When she realized that I was holding firm, she listed suggestions one by one:

-Come to Parker Miller for opening night of Into the Woods (I promise I won't even talk to you).

-Have him over for dinner and show him how to make homemade fusilli. Little did she know that Simon likely already knew how to do this.

-Dinner and a movie.

-Dinner at Lola's (it's worth the hype).

As if I didn't know that...None of her suggestions worked for me. And then I had the perfect idea.

I sent Simon a text Thursday morning.

I'll pick you up at six, send your address please.

Do you have a record? What is your driving style? He asked with some laughing face emojis.

He did have a reason to be concerned, but I wouldn't let him know that. He was working late and suggested that I pick him up at the restaurant.

When I got there he was waiting outside for me, flowers in his hand. He had on khaki dress pants and a form-fitting blue and yellow gingham button up shirt with the sleeves rolled up just below his elbows. I looked at the flowers more closely and noticed that they were peonies. My favorite. Did I tell him that?

He got into my low-end SUV and took a look around, checking out the pile of odds and ends that filled the floor of my backseat.

"What?" I asked defensively.

"They say a car can tell you a lot about a person."

"Oh, is that right? And what is my car telling you?" I asked.

"That you are a very busy woman that has something in this car that can rescue you from almost every situation," he laughed. "Where are we going, anyway Miss Sylvie?"

"You will just have to wait," I said as I took off, heading towards the beach.

I took a left two blocks before the beach access road and pulled into the back of a small free-standing shop.

"What in the world?" he asked, looking around.

"You'll see," I said knowing that all his questions would be answered once we walked around to the front of the building.

"A nail salon?! Sylvie, you're taking me to get my nails done?"

"Don't knock it til you try it," I said.

We stepped inside and Jennie smiled at me pointing to the two pedicure stations with warm water and bubbles filling the tubs.

"I'm sorry Sylvie, but I'm not getting my nails painted, I am drawing a line here," he was still smiling but I could see the discomfort on his face.

"Relax, no polish. You are getting a spa pedicure that I promise is going to blow your mind and your feet will thank you after that horrendously challenging hike on Saturday."

I showed him how to get into the chair and his technician helped roll the sleeves of his pants up. I grabbed the remote attached to his chair, powering on the massage settings.

The technician pushed the side arm down next to him, locking him into his seat. She had a bin on wheels with different types of scrubs and lotions lined up for him. I could see his eyes darting around trying to decide what exactly he was supposed to do.

"Just lean back and enjoy," I said as I handed Jennie the nail sample of the color I had selected for my toes.

"I'll be right back," she said, winking at me.

When she returned, she held a tray with two glasses of champagne and a bottle beside it.

Simon's eyes went wide.

"Yes please," he said as he passed a glass to me and kept one for himself.

"Ok, I'm starting to get it," he said as the young woman pulled his right foot out and onto a towel, cleaning his toes individually and filing down his nails.

"Beautiful feet you got there," I laughed.

"Never in my life have I been more grateful to have relatively normal looking feet."

I laughed. We were there for about an hour. By the time we were done, the champagne was gone and we were both smiling and relaxed.

"What's next?" he asked. "I'm starving!"

"Me too! I have reservations at Lola's for seven thirty. It's two blocks from here."

"Amazing. I want you to have fun too. Why don't we agree to share an Uber home, that way you don't have to worry about driving after?" he asked after I insisted on paying for our pedicures.

"That's very presumptuous of you Mr. Simon."

"I meant, to share the same car but I will have him drop you off first, and then bring me home!" he said defensively.

I just laughed. I was one step ahead of him and had already thought of that too.

My phone beeped.

Holy shit. Connor Steer is at the play. Why is he so hot? I'm going out tomorrow night with Kara and Marley. Girls night. You In?

I laughed, not quite ready to respond to Selena.

I had to hand it to her, she was right. Lola's was a perfect date spot. Why did I think this was only a singles joint?

Simon and I shared a platter of oysters as an appetizer and we both ordered seafood dinners from their list of specials. Conversation was easy and I spent most of the meal staring at his lips. He had grabbed my hand multiple times during the pedicure and I could feel Jennie staring up at me. I had refused to make eye contact with her. But it felt good. His hands.

He had ordered a bottle of Chardonnay and made it clear that we were not arguing over the bill; he was paying. I wasn't exactly made of money, so I let him know that I came in peace.

By the time dinner was over, I was tipsy and happy and maybe a bit smitten. I didn't want the night to end, but I also thought about what Selena would do in this situation - which was a little bit gross, I mean, I didn't need to think about her with Simon. Ick. The point was that she wouldn't be inviting Simon back to her house after the second date.

"Should I order a car?" he asked as he signed the bill at the table.

"Want to walk the beach or something first?"

He looked up at me and smiled. I don't think he was quite ready to say goodbye either.

We removed our shoes and walked down the steps that led to the beach. I held his hand, noticing how empty the beach was. Aside from an older couple with their dog and a man with a humongous pair of headphones jogging along the water, we had the beach to ourselves. The sun was just barely out, minutes away from disappearing below the horizon.

"I worried you might be a serial killer on Saturday, but if you didn't kill me on the top of that desolate mountain, I feel like I'm probably safe on a quiet beach," I blurted out.

He laughed.

"I never thought of that. Shit. Sorry, I guess a hike on the first date can be slightly creepy."

I laughed.

"I'm teasing! Kind of!"

We remained hand in hand walking along the water where the water meets the sand. Enough to feel the cold, wet sand left behind, but not the water.

He stopped, tugging at my hand to stop with him. When our eyes met he turned and wrapped one of his hands around the nape of my neck, gently pulling me towards him. He kissed me, slowly and gently. We could have been there for hours or minutes, I wasn't sure.

Suddenly I was whacked in the back of the legs, falling further into Simon's arms. My knees were inches from the cold sand, I stayed bent over, stunned and unsure of what just happened.

"Oh my God, are you ok?" asked Simon.

I turned, honestly expecting to see one of Tonya Harding's hitmen, but instead I saw a ninety pound Labrador Retriever with a tennis ball in his mouth. As I began to stand up I looked past him and saw a man running in our direction.

"I am so sorry. I threw the ball and the wind just kind of took it. Are you ok?"

I was now fully upright and shaking out my legs to make sure nothing was displaced or broken.

"Yes, yes, totally fine. Just surprised me."

"Cmon Frankie, let's leave these nice people be," he said while grabbing the ball from his mouth and throwing it in the opposite direction.

Simon was smiling at me.

"You fell like you had been shot," he laughed.

"It felt like someone whacked me with a pipe in the back of the knees!"

We laughed and continued our walk. The sun had just about set and we both knew it was time to order a car.

The ride to my apartment was quiet, but the questions bouncing around my brain were loud. What was the right thing to do? I knew that I wanted to invite him up, but was it too soon? I didn't want to do this wrong.

I pulled out my phone, tilting it towards the door and texted Selena.

Quick, I need help.

What?! Are you ok?

Yes, totally fine. In cab on way home from date, with HIM. Do I invite him up? Is it too soon?

Oooooh, wow, you really are putting a lot of thought into this. It's a first. You must really like him.

Hurry the hell up, what would YOU do?

Is this your second date?

Yes

It's one date longer than you usually wait, Sylv. No offense... But I say do whatever feels right. I'm not convinced that 'my way' is right anymore...Also, don't forget about my text (up) about tomorrow night!

She was relentless about this girls night. Had she turned into a party girl?... Was she becoming a slut? A hussy?...No judgment of course.

It was Thursday, and I'm sure Simon has to work tomorrow too. We were now parked in front of my building.

"Sir, I'm just going to walk her to the door, please wait as I'll be right back," Simon said.

When we got to the main door of the building I turned to look at him and nearly bumped my head into his chest.

I looked up at him. He was smiling.

"I really want to invite you up...but-"

"I'll stop you there. I really want to come up, but we both have to work tomorrow, and I really want to go about this right," he said sweetly kissing the bridge of my nose. "Can I see you this weekend?" he asked while wrapping his arms around my waist and pulling me into him.

I nodded, and grabbed the top of his shirt pulling him towards me in a kiss that I was sure would leave me on the top of his mind.

Chapter Twenty-Five

SELENA

Opening night went off without any surprises. Tanya and Adam were right, Little Red Riding Hood's performance stole the show. She was incredible and worth the price of admission (and the sixty hours I spent making the costumes).

What did come as a surprise however was passing by Connor Steer in the hall during Intermission. I was making my way from my seat to the backstage Holding Room to check on all the costumes when we locked eyes for a brief moment. I'm sure he needed a minute to place who I was, but I recognized him the second I saw him.

I was rushing to get backstage so I did not have a chance to do more than wave hello to him. What was he even doing there? Did he have a kid in the play? Was he married? Divorced?

I spent the second half of the show peering around the audience in hopes of locating him, but it was hard to see past the two rows in front of me.

Tanya texted me after the show to let me know that all the costumes were in tip top shape and that I should not feel like I had to attend the remaining performances. I was thankful for this because even though the show was really good the first time, I thought it might lose its appeal from here.

With the weekend opening up I had taken the initiative and made plans for a ladies night on Saturday. Kara and Marley were in and said they would reach out to a few other single friends that might want to join us. I assumed that Sylvie would jump at the chance to go out with me so I was shocked when she did not respond to my text.

I was convinced that I was ready to truly put Jack behind me and maybe take a crack at my first true no-strings hookup? A one-night stand would be ideal, but I figured babysteps might be best, and begin with a drunken kiss that did not involve the exchange of any personal information or future plans.

What was up with Sylvie the past few weeks? I pulled my phone out to see if she had responded to my earlier text. Nothing. She had no problem texting me about her plans to seduce her date, but nothing about girls night.

She had begged me countless times to join them for a girls night, and although I occasionally went along for the first few hours to check the box, here I was, ready to be all in and she was ghosting me.

I was impatient.

Sylv, what's your plan? Are you in for tonight?

I saw the three dots pop up on our thread and then disappear. She was being so weird.

You're being weird.

Apparently I had no filter today. I put my phone down on the table and grabbed Queso's leash for his final walk of the day. We stepped outside and were greeted by a late afternoon sun. The fruit trees lining the apartment complex were blooming white miniature flowers. I could hear the bumblebees buzzing overhead. I added two extra blocks to our walk and by the time we returned home Queso looked up at me in disgust, tongue hanging out the side of his mouth.

As I entered my apartment I saw that I had two missed calls from Sylvie.

That's more like it.

She also sent a text.

You're awfully pushy. Yes, I'm coming. I probably won't stay late, but I'll pick you up at seven and we can head over together.

It's like she stole all my lines and all my moves. Was this some sort of punishment? Was she trying to show me what it was like to be around me?! I get it. Point made.

Kara lived downtown just around the corner from the strip of bars, self-proclaimed as the 'best' on a Saturday night; so we were meeting at her place at seven for a pre-bar cocktail. This seemed overly indulgent to me, but my goal was to keep my inner thoughts to myself tonight. I had to focus on the fact that it would save me some money and likely be the only time I'd actually get to catch up and talk to the girls.

Sylvie and I met downstairs to wait for our car. When I caught up to her it was like the scene in The Parent Trap where the twins had secretly switched homes. I looked like Pretty Woman pre-Richard Gere and Sylvie looked like she was going to midnight mass.

"Ummm, a turtleneck? On a Saturday? In late April?" I asked her.

"Well, I didn't realize you owned bootie shorts, so I guess we are both surprised," she quipped back.

I looked down at my shorts. I made them earlier in the week knowing that the air was warming up and they would look perfect with the new wedge heels I had picked up at the consignment shop downtown. I was pleased with them and refused to let Sylvie's comment take me down.

When we got to Kara's there was a large group, including Lily, Chloe and her friend Camden all gathered in the kitchen. Camden was mixing drinks and taking requests. As we stepped inside the room to join them, their eyes darted from Sylvie to me, and then back again.

"Enough already. Camden, can I have something, anything actually please."

After about ten seconds everyone had moved on and went back to their mini conversations.

Sylvie eventually leaned over and whispered in my ear, "You look great, I want a pair of those shorts."

When we arrived at the Tap Room it was nearly nine and the band had everyone out on the dance floor. We stopped at the bar to grab drinks and then shimmied out onto the dance floor. I noticed that Sylvie had ordered a club soda.

I bounced over to where she was with Marley and whispered into her ear.

"Club soda? Should I be worried that you're making me an aunt?"

She looked repulsed, then disgusted and then pretty angry.

"Nope Selena, I've seen you pretend this was a vodka tonic for most of your adult life, I'm not sure why my doing it is now a problem."

I shrugged and decided her negative energy was really bringing me down and wiggled my way back to where Kara and the rest of the girls were dancing.

As I moved I searched around the room, looking through the packs of single men. I was at a really hard age. It had become difficult to tell the difference between a twenty one year old and a twenty seven year old, so I decided to focus my energy on the men that were likely in their thirties. Which I quickly realized was a losing strategy since there were so few of them.

I was back at the bar when I locked eyes with a man that I guessed was in his twenties. He wore loose fitting jeans with a tight tee shirt and an unbuttoned flannel. His hairline sat a few inches back from where I had to believe it first began. He needed to shave, but I understood his vibe. He was rugged.

I continued dancing but made sure to look back at him a few more times. The final time he was gazing in my direction again and smiled at me, lifting up his drink in my direction. I smiled back and took a sip of my beer. When I looked back again he was motioning for me to come his way.

I leaned over towards Kara.

"I'll be right back."

She nodded, disinterested in my whereabouts. As I walked across the dance floor, a hand grabbed my shoulder. It made me jump.

When I turned I saw Sylvie.

"I'm heading out, are you going to be okay to get yourself home?"

"What time is it?"

"I don't know, like ten," she said, defensively.

What the hell, Sylvie was leaving at ten? On a Saturday?

I was too anxious to make a connection with the man waiting at the bar for me to argue.

"I'm fine, text me to let me know you got home ok."

She smiled clearly relieved by my lack of pushback.

I had just enough alcohol in me to add a little sass and go from my casual, timid walk to more of a strut. A fashion walk even, as I made my way across the dance floor in my fancy bootie shorts, eyes still locked with this mystery man.

As I got closer to him, only steps away, it became painfully clear that this man was a Mona Lisa. He was much more handsome from across the room.

"Hey there, I'm Paul," he said while extending his right hand. "Can I buy you a drink?"

I smiled back at him and he returned the smile, exposing a crooked grill of teeth. He had an extra tooth just observing from the roofdeck of his gums. *Jesus I was being an ass. What a superficial bitch.*

"I'm Selena. Any light beer is fine."

"I've never seen you here before," he said while leaning over to get the bartender's attention.

"Yeah, this isn't usually my scene."

The bartender was now talking with him, clearly they were friendly.

"I take it you come here a lot?"

"Yup, pretty much every weekend," he said with a proud smile.

I took a deep breath. Maybe I just needed another drink. I'm sure he's not actually revolting and slimy. I'm being hyper-judgemental and it

He interrupted my thought by handing me a beer.

"You know what, Paul, want to do a shot?" I asked while flagging down the bartender and ordering two lemon drop shots before he had a chance to respond.

When I looked back at him, another huge smile broke out across his face. *Oh my God, those teeth!*

"So Paul, what do you do for work?"

"Well, I'm in between jobs at the moment. I was a foreman but my boss was a total jackass."

Red flag, red flag, red flag Selena. Abort.

I looked across the room hoping that I could make eye contact with Kara or Marley and they could come save me. I kept my eyes wide, begging for them to understand my rescue cry. Instead, Kara looked over at me smiling wide, giving me a thumbs up from across the dance floor.

Our shots had arrived. I picked mine up and had already licked some sugar off the rim when Paul lifted his glass up for a *cheers*. I threw it down so fast that the lemon was in my mouth before I had time to shutter from the swig of vodka.

"Want to get out of here?" he immediately asked.

Oh dear. How did I get myself into this situation? But isn't this what I wanted? I mean, Kara was still across the way giving me a thumbs up. Was I being too picky?

I paused, faking a momentary lapse of deafness.

"Selena, want to get out of here?"

Shit, that was loud.

"Umm, well, I'm with my friends, so I really can't leave," and just as I was putting my beer bottle down on the bar I felt a huge, heavy body fall into the back of mine.

I was able to jump forward and quickly turned to see what the hell that was. The volume in the bar had drastically increased and then the band suddenly stopped playing. There were three younger guys in an absolute brawl. I was backing up when a bottle shattered right in front of my feet.

"Ouch!" I yelled expecting to turn and fall into the arms of Paul and his wild mouth of teeth.

I did a double take, turning and looking everywhere for this man that I had just shared a shot with AND been invited to leave with. He was nowhere to be found. Why was I even surprised?

"Miss, are you ok?" One of the bartenders had leaped over the bar and was standing in front of me while the bouncers ejected the three men from the bar despite their protests.

"Yes, I'm ok."

"You're bleeding," he said, pointing down at my feet.

I looked down and saw blood oozing down the front of my leg, a piece of glass wedged into my shin just above my ankle.

"Oh my God!" I yelled, panicking.

He crossed back over the bar again grabbing a roll of paper towels. He pulled some off and ran cold water over them.

"Here, you can pull it out with this," he said.

"I'm not pulling it out! Are you crazy? I need to get to a hospital. I can't even think about how many germs are burying themselves inside my leg as we speak."

"It doesn't look very deep, Miss. If you'd like I can take it out for you," he offered, apparently he was also a freaking doctor.

"Absolutely not, I would ask you to call an ambulance, but I know how expensive that is out of pocket," I started.

"Selena! Oh my God! Are you hurt? Are you okay?" Kara asked as she and the rest of our group began to surround me.

"No, I need to get to a hospital," I said, pointing down at my injury.

"Oh man, you just need to pull that glass out, I don't think it looks too bad," said Camden.

"I'm sorry Camden, I thought you were in advertising sales, I didn't realize you were an ER doc," I said.

He stood up straight, looking at me, as if to decide if I was serious or kidding. I was serious, (FYI).

"Can someone call an Uber? I need to get to Saint Matthews ASAP," I said watching the blood trail down my leg.

Chapter Twenty-Six

SYLVIE

Simon was picking me up today at ten for what he promised would not be a hike. We had squeezed in as many dates as we possibly could, but between school and our jobs, life was busy. He suggested I dress casually and be ready for anything. I had let myself sleep in until nine so I was scrambling a bit to be ready for the day.

I had not anticipated picking up Selena at Saint Matthews ER last night for what appeared to be a really bad boo boo. She was convinced that a glass shard was going to require stitches, a tetanus shot as well as a round of antibiotics, but the staff there assured her that antiseptic and a bandage was all that was needed. It was exhausting.

I waited for Simon's text to say that he was out front and sure enough one came in right at ten o'clock.

Out front! No rush.
Be right there.

When I got to his Jeep there was a beautiful bouquet of white daisies waiting for me on the passenger seat. They were rolled together in decorative tissue and then wrapped with a burlap string.

I smiled and leaned in to kiss him on the cheek.

"Thank you, they are so pretty."

"So are you. Buckle up," he said, turning over his left shoulder to search for oncoming traffic.

"What are we doing today?"

"Are you up for a visit to the City?" he asked.

"Always! But I would have dressed a little nicer," I said, staring down at my Birkenstocks and casual sundress.

"You are dressed perfectly, trust me."

"Well can you tell me what we're doing?"

"Fine," he said, smiling. "We are starting the day out by visiting Giueseppi's II in Greenwich Village. I need your help making some design decisions. And clearly we need some work on the name," he laughed.

"My help? Oh boy, what makes you think I'm qualified?"

"Beautiful people usually know their way around beautiful things..." he trailed off.

"This is so exciting! What types of decisions?"

"Well, I am having all of our booth seats upholstered, so I need help with fabric selection, lighting, linens and I think I want to do some wallpapers down the hall and into the bathrooms."

I squealed, I couldn't help myself. This truly sounded like so much fun. Selena would be so jealous. While I never got into the family's passion of creating, and appreciating high fashion, I sure did love design.

He smiled at me.

"Don't worry, we have brunch reservations too."

"Speaking directly to my heart," I said, laughing.

"What did you do last night?" he asked.

"Ugh, my twin is single for the first time, in what feels like forever and she dragged me out with her friends. I only lasted until ten, but in typical Selena fashion, her night ended in an unnecessary trip to the ER."

"Oh my God, is she okay?"

"Oh yes, totally fine. She literally had a cut," I laughed.

I pulled out my phone and shot her a text.

I hope you're feeling okay today. I'm out for the day but will be back later if you need anything.

Tell me you're with that man again, and so help me God if you don't start to spill...

I smiled deviously, putting my phone back in my bag without a response.

We pulled up to the train station in town and Simon stopped to grab an oversized backpack from his trunk.

I looked at him quizzically, wondering if there was a shovel in this bag.

"What? I have most of the samples with me! Don't worry, I will not be schlepping this around with us all day long."

"I wasn't worried about THAT!"

"Oh, no murder weapons inside either, promise."

We laughed and found seats on the train. Leave it to Simon to time it perfectly.

"Ahh, today is just what I needed," I said, looking out the window.

"Everything okay?"

"Yes, and no. I've been running numbers at my family's shop and I just don't see things getting better. As it is, my mom and I are grossly underpaying ourselves, I just don't see how we retain our clients if we start raising our prices," I trailed off.

"I'm sorry, that's such a mood killer, let's talk about something else. Anything else, actually," I added.

I turned back from the window, looking at Simon.

"Show me what's in that bag!"

He laughed.

"You'll have to wait until we get there Sylvie, no spoilers! But in all seriousness, that's a lot on your plate. I'm totally down for talking about it."

I shook my head, rejecting the opportunity, but grateful for the offer.

Chapter Twenty-Seven

SELENA

My 'Girls Gone Wild' night was a complete bust. I drank too much, met a total loser and convinced myself that I was going to need a leg amputated. Pretty much par for the course, but regardless it was still dreadfully disappointing.

I had absolutely zero interest in another night out tonight, but I did not want to spend my day home alone. I decided I would start the day by visiting Nonni. I knew my mom and dad would be there later, and Sylvie and I would have dinner with her on Monday, so why not give her extra time with family?

I swung by her favorite bakery and grabbed her a slice of tiramisu. When I opened the door to the Memory Care Unit I was met with organized chaos. The staff was cleaning up the tables from lunch and most of the residents were either back in their rooms or watching television at the end of the hall where episodes of The Lawrence Welk Show played on repeat. My eyes stopped when I spotted my grandmother still sitting at a table across the room. Who was she sitting with?

I took a few steps closer and a loud voice boomed.

"Sweetie pie! Are you coming to my game?"

It was Walter, yelling in my direction.

He whispered something to Nonni and she smiled.

I hadn't seen her smile in weeks.

"Hi Nonni," I said while pulling a chair out.

"Nonni?" she yelled and laughed, looking at Walter. "She thinks I'm old enough to be a grandmother?!"

Walter laughed.

A knot rose up to the top of my throat.

Our family had been forewarned and coached on how to handle these situations, but nothing can truly prepare a person to pretend to be a stranger to their loved one. Nothing. I swallowed my sadness down, roughly.

"What are you two up to?" I asked.

"Well, we're going to the game!" Walter yelled as if I was still across the room.

One of the nursing assistants came over and put her hand on my shoulder, and whispered into my ear.

"You are doing a really great job," and squeezed my shoulder.

Her words, or maybe just her touch immediately triggered tears. I refused to let them fall, and I also refused to confuse my Nonni by letting her see them.

I laid the bakery bag onto the table.

"I brought you two some dessert, I thought maybe you would want to share."

I pulled the tiramisu out and handed Nonni a plastic fork and then handed the fork I had intended for myself over to Walter.

"Mmmm, did you make?" Nonni asked.

I paused.

"Yes, yes I did."

"Mmmm this is delicious," yelled Walter.

"*Molto bene*," said Nonni.

I sat with Nonni and Walter for another ten minutes and then the nursing assistants came to the table and suggested that they go back to their rooms to rest. I didn't think that I could handle the pain of being one on one with a Nonni that didn't know who I was. So I said a casual goodbye to both of them.

When I was a few steps away, Nonni spoke up.

"Come back soon Selena."

I stopped, this time the tears coming back to my eyes and pouring down my cheeks.

"I will Nonni, I will see you on Monday."

Chapter Twenty-Eight

SYLVIE

The restaurant was absolutely beautiful; tucked in a brilliant corner of the Village, flanked by some of my favorite brunch spots. Although the space was previously a restaurant, Simon and his team were in the process of moving walls and opening the kitchen up to the main dining room. Arches were added to doorways and the floors had been swapped to a terracotta that was sure to incite the feeling of *Old Country*, as Papa would have called it.

We spent about two hours touring and working through all of his samples. I couldn't believe how much he truly wanted my opinion on so many decisions. We often agreed and when we didn't he would pause and listen to my reasoning. I wasn't even sure why I was standing so firmly behind some of my choices. But as I reminded him, he knew his Holly, CT restaurant better than anyone, but meals out in the city were kind of my specialty. I think I even had him convinced to add a specialty brunch to his weekend lineup.

My absolute favorite part was picking out wallpapers for the hallway and restrooms. It was going to be such a vibe.

He had just put all the samples back into his bag and left it in the back office, when he grabbed me by my hand and brought me behind the empty bar.

"So I have one final decision that I need your help with."

He opened up the wine fridge and pulled out three different bottles of bubbly drinks. He must have thought this through as there was a tray of champagne flutes on the counter of an otherwise empty bar.

"Oooh, this looks like the type of decision I'm really good at," I said flirtatiously.

He opened all three bottles and poured us each three generous glasses.

"Let's start with the rose," he said, raising his glass to mine.

By the time we finished all three samples it was clear that I was operating on an empty stomach.

"So you take me on a date and use me for free advice, what's in it for me?" I asked taking a step towards him.

My hands had conveniently found their way to his waist and before I knew it they were traveling up his midriff to his chest. This was a solid man. I could feel his strength through his shirt.

His breath was warm and smelled of the sweet prosecco that ended our tasting. He leaned forward, kissing me. I kissed him back and wondered how we might ever stop.

He pulled away, grabbing at my hand, and pulling me towards the back of the restaurant. I followed him into his office.

I was suddenly sure that the Board of Heath would not approve of what was about to take place in this beautiful restaurant.

Chapter Twenty-Nine

Selena

When I arrived at school on Thursday morning there was a note taped to my door from Principal DiMatino.

Please come to my office when you get in.

Hmmm. I was completely puzzled. He had never left me a note like this before.

We were halfway through the last quarter of school and the warm May air had the kids extra excited for the prospect of summer. Art class seemed to always be where most of the students relaxed, socialized and shared their excitement for summer break. Although I often had to threaten them with a visit to the principal's office, I had yet to actually send anyone this year.

I unlocked my classroom and put my lunch bag and purse in my closet. I made my way down the empty hall only seeing a few fellow teachers as they arrived for the day.

His door was open, but I knocked quietly to get his attention.

He looked up and smiled at me, his face quickly turning more serious.

Was it my mom? Nonni? Sylvie? Oh my God, did someone have a heart attack?

"Is everything okay, Mr. DiMatino?" I could hear the panic in my own voice.

"Selena, you know you can call me Will," he started. "I hate having conversations like this, and I especially hate having them with wonderful teachers like you," he stated.

I stared at him, nodding my head, willing him to hurry the hell up and tell me what this was all about. He gestured for me to take a seat.

"Cullen Summer," he started, looking up at me for a reaction.

His name alone brought back the frustrated emotions of the previous semester. Cullen was a self entitled problem child at Parker Miller. Rules did not appear to apply to him. He spent the entire third quarter doing absolutely nothing in my Ceramics class. He did not start or finish a single project. He instead sat on his phone playing games and watching videos and distracting the entire class. I had copied Mr. DiMatino on multiple emails that went home to his parents, alerting them to his behavior.

"Yes? What about Cullen?" I asked.

"Last night I had a meeting with Mr. and Mrs. Summer. They believe that the D you gave Cullen last quarter was unfairly assigned and are threatening to sue the school for defaming his character," he said, rolling his eyes.

"Defamation of character? He deserved an F!"

"I know. They are claiming that his transcript will now be an inaccurate representation of him when he goes to apply to colleges."

"My grade would be the only accurate representation of his character!" I said, raising my voice. "That entitled little..." I started to mumble quietly under my breath.

"This sadly is not our first experience with a family and teacher in this exact situation. We have only had one parent go so far as having their attorney send us a threatening letter. We have found that if the parents see us take action, they back way down."

Take action? He has to be kidding me. I looked down at my lap, my pointer finger now tracing the nails of my other hand, while my heart rate picked up.

"Selena, we are going to amend his grade to a C-"

"You have got to be kidding me," I said, cutting him off. "Look back at the emails, they are all in the portal. I copied you, I gave his parents at least one note every two weeks letting them know that his behavior and lack of work was unacceptable and that he was going to fail my class. They knew about the situation."

Hot tears stung the corners of my eyes. I blinked rapidly to keep them from trickling down my face.

"Yes, I pulled those up for our meeting last night but their response was that because they did not respond, it proves that they did not in fact see these notes. Look Selena, I know it's crap. It's total crap. And frankly, this is the worst part of working at a private school. Selena, you're going to have to take a leave of absence for the rest of the year. You will be paid, and I will make sure that the rest of the faculty are aware of the circumstances."

"A leave?" my voice was now loud enough that his secretary, Mrs. Henstead stood up and shut his door quietly.

"Unfortunately, Cullen's mother is a very powerful and influential woman, Selena. My hands are tied with this one. I spoke to the School Board and it really is our only option."

He paused, looking at me. I was standing now, tears streaming silently down my face.

He stood up behind his desk.

"What are the kids going to think? What is everyone going to say about me? This is absolutely humiliating, you have to understand that? You're going to let some bratty seventeen year old dictate the choices that you make as a principal?"

He said nothing, sadness spread across face but the kindness in his eyes reminded me that this was not his fault.

"A sub is on her way. If you could be so kind as to show her where your supplies are located and how to work the kiln. Your job will be waiting for you in the fall, Selena, and I will be in touch often. I know you can't right now, but I hope in another week or so, when you are less angry you can use this as an opportunity to extend your summer break a few weeks, maybe try something new?"

I looked up at his clock, knowing I only had twenty minutes before all the students arrived. I wanted to be out of here by then. I made my way over to the door and I paused, turning to look back at him. He knew this was unfair but his hands were tied. I knew he did not enjoy this part of his job. But still, I could not bring myself to say anything to relieve him of the guilt he undoubtedly felt.

Chapter Thirty

SYLVIE

Simon and I spent the next three weeks sneaking in every free moment we could together. I had yet to invite him to spend the night, I wasn't quite ready to risk bumping into Selena. I wanted him all for myself. But we had spent many nights at his apartment. As many nights as our schedules would allow at least. We even sat in separate rooms with our computers logged into evening class, texting each other funny lines and convening in the bedroom at the first sign of a break.

His apartment was on the other side of town, closer to *Giuseppi's* and close enough to *La Sarta* that I had started to pack an overnight bag in anticipation of my commute the next morning. Sleeping beside him had become my absolute favorite. Never had I met a man who I was excited to wake up beside, let alone move onto breakfast with, and occasionally lunch. Fine, dinner too. This was all new territory for me; it was terrifyingly beautiful.

His apartment reflected how little time he truly spent there. It had all the basics but absolutely none of the comforts of home. One night he took me shopping and asked me to help him pick out throw pillows and blankets and new bedding for his room. We got him new mugs and glasses, towels, some rugs and some fancy soaps and shampoos.

He wanted me to feel at home. He said he wanted to see my stamp everywhere he possibly could. He was undeniably sexy but I was unprepared for just how thoughtful a human being he was.

We did two separate trips to restaurant supply stores, continuing to outfit his new restaurant with chairs, flatware, and I even convinced him to include bowls of my favorite sugar scrub in the bathrooms. I felt instant pride anytime he showed me progress pictures of the space, knowing that my decisions were playing integral roles in the look and feel of what was sure to be the next successful spot in the Village.

Despite Selena's pleas and my mom's persistent questions, I had managed to keep Simon all to myself for two full months. So, on a Sunday night in late May while snuggled up on his couch watching NBA playoffs, Simon suggested we meet his brother and his wife out for dinner and I absolutely panicked.

"My brother Dom and his wife Katie want to meet you."

I paused, not quite sure how to respond.

"Oh, really?" was all that I could get out.

"Yeah, I really want you to meet them! They're fun! And I know they will love you," he said convincingly.

I smiled at him, unsure of what I was so afraid of. I had never brought someone home to meet my family. Aside from my senior prom date, and all of Holly knows how that turned out.

My family did not know my type. They did not know how I behaved around a man. But they definitely, definitely, have been waiting for this moment. Add in the fact that Simon was a second generation Italian (not from Sicily)...I knew that their reaction would be A LOT. I was in no rush to expose him to that.

His eyes darted up and down my face.

"If it's too soon Sylvie, we can wait."

"No, no, I'm excited to meet them," I said, forcing a smile onto my face. Truthfully I was excited to meet his family and learn more about him, it was just my family I wasn't quite ready for.

"Great, they'd like us to come for dinner next weekend if that works for you! They live in the City. I figured we could make a weekend out of it. I went ahead and booked us a night at the Hudson Hotel; I know you love a good brunch-- AND I reserved a table for the two of us the following morning at a Jazz brunch in Soho."

I raised my eyebrows.

"I know it's a bit presumptuous, and I have until Friday to cancel both reservations. So like I said, there is no pressure," he said, now pulling me onto his lap and burying his face into my neck.

"You really think of everything, don't you? Well there is no way I can say no to brunch. Twice. It's truly my weakness. I can't wait," I said, and meant it.

I remained on his lap, straddling him but pulled my body off of his chest. Staring down into his eyes, I leaned over, playfully kissing him. He tried pulling me in tighter but I pulled back against his gentle force.

"Playing hard to get are we?"

I got off his lap, standing up, one of my hands grabbing his. I turned myself away to hide the enormous smile that had taken over the entirety of my face. When was the last time I was this happy? Have I ever been this happy?

He followed my lead as we walked hand in hand into the bedroom.

Part Two

Chapter Thirty-One

CONNOR

I could not stop thinking about the beautiful sister from Elsie's shop. I kept coming up with excuses so I could stop by and pepper her family for intel, but realized how absolutely absurd that would be. What I did know was that she was a teacher, and hard at work for an upcoming theater production, so when my niece joined us for dinner last Sunday and shared her role as Little Red Riding Hood I felt like fate had interceded.

"Brooklyn, is there a Cinderella in your play?" I had asked her, certain that I had seen a Little Red Riding Hood costume in production that day at the shop.

She couldn't hide her shock that her uncle could be so well informed. I committed to attending opening night and she was absolutely thrilled.

"What was that all about?" Sarah had asked me.

"What? Can't an uncle, a godfather, be there to support his talented niece?' she let it go with a roll of her eyes.

I had left New York and moved to Holly four years ago when my sister Sarah lost her husband, Bryan, to pancreatic cancer. He was diagnosed and within six months we said goodbye to him. She was left a widow with a twelve, ten and six year old. With both of our parents deceased the guilt of living alone in the city was overwhelming. I was able to sublet my apartment in the Lower East Side and rent a beautiful apartment directly overlooking Holly's harbor. The commute was not always ideal, but knowing I could be there in a pinch for Sarah and the kids made it worth it.

One perk of living in the suburbs was definitely the bike trail access. My bike and I knew the path along the East River Greenway better than anyone. Despite the scenic views, the terrain made for a flat, easy bike ride. I was thrilled to invest in a mountain bike and hit the trails out here. My body took months to adjust to the hilly rides and I had learned the importance of trail maps and markers the hard way.

Sarah's kids were older now and although the grief would always be there, Sarah had adjusted to life without Bryan. Her kids were fairly responsible and more independent than most kids their age, and Sarah was even dating here and there. I could not believe that Brooklyn was sixteen and out there driving. Once she passed her driving test I surprised her (with Sarah's permission) with a used Honda. She was thrilled.

Sarah had been pushing for me to return to my life in the city, suggesting that my marital and paternal clocks were ticking. She wasn't wrong. I was ready to settle down. The dating scene had felt old for years, but most of the single women in Holly were either too young, or divorced, or too old. I rarely hung around the city long enough to have a social life there, but I was lonely and needed to find a better balance.

It likely was time for me to move back to my city apartment. My agreement with the current tenant was six months' notice to vacate. Nearly every morning I woke up thinking that I would send that email... However, I had yet to pull the trigger.

The play came and went without incident. Brooklyn was the star of the show and I'll forever be grateful that I showed up that night. Brooklyn shined. I did see the beautiful costume designer in the hall during intermission and I swear we locked eyes, but she took off in a rush before I had the chance to approach her.

I knew I was concocting a story between us that truly didn't exist, and I would never consider myself a romantic, but there was just something about her...and I found myself wanting to know more about her.

I had never been more hopeful that my firm would send some new clients my way that would result in new suits needing alterations. I had even put a bug in Jen's ear at the office suggesting I be in charge of all the fashion slash designer clients. She raised an eyebrow questioning me. All I could do was smile and walk away.

At the ripe age of thirty four I was joining the ranks of some of the more senior attorneys in the office. The only more senior staff were the partners, or the attorneys that knew they didn't have a shot at ever becoming one. I had started with the firm immediately after grad school and had been on the partner track ever since. Rumors swirled that I was up for partner in the next eighteen months but I refused to acknowledge them and change any of my work behaviors.

I've seen attorneys absolutely kill themselves trying to cross the finish line to partner. I refused to stay in the office just to outlast other associates. I preferred to bring my work home on the train and finish out my workday there, and it served me. My clients were happy and my Managing Partner was pleased with my work.

Having unintentionally carved out a niche sector of our client list had certainly had its advantages. A couple of the designers had even taken to sending me menswear for events that they expected I attend. Events weren't really my thing, but I was getting the hang of it. I had just about perfected my Irish Goodbye.

Summer was right around the corner and some of my new clients let me know that their events would nearly all relocate to the Hamptons. This made things about one hundred times more difficult. Holly was not an easy commute to Long Island. Although many thought the ferry service was a relaxing way to avoid traffic (which it was), it also meant operating on someone else's schedule. I was too old, too impatient and too tired to live that way on the weekends.

There was no possible way I could get my apartment back in time so I was investigating other options. The summer rental prices were ludicrous and I was too late to jump in on any house-shares.

Trevor Morrissey, a fifth year associate, had offered his couch to crash on when needed so it was a relief to know that regardless of what I came up with, there was a fallback plan. But much like being too old and impatient for the ferry, I was too goddamn old to be sleeping on someone's couch too.

The only way to avoid all of it was to come up with an excuse for missing most of the summer events.

Chapter Thirty-Two

SIMON

When I walked into my office in our Holly restaurant on Monday morning I knew that my grin would be a giveaway to the amazing day I had spent with Sylvie yesterday. I had never in my life met a woman like her. I was so excited to confirm our plans with Dom and Katie.

I had noticed her confidently walking into Giuseppi's on Thursday nights for years. Her beauty caught nearly every man's eye in the bar but the sexiest part about her was that she looked like she could have cared less about the attention. Her focus always appeared to be on having fun with her friends.

She even stepped out of my Jeep with full confidence at Mount Maple, despite never having hiked a day in her life. But as I've gotten to know her I've noticed that a lot of that confidence is a show. She was a beautifully confused woman, unsure of what she was supposed to be doing with her life. She was compelled to give up or at least put on hold her future for her family, and there was truly nothing sexier than that.

I was beginning to see what felt like a truly authentic version of Sylvie during our conversations about the new restaurant design. She was so confident and excited, and creative when making selections; in fact, she had some suggestions that had never even crossed my mind or my architect's mind. Ideas that I wanted to investigate. I was constantly thinking of what I could ask her for help with next. She had completely transformed my apartment in one trip to Target. She made me excited to come home, but that was mostly because she was often meeting me there.

Don't even get me started on my office in the Village. I would never view that room the same again.

She was an unbelievable woman.

KNOCK, KNOCK.

I looked up. My seventy-four year old father was standing in the doorway. He was shorter than me, stocky, with a classic comb over to hide his bald spot. His face had the lines of a full life but the youthfulness of his eyes reminded me he still had so much ahead of him. He had a stack of folders and he motioned with his head to meet him in the hall.

My father had semi-retired two years ago but his name was still associated with all aspects of the Holly restaurant. Retirement was a loose term since the portfolio of commercial properties that he had invested in over the years kept him busy day-to-day. He was the primary owner of all the commercial real estate (although my name had been added to the deeds) and aside from the new restaurant, no major decisions were made without running it by him.

"Mr. Brewer and Ms. Gorman are waiting for us in the break room."

I nodded. Don Brewer had been my dad's attorney since I was old enough to walk. Martha Gorman was our accountant's wife and now our commercial real estate agent.

The plan for today was to go through each of the properties we had identified to sell and put together letters for all our tenants. Martha had done the market research to come up with sales values for each property so that in the letter we could offer our tenants the opportunity to purchase the property before it hit the market.

Most of the tenant relationships were my dad's. He had 'retired' from the restaurant but stayed busy managing his properties. Some of his tenants had been with him since I was an infant and it was clear that some of these letters were hard for him to write.

He had worked with Martha to craft a specific letter for each tenant. He passed them around the table for review and had left a space for my signature next to his on each of them.

As I sifted through the letters, one of them caught my eye. I realized I had been holding my breath. I turned it over multiple times and my dad was now looking at me funny.

"What is it Simon?" he asked.

I didn't even know what to say. I looked down again, rereading the name the letter was addressed to: *Elsie Rossi.*

My heart rate had picked up and I felt completely helpless.

I held the letter up so that my dad could see it.

"This property," I started, still unsure of what I was even asking. "Do we really need to sell this one?"

"Why?"

I looked over at Don and Martha.

"Dad, can we step out for a minute?"

I could tell that I had made everyone in the room uncomfortable, I couldn't get out of there fast enough. We stepped out and my father shut the door behind us.

"What is going on?"

I cleared my throat, looking down at my shoes.

"I think I am dating Elsie's daughter," I responded, still looking down at my feet.

When I looked up my dad was staring at me, bewildered. Stunned, actually. I hadn't mentioned my dating life to my father in years. Mostly because it had been nonexistent. I would go out here and there but nothing even close to serious. He would bring it up from time to time, but when I let him know my focus was currently on the business, he didn't dare argue. He would occasionally remind me that it was possible to have both: a life and a successful business but we both knew how hard that was, so he didn't push.

"You're dating Selena?"

"No! I'm dating Sylvie!"

"Sylvie doesn't date," my dad said very matter of factly.

"Wait, you know Sylvie?"

"Of course I know Sylvie. I have known that family since before the twins were even born. This is the hardest letter for me Simon. I'm sorry that it is now difficult for you as well. But unfortunately we have to separate our feelings and our personal relationships for the business," he said.

I let out a long deep sigh and opened the door back up to the break room.

We were in there for hours, looking through letters and comparable commercial properties. We were going to give each tenant three weeks prior to putting their properties on the market. I had no idea what this would mean for Sylvie's family. Maybe this was the push she needed to move on with her career? Maybe she might eventually thank me.

But I knew that there was going to be a lot to come before the possibility of gratitude...

Part Three

Chapter Thirty-Three

SYLVIE

It had been two weeks since my mother received a letter from her landlord informing her that the building that housed *La Sarta Tailoring* was going on the market. He was kind enough to offer her the first right to buy the property which also held six apartment units above us and was hitting the market for a cool 1.4 million dollars. The letter was emotional, and the landlord hand delivered it himself on a Monday morning before I had arrived at work.

We had spent the last two weeks going over our options. There was no possible way we could afford to purchase the building, that was for sure. We had hired a local real estate agent to show us comparable commercial rental properties, and it was painfully obvious that we had the lowest rent in town. All these years, my family had been great tenants, but we had also been very well taken care of.

My mom was emotional when she called this morning to share that we were unable to purchase the property and that the holding company could move forward with marketing the property. I was sick over it. The decades of sweat and collective memories housed in this building were irreplaceable. I had stayed up late every night combing through all the options to keep *La Sarta* (and my mom) afloat.

My evening classes were over but I was so focused on supporting my mom and helping with Nonni that my relationship with Simon felt like it was put on ice. Over the weekend he seemed different. He was quiet and it felt like he had a wall up. I had so much of my own stuff going on that I didn't even bother to read into it.

He hadn't asked me a single question about myself, so I didn't bother sharing the pressing news with him. We talked about the weather and the news and other boring things that one might discuss on a first date that you did not plan on seeing ever again.

I wasn't sure how we had gone from two months of red hot intimacy, to such a lousy weekend, but I truly did not have time to care.

Selena had her own bag of issues which admittedly were tough on her ego and I could see her questioning her life choices. Luckily school was out so it no longer felt so odd that she wasn't working. She was meeting us at the shop for what felt like our five thousandth brainstorming session. I had stopped on the way to grab coffees and muffins, desperate to put a smile on my mother's face.

When I arrived, my mom and Selena were already there. They had brought chairs over to one of the workstations and my mom looked nervous.

"Who wants muffins?" I yelled as I used my hip to keep the front door open while I swung the tray of coffees into the shop.

"Sylvie! You didn't have to do that!" my mom said. She had stood up to help me carry everything over to the table. I was surprised when I looked over and saw my dad sitting next to Selena.

"Oh, hey dad! Not used to seeing you here! You can have my coffee," I said, bending down to give him a kiss on both of his cheeks.

"Sylvie, we want to talk to you," my dad said, motioning for me to sit down.

I looked over at Selena, asking her with my eyes *what was happening*.

"Okay..."

"Sylvie honey, we feel so terribly about the position that this unfortunate situation has put you in," my mom began, already fighting back tears.

I looked at my dad and Selena's face, trying to get a read on the room. They looked like they were at a funeral. Like my mom was just about to tell me someone died.

"Wait, I'm sorry to interrupt. I don't understand, why are you worried about me?!"

"Sylvie, you gave up everything to work here. You skipped college, and completely jumped into our family business," said Selena. "This must all be so overwhelming."

For the last two weeks Selena has been treating me differently. She had practically been tiptoeing around me, asking if I needed anything or wanted to talk. I was honestly so consumed with coming up with a plan to save my mom's business that I didn't have time to question her motives.

"ME?!" I asked again, this time my voice was louder.

"Sylvie, we have a plan to financially support you while you figure out a new path," my dad started. "Mom has friends that own similar shops and we have full confidence that we will be able to find you work, it is just going to take some time."

"Time out," I said, making the hand motion as if I was a basketball referee. "I'm fine. Let's not worry about me, let's focus on a plan for mom."

I looked over at my mom who was holding a handful of tissues, frequently wiping underneath her eyes.

"You must understand *bella*, I would have never brought you into this business if I thought there was a possibility of all of this," she motioned her hands around the room. "It was irresponsible of me to think Mr. Carlino would own the property forever, or that our rent would never increase."

"I'm sorry, Mr, who?"

My heart was now pounding out of my chest. Surely that was a popular name.

"Carlino. Joseph Carlino is a good man, honey. This is not his fault," my mom said, misunderstanding the question.

I shook my head, trying to bring my focus back to the conversation at hand.

"Mom, I'm worried about you. This is your business. I am not worried about me."

"I will be fine. Dad and I talked, we are going to transform the dining room into a work studio and hopefully I will keep most of my clients. I will no longer offer dry cleaning and I don't see how I will be able to afford to pay you," she said, her voice nearly a whisper by the end.

"Really?"

Why hadn't I thought of that. It was perfect, genius even.

"There are all sorts of jobs at the school that don't necessarily require a degree," added Selena.

"So mom, you are ok? You will be able to continue to do what you love?" I asked, relief washing over.

"Sylvie, yes, I'm fine! It's you I'm so worried about."

I slouched back in my chair. My smile grew bigger as I sat there thinking about everything we just discussed.

"What the hell Sylvie?" Selena asked.

I didn't even know what to say. I still did not want to hurt anyone's feelings, especially my moms, but I could have screamed with relief.

"I'm going to be just fine guys," I said calmly, with a twinge of excitement.

All three of them looked at each other, puzzled.

"Mr. Carlino said we can stay here rent free until the property has been purchased, so we are not in a rush," added my mom. "He also told me that you will be able to collect unemployment while you figure things out."

I nodded.

"I think this is a blessing in disguise."

"Huh?" asked Selena.

"I love working with you every day mom, but this isn't my dream. I just jumped in to help you and Nonni. I was never going to be able to work with machines and fabrics like you and Selena can. And if I'm being honest, I really don't have a desire to."

My mom looked shocked.

"Come to think of it, I have noticed how bored you look when I come in here," added Selena.

"Is that true, Sylvie?" I could see the hurt in Mom's eyes.

"Kind of mom," I was done with the lies and the secrets. "I've been taking online night classes. I just finished my third semester."

"What?!" asked Selena. "I knew you weren't taking Spin classes! Why wouldn't you tell us?"

Now Selena looked hurt.

"Because of this," I said pointing to my mom and back at her. "I knew you guys would take it personally and be sad that I didn't love what I was doing. I was so afraid I'd hurt you. But truth is, I want a degree. I don't know exactly what I'm meant to do with it. But I really like the business classes I've been taking."

Nobody said anything for what felt like an hour. The silence was uncomfortable.

"I'm really proud of you," said my father.

He was a quiet and humble man. I had seen him angry maybe four times in my life. He wasn't a man that needed attention, or credit, or much of anything. Well, food. Don't let him miss a meal. But he was such a quiet, and easygoing man. His words gave me goosebumps.

"I'm proud of you too," added Selena, grabbing my hand to squeeze it.

"I'm so sorry that you didn't feel like you could tell us," started my mom. "But I also understand why you didn't. It's because you're such an amazing daughter, Sylvie. You put us first and you second, and it's time for that to change." she added, standing up to give me a hug.

I'm not an emotional person. Compliments do not make me cry. I have no idea what was going on today. I had to imagine some dust had lodged in my eyes at that exact moment..

We all looked up as the front door's chimes clanged together. There was Connor Steer, at the front of the shop, visibly aware that he was interrupting something serious.

"Nothing to see here Connor, just your typical emotional family meeting on a Friday morning!" I yelled out, still wrapped in my moms arms.

"Wow, I'm so sorry to interrupt! I just wanted to drop off this new suit," he said, placing a garment bag down next to the register. "You've got my measurements, right?" he asked mom, clearly anxious to get out of here. Selena chose that moment to pop out from behind our dad.

Connor stood up straight. "Hey," he said directly to Selena, as if they were the only two in the room.

"Hey."

"I'm really sorry to interrupt," he repeated, standing there awkwardly.

"Selena, why don't you walk Connor out and let him know of the upcoming changes that he can expect," my mom said, winking at her.

Selena's eyes bugged out a bit, her head tilted to the side. A smile quickly washed over her face as she made her way out the door, with Connor following right behind her.

Chapter Thirty-Four

SELENA

I stepped out onto the street, anxious to get as far away from my family as possible. I motioned to a bench two businesses down so they were weren't able to spy on us from inside the shop.

"I'm so sorry about that. My family has a flair for the dramatic."
Connor laughed.
"What's going on? Things seemed tense in there."
"Understatement of the year. Long story short, our building is being sold. My mom has been panicking about this putting my sister out of work, and turns out Sylvie has been stressing over my mom being out of work. Surprise to us, Sylvie doesn't even want to work there anymore."

I stopped, suddenly realizing I was telling him way more than he needed to know.

"It never seemed like Sylvie was ever thrilled to be here, she usually looks pretty bored when I come in," he added.

"I'm sorry, I have no idea why I told you all of that. And yes, now that I think about it, I agree on Sylvie."

"Oh my God, selfishly, who is going to take my clothes and make me look like I belong anywhere near the fashion world?"

"Well, good news there! My mom is converting a room of her house into a tailoring shop, so she can still keep you fancy. You'll just have to drive two miles that way," I said pointing away from the harbor.

"Phew!" he laughed. "How have you been doing?"

I could feel my cheeks heating up thinking about our last encounter.

"Oh, I'm good. Over it. Sorry about that last time, you caught me-"

He interrupted.

"Your costumes were incredible, Selena."

He said my name again. I had never been more aware of my actual name. It stood out from any other thing that came out of his mouth. It felt so personal, and dare I say, romantic?

"Oh that's right! I'm sorry I couldn't stop to say hi to you that night. I was running backstage to check on how everything was holding up during the show. What were you doing there, anyways?"

"My niece, Brooklyn. She was Little Red Riding Hood," he said, beaming with pride.

"No way! She carried the entire show!"

"Right?! That is what I told my sister Sarah, too!" he laughed. "But seriously, you're so talented. I hope those art students of yours know that."

"Oh, you have no idea..."

He smiled down at me, our eyes locked. The distraction was just what I needed to stop from spewing out my disastrous professional situation.

"Well, I better get back to this very serious family meeting, which turns out isn't all that serious after all. Thankfully!"

We both stood up from the bench at the same time, awkwardly unsure of what to do next.

"So, think you're up for that date now?"

"Now?! Well, I-"

"Not now, now. Soon. Like, maybe this weekend? Could I have your number Selena?"

I laughed, of course he did not mean now, now.

NOT AS IT SEAMS

We exchanged numbers, not committing to any specific plans.

"I will shoot you a text tonight when I get home from work, we can make plans then. Does that work?'

I smiled, letting him know that it sounded just perfect.

Chapter Thirty-Five

SYLVIE

The weight I had been carrying for months, maybe years, had been lifted. I was so relieved and had never felt more free in my life. However, this did not diminish the fact that I had absolutely no plan, and my savings account was the equivalent of six months rent.

After our family meeting I had spent most of the day researching how to file for unemployment so that I had some help while I figured my life out. Afterwards, I sat at my desk, rehashing our conversation from earlier. There was one thing, one name that had stood out to me. I couldn't seem to let it go.

Mr. Carlino.

I pulled up my emails from Simon, to confirm the spelling.

There it was.

Simon Carlino.

"Mom, how do you spell Mr. Carlino's name?"

"Why *nipotima*?"

"I want to send him my own personal note, also remind me of his first name?" I lied.

"Joseph, C-A-R-L-I-N-O."

I nodded, immediately typing his name to my computer's search bar.

Apparently that was a popular name.

I then searched *Joseph Carlino, Giuseppi's, CT*. Within seconds a picture of Simon and an older, shorter, balding man appeared on my computer. I clicked on the first article. "Joseph Carlino, Holly, CT restaurateur and real estate developer," and I immediately recognized him.

It was official. This explained Simon's behavior over the last two weeks. He must have known when the letters were going out. In fact, he must have known this entire time. He'd also hid the fact that he knew me from Ladies Night...clearly this guy was great at keeping secrets. I was angry but mostly I was sad.

I couldn't remember the last time a man made me feel like this: so small and kind of stupid. I sat at my desk staring at my screen literally trying to think back to the last time... PROM! Prom night, our junior year. My date was Eddie Pullman. I wasn't even convinced that I liked the guy, but he was good looking and I was excited to be his date and he appeared excited to be my date. Next thing I knew he was grinding Antoinette Kuppo, the foreign exchange student on the dance floor. I was humiliated.

Okay, not really the same thing. But I was also quite angry then too, so kinda similar.

I decided to refocus my energy and pulled up my admissions packet that I had saved in a special folder in my inbox. I clicked on the 'Career Services' section and was brought to a long list of student services. I clicked on one and saw that there was a Career Counselor assigned to me. I decided to shoot him a note.

Dear Mr. Siver,

I am a student in UCONN's remote evening program. I have been juggling classes in addition to working at my family's business, but we recently found out that our family business is closing. Although change is hard, I am looking forward to starting out again and trying something new. However, without a full degree I feel very limited.

I was wondering if you ever work with students like me that are looking for jobs while still attending classes?

I am a hard worker and know that I will do well wherever I land!

Thank you in advance,
Sylvie Rossi, Student ID #459285

I spent the rest of the day sitting beside my mother while she worked and wrote out ideas for how to let our customers know of the upcoming changes. We worked on a sign for our front window as well as a note to mail out. We also came up with a game plan for how we'd deal with our current vendors and those that would continue working with my mom once her workshop was at home.

I could see this gave my mom a sense of relief. She looked so peaceful and relaxed; her body so perfectly molded into the chair as she sat in front of her sewing machine. She was humming and so was her machine!

When I got back to my desk I had already received a response from Mr. Siver. He let me know he was there to work with me on whatever I needed and sent some links for personality and interest tests that would match me up with jobs that would be 'fulfilling and profitable.'

The quizzes on Tiktok were my absolute favorite so I could not start these career ones fast enough. According to the personality test I should be out of the office and spending time with people. I would not be happy sitting in a cubicle or behind a computer all day. *No kidding!*

The irony of the career test results were not lost on me.

There was a long list of suggestions, but at the very top was 'Design.' The list included Interior Design, Furniture Design, Fashion Styling, and went on and on from there. It also suggested retail or front of house in Hospitality.

I sat back in my chair, scanning the list over and over again, hoping I would feel a strong gravitational pull to something.

I'm not an idiot. I know that testing high for these careers, and having an interest in them would not result in some fabulous job offer. But it was giving me hope. And to be honest, I needed hope.

All of it immediately brought me back to the multiple Sundays spent inside Simon's new restaurant. I absolutely loved helping him make choices. All the catalogs and samples were thrilling. I had even convinced him to move away from some of his initial plans. And he actually listened to me! Or did he just feel bad? Maybe he hadn't even ordered my suggestions, it was probably all a big ruse.

I was pissed.

"Mom, I'm going to head home."

She looked at the clock, it was four, an hour earlier than I usually leave.

"Of course honey, there is no reason for you to do full days here. In fact, get out of here!" she motioned to the door.

I grabbed my bag, gave her two kisses and was on my way.

I stepped out to a beautiful Friday afternoon.

I looked down at my phone. Nothing from Simon all day.

Screw this. Blocked.

Sleen, I saw that Lola's has a Happy Hour tonight, you game?

The three dots were on my screen within a second of sending the text.

Ummm...yea!

Be ready to leave at 5:00.

Yay! A sister night!

I couldn't help but smile, her predictable cheesiness was exactly what I needed.

I was home in five minutes and pulled together one of my favorite outfits. It was a slim fitting sleeveless blue mini dress that I accessorized with a patterned belt that lay loosely on my hips. I grabbed my favorite pair of oversized earrings and a pair of nude wedges. I hit my hair with the blow dryer to bring back some of its fullness and body. Before I had time to sit down and realize how tired I was, Selena was knocking on my front door.

Chapter Thirty-Six

SELENA

Something was up with Sylvie, I had no doubt. I'm sure the stress of the unknown was weighing on her, but my sister senses told me it had something to do with the mystery man that she had been dating. I knew better than to push her for information, so tonight I would go along for the ride and hope that she would come out with it when she was ready.

We got to Lola's early enough to secure an indoor table along the wall with raised windows overlooking the Harbor. The air was warm but the breeze made it the most perfect night. The Happy Hour menu was small but served its purpose. We both ordered a glass of sangria and a tray of oysters to share.

Sylvie was distracted. She was constantly looking over my shoulder, scoping out the crowd. Was she looking for someone? Was 'he' here?

"Who're you looking for Sylv?"

"What? I'm not looking for anyone... I'm just checking out the crowd. So far, it's a bunch of couples," she said followed by a frustrated groan.

Clue number one that Sylvie was clearly back on the prowl. I refused to grill her, I would be patient and wait for the sangria to work its magic.

Tonight's impromptu plans were the perfect distraction from anxiously awaiting a text from Connor. I pulled my phone out and looked one last time. It was only five, I'm sure he was still working and I refused to feel so desperate. For the first time in my life I was committed to not committing. I was going to play all the games that I had watched my friends and sister play for years. I was in charge.

By the time the waitress came back to take our third drink request I was over the sweetness of sangria. Happy Hour was just about ending and I had no idea where this night was going to take us. We both ordered a vodka tonic and decided to close out our dinner tab to go join the party out on the restaurant's patio. There was a two person band strumming guitars and singing, and the crowd was definitely feeling good.

"Let's hang out over here," Sylvie said, pointing to a corner that was conveniently tucked behind a large group of men, clearly fresh out of work.

I smiled and raised one eyebrow at Selena.

We pulled out our phones at the same time, a text from mom had come in.

Hi girls, don't panic, all is fine. I'm in the hospital with Nonni. She had a fall. They were concerned that she broke her hip, but x-rays are clean. She is very confused. She has been calling me Carol, but we are both fine and I should be bringing her home soon. XO

She added a few happy emojis to the end of her text.

"Carol?" Sylvie asked me. "Where does she even come up with this stuff? I miss Nonni."

"I know, do you think we should leave?"

"It doesn't sound like there's anything we can do, they will both be home and exhausted in a few hours. Nonni would want us to have a fun sister night," Sylvie added, pulling my hand to join her on the patio's dance floor.

It was around ten when I looked at my phone, feeling completely exhausted and ready to call it a night. Still no word from Connor, and I was ignoring the disappointment as best I could. Sylvie and I had talked to multiple groups of men throughout the night, but none of them interested me. I looked over and saw her cozily chatting up a man along the patio's railing. She was way too good for him.

I walked over and gently tugged at her arm, pulling her away.

"I'm ready to head out Sylvie."

"Ok, I think I'm going to stay," she said.

I rolled my eyes and looked over her shoulder at the man leaning against the bar.

"Sylvie, I don't know if it is the alcohol, or if you just truly have no idea how gorgeous you are..but that guy? He's a dog! Let's go!" I said, now forcefully grabbing her arm.

Luckily she didn't put up a fight.

I called an Uber and we sat on a bench along the side of the restaurant.

"What's going on with you Sylv? It seemed like things were going really well with the mystery man. It was the happiest I've seen you in a long time."

'Yeah, well let's just say he is full of more mystery than I am interested in."

I waited, hoping she would explain.

"He owns mom's building, the whole thing is gross."

A black Honda Accord pulled up with an illuminated Uber sign in the window. We confirmed that the license plate matched the app in my phone and both got into the back seat.

"What building?"

"The shop Sleen. His family is selling our building."

"Oh my God," I tried to catch the expression on Sylvie's face as she talked about it. As we passed under street lights I could see the pain, the hurt. I have never seen her like this.

"So you're sure he knew that was our family's?"

"Yes, he's been weird for like two weeks."

"Have you talked to him about it?"

"No, and I'm not going to," she said very matter of factly.

We were both drunk and tired, now was not the time to press.

As we got out of the car and entered our apartment building I looked down at my phone, checking for any missed texts from Connor. Nothing.

"I'm going to go see Nonni tomorrow if you want to come, no pressure," said Sylvie.

"Perfect, text me when you wake up."

Chapter Thirty-Seven

SYLVIE

I was woken by the buzzer for my apartment at nine. I quickly looked at my phone to see if it would provide any clues as to who it might be, but instead only saw a check in from Selena and a very long text from my mom.

I pushed the buzzer, "Hello?"

"Flower delivery for apartment 214."

I buzzed him in, "Come on up." Who in the hell was sending me flowers? I hadn't received flowers since what's his face, the bouncer at Noah's had sent me an arrangement with an invitation to dinner. Which I graciously ignored.

I threw a robe around me and answered the door before the young guy had a chance to knock.

A dozen roses. Real original. I placed them on my counter and grabbed the card as I made my way to my espresso machine.

Sylvie - You have to believe me. I had no idea that your family's business was part of my father's sell list until the letters went out! I didn't even know he owned it. I feel terrible and understand if you never want to speak to me again. However, I really really want to see you, talk to you, explain... please unblock me. I can tell you blocked me Sylvie. Simon

Wow. Ballsy. I had blocked Simon. I had to admit, I did not expect to hear from him, and I certainly didn't expect him to call me on it. I read through it three or four times. Each time a new emotion hit me in the gut, but mostly I missed him.

I opened up my contact list, my thumb hovering over his name. If I did unblock him, what the hell was I going to say? Don't worry about it, I'm sure tons of relationships are built off of one destroying another family's inherited business? I mean, look how great things turned out for Romeo and Juliet?

What was the point?

I left my contacts and moved back to my messages. Time to see what my mom was spewing at such an early hour. It was to both Selena and I.

Girls, I know you're planning to see Nonni this morning. Thank you. It means a great deal to me that she has other family members that love her like I do. Please don't mention what is happening with the shop. I think if she was lucid enough to understand it might send her over the edge. I hate to ask, but we might have to carry on and act like no changes have been made. She has a new friend named Walter. He's very loud, but he seems to make mom smile, so go with it! Thank you bellas. Ti amo tantissimo.

The next text in the group was from Selena.

That makes sense mom. Don't worry, we've got it. Walter is a funny man. Sylv, text me when you're ready to go!

Let's plan to leave at ten. I responded.

Selena drove; the car ride was suspiciously quiet.

"Ok, what's up?"

She looked over at me as if taken aback by my question.

"There's just a lot going on. This whole break from work thing. It's not just humiliating and infuriating, but it's also a bit eye opening. I think I'd be better off in a public school maybe... I mean, I guess there are some perks."

I paused, knowing that she would eventually continue.

"I haven't been checking my school email much, cause, well ...screw them. But I was bored this morning and checked it. A parent, who I've never heard of, her name is Lea Campbell, well, some high society woman, emailed me. She acted like I was supposed to know who she was. Apparently she had admired my costumes at the play and wanted to talk to me about creating something custom for her."

"What? Selena! Lea Campbell? She's huge! That's incredible!"

"Look, I know you're going through so much right now, and I know that mom is overwhelmed between Nonni and the shop," she trailed off, still not smiling.

Again, I sat in silence, giving her the space to continue.

"But my visits to the shop were often the highlights of my week. I love being an art teacher. Ok, fine, I sometimes like being an art teacher. This year, not so much...but knowing I had the shop to go to and mess around with scraps and use all the machines and forms. It just kind of rounded out my week, you know? And now I have this opportunity, that I would normally be absolutely freaking out over, but I'm not even sure where I would work and what equipment I would have to use."

I nodded. "That makes total sense Selena. I know going to mom's house won't be the same as the shop, but I know that mom will want you to still come by and help yourself to her equipment to create your amazing designs!"

"I know it's weird, but sometimes I would go at night or on the weekends when it was closed, and pretend I was like a designer or something. I know it's stupid-"

"That's not stupid Selena. How often do you use your kitchen table?"

She turned to look at me like I was crazy.

"I don't know...I mostly use it to fold my laundry."

"What if we put that in our storage unit in the basement and started to build out a little workshop in that nook of your apartment? Mom can't take all of the equipment and forms to her house, she already told me how she is going to have to downsize her operation."

A smile broke out across Selena's face. Her eyes remained on the road.

"You know what? That sounds kind of amazing!" she said as we pulled into The Springs of Holly Valley.

I ran over to her side of the car and gave her a squeeze as she got out of the car.

"I cannot wait to see this new space come to life, Selena! You've got this! It's going to be different - but it's going to be ok," I said assuringly.

Selena grabbed a mysterious bag from her trunk on our way in.

"Whatcha got?" I asked her.

"Just some stuff for Nonni and Walter," she smiled.

We spent the next forty five minutes listening to Walter repetitiously tell stories as we sat with him and Nonni at a dining table, sipping coffee. Nonni did not appear to know who we were but allowed us to give her a polite hug. Selena had created a bag for her to attach to the front of her walker. She used fabric from one of Nonni's old quilts, and for a second, it seemed like she recognized it. But as quickly as it came, the look was gone from her eyes.

Walter on the other hand greatly appreciated the extra large baseball tee shirts that Selena had picked up at a closeout sale for him at Big Al's. I did not understand what made her get them until Walter stood up to grab his cane and saw his belly busting out of the bottom of his much too small shirt. Selena noticed things that we all noticed, the only difference was, she generally did something about it. Selena was a doer. I wanted to be more like her.

On the ride home Selena had stopped for coffees and I could tell that she intentionally took the longer route home.

"So, do you think YOU'RE ready to talk about it?"

"Talk about what?" I asked, casually. And no, I did not want to talk about any of it if I was being honest.

"There's a lot to choose from Sylvie, night school, work plans, the man that clearly just hurt you."

I turned, looking out the window. That last part stung.

"You know, you don't need to hold it all in. You can trust me. Nothing will get back to mom."

I sighed, "I know."

"Why did you keep college a secret? I am so proud of you for going, mom is too. Why would you think you couldn't share that with us?" Selena asked, the hurt coming through in her voice.

"I just didn't want to upset mom. And I didn't know - I still don't know what exactly I'm trying to accomplish by going. I just wanted to have options. I've been bored stiff at the shop. For years. I'm not like you Selena, I have no desire to sew, I get no joy from making fabrics fit bodies-"

"I know Sylvie, I've noticed how unhappy you've been," she interrupted. "I'm so sorry that you felt like you couldn't talk about it with me. I mean, I complain about my job to you like every day!"

"I'm sorry too, I just feared it would send mom into a tailspin. Her plate is so full with Nonni and the shop. I didn't want to put you in the middle."

She grabbed my hand and squeezed it.

"I get it. Now onto the mystery man," she was looking over at me.

"I really don't want to get into it. We met in class. We had to do a project together. I thought he was a complete ass, but turns out he was ten times nicer and thirty times hotter in person," I said, quickly realizing I was saying too much.

Screw it.

"His family owns Guiseppi's..."

"Wait, like, *Ladies Night* Giuseppi's?" a smile creeped across Selena's face.

"What are the odds, right? He pretty much runs it now and is starting a second location in the city, but in order to afford it, his father is selling off a bunch of commercial properties in Holly."

"So did he know the whole time that he was about to sell our shop?"

"Well, I'm not entirely sure. I haven't talked to him about it."

"Sylvie! You have to give him a chance to explain, no? Has he reached out?"

"Yes, I mean, I'm guessing he has. He did send flowers this morning. But since I blocked his number it's hard to really know what's going on."

"Seriously? You have to talk to him! I mean, let's be honest...it seems like this whole situation is a blessing in disguise? I mean, it forces you out of a job you really didn't want, no?"

I hadn't let myself think of it that way. Although I knew deep down it was the truth, it COULD have been something that really destroyed my family.

"Like I said Selena, I really don't want to get into it..."

I was so grateful that the conversation would end no matter what as we had just pulled into Selena's assigned parking spot.

Chapter Thirty-Eight

SELENA

When I walked in I stopped in the doorway to my apartment, slowly looking around. Sylvie was right. If I got rid of the kitchen table I had two big walls and a decent area to work out of. I would have to find a way to tuck things away and keep it tidy or else it might drive me crazy to walk into a mess everyday, but there were bins and containers for that.

I took a seat on my couch and pulled out my phone. I had heard several text messages ping on the drive home.

My heart skipped a beat when I saw that two were from Connor Steer.

Selena! I am so sorry that I didn't reach out yesterday. I had an emergency come up at work late in the day - I was in the city until almost 9 and I thought it was rude to send you a note so late at night - but I also realize it was rude not to text when I said I would!

The second note looked like it arrived immediately after.

So anyways...sorry to ramble. I'd love to chat and make plans to get together. What does your evening look like tonight?

My insides were swirling and I was so grateful that Sylvie was not there to see the smile that was currently holding my face hostage.

What would Sylvie do? I paced back and forth in my small one bedroom apartment.

Hey Connor. No problem. I'm busy tonight, definitely another time.
I hit send.

Never in my life had I played hard to get. I regretted the text as soon as I sent it. I had absolutely zero plans for the night. Kara had invited me out but after the debacle with flying glass and my ER visit (it was healing beautifully thanks to my daily first aid routine) last time, I was really not interested in another girls night out.

He replied immediately.

No problem, tell me when is good for you, and I'll make it work.

Hmmm...I didn't want to wait until next weekend. I couldn't. What if he went out tonight and met someone? Fell madly in love and forgot I ever existed?!

Well my Sunday is wide open...

Perfect. Do you like the water? I was thinking I'd rent a boat down at the harbor, we could make a day of it?

My jaw dropped. When Jack and I had started dating he had positioned himself as a rugged adventurer. In fact part of his online profile read: "City man with an Upstate Heart. On the weekends you can find me bouncing from one outdoor adventure to the next." What a bunch of bullshit. I had told and hinted to Jack dozens of times that my dream date was to bring a picnic onto a boat rental and head out to Boater's Island. I had never actually been there, but I had seen plenty of pictures of friends with their boats moored, partying and relaxing for the afternoon.

Sounds perfect. I'll pack a picnic.

And so do you Connor. You sound absolutely goddamn perfect.

My phone started to ring. Oh my God, was it him? I looked at the screen, it was Tanya.

"Hey!"

"Enjoying your break Selena?"

"You know it!" I responded animatedly. "I was actually going to call you, I checked my school inbox this morning and I had an email from a

Lea Campbell. She said she loved my play costumes and asked if I would be interested in creating something custom for her!"

"Holy shit Selena! This is major! I hope you said hell yes!"

"Do you know who she is?"

"Do I know who she is?...Seriously? Don't you!"

"Umm, no," I responded. Should I be embarrassed to admit that? Sylvie had mentioned on our way to visit Nonni that she was 'huge' but that was the extent of it.

"She's the President of the Tribeca Film Festival and their production company! Her job is about as public as they come in New York! She's constantly being photographed!"

"Holy shit."

"Umm, yup."

I was now pulling out my laptop to Google her. She was stunning. She was a long, lean Black woman with legs for days. She had a size two figure and would be a dream to dress.

"So what's up?" I asked her.

"Well I remembered you saying you wanted to do some traveling this summer, possibly spend some time at the beach?" she asked.

I was immediately ashamed because I *had* said that. I *had* intended on doing that, but had done absolutely nothing about it. Between everything going on with Nonni and the shop, I had completely forgotten about my plans for a 'summer of me.'

"Yes?"

"Well one of the girls that I went in on a house share with has to leave in three weeks, her room will be available to you for July and half of August if you want it! Our house is adorable. It's in Easthampton, we can walk downtown AND the caterer that I'm working for needs extra hands, so you can even make some extra cash while you're here!" she exclaimed, excitedly.

"Wow, that's a really great offer. I have a lot going on at home at the moment. Can I think about it? When do you need an answer?" I was panicking. "Is the house clean? What are the other roommates like?"

"There are three of us here. My friend from college, Maura and her brother Tommy. Maura is a teacher too. Tommy works from home, no clue what he does, but I haven't seen much of him. House is super cute and clean. There are three bathrooms so we don't feel like we're on top of each other. Rent for the six weeks is forty five hundred. I don't have a ton of time to fill the spot, hate to rush you, but I probably need to know by tomorrow."

"Ok, no problem. Thank you so much, I'll give you a buzz tomorrow!"

I put my phone down and walked around my new 'design studio' that hugged the exterior of my living room. I brought my laptop back out and composed a reply to Lea Campbell.

Dear Ms. Campbell -

First, thank you so much for your kind words regarding the costumes. It was an absolute pleasure to work with the play's staff and performers. I truly enjoy design and creation and would be delighted for the opportunity to create something custom for you. Just let me know how you'd like to proceed. If you prefer to give me a call, I have included my phone number at the bottom of this note.

Best -

Selena Rossi

My first custom design assignment and a date with the sexiest man in Holly. All in the same weekend. It felt like life was making a drastic turn around.

My mom had put together a scrap basket in her new workspace so that I could stop by and grab it at any time. I decided to take a ride over there to see if she had anything that might inspire a new outfit for my date tomorrow with Connor.

Chapter Thirty-Nine

SYLVIE

The flowers were a constant reminder of the unfinished business I had with Simon. Was it unfinished? I would normally just forget about him, move on...leave him in my past. But there was something stopping me, something keeping just the smallest bit of door open.

Although my mom was moved out of the shop, I was going to keep it open for the next two weeks in case there were clients that had not received our phone calls, emails or postal letters. I was also putting together a simplified invoicing system for her. Her business was going to be much smaller without the dry cleaning component, but still, this part of the business was foreign to her and I knew there was going to be a definite learning curve.

I also needed to use my time alone to get my own shit together. I had secured my status with the unemployment office, the cushion of those biweekly payments was a welcomed relief, however, it was not nearly enough to relax fully.

It was Sunday and I was up before eight, looking in the Sunday papers for employment opportunities, scanning the UCONN career site and countless online classifieds. I was overwhelmed. I did not want to just take something to say I had a job. I did that once, and look where it got me. This time I needed to be thoughtful, methodical. I had updated my resume and found a way to gracefully suggest that my college diploma was just around the corner.

My phone dinged.

You up, buttercup?

Selena. I had learned years ago to silence my phone to avoid being woken up by my sister. She was such a morning person. It was annoying and refreshing all at the same time.

Believe it or not, yes I am.

My phone immediately began to ring.

"Yes, Selena..."

"Well good morning to you too, sister. I have a crazy thought I want to run by you."

"Okaaay..."

"You know my teacher friend, Tanya?"

It took me a minute but I did remember meeting her and Selena for drinks a few times over the years. She went on before I had a chance to answer.

"Well, she called me yesterday and offered me a room in a house share in the Hamptons!"

"That's amazing Selena!"

"Oh, well, yea, but I'm calling you because I think you should take it!"

"What?! Why me? You have the summer off, you're single, you're free Selena! You should go!"

"Yea, I've thought about it a lot. I really don't want to. It just doesn't seem like a situation where I would thrive. I did the roommate thing in college, it was fun, don't get me wrong, but I don't need to do it again. Summer is my time to design and create, and who knows what this high society woman wants from me, I'm honestly hoping it's something very time consuming! This is YOUR chance - go live outside of this town, share a house, do new things, meet new people Sylv! She even has a summer job waiting for you as a caterer! You deserve this!"

My heart rate had picked up. So many thoughts swirling around my head.

"This is really the nicest thing you've done for me, Sleen, it's an amazing offer. Which is why you should take it!"

"For the final time Sylvie, I do not want it. I already asked her if it was okay to offer it to you and she was thrilled by the idea of it. But she needs an answer by the end of the day. The sublet is for six weeks, beginning July first. Seems like a no brainer, but if you need time to think, take it. I told her I'd have an answer for her by seven, so don't think too hard!"

I hung up and immediately crawled back into my bed, staring up at the ceiling while I digested the decision ahead of me.

If I went, was I running away? Was I avoiding the problems at hand? I pulled up my calendar on my phone, classes did not resume until the first week of September. I had no job, no relationship, nothing stopping me from saying yes. This was my chance to get out of this town, meet new people, try new things... but with the comfort of knowing it was temporary.

I pulled out my phone.

I'm in. Send me Tanya's number so we can make plans. Thank you so much for sharing this with me - you're the best! I'm so excited!

Chapter Forty

SELENA

I had mixed emotions about Sylvie leaving for the summer. She has been my lifelong built-in friend. But I knew that she needed the opportunity way more than I did. She had to get out of here and see that there was a big huge world waiting for her.

Visiting my mom was a perfect distraction. And her scrap basket made it worth the trip. She had just hemmed a beautiful metallic dress and had about a foot of material chopped off and into her basket. I added it as a flowy panel to the back of an otherwise plain white tee shirt. It would dress up what was once a very basic outfit that I had planned for the boat trip. It wasn't quite warm enough for a bathing suit, and I was sure it would be cooler on the water, so I paired it with a short, but loose fitting pair of cut off jean shorts and a casual sandal. The white made my olive skin pop.

I spent an embarrassing amount of time at the grocery store trying to plan a romantic picnic to impress Connor. I had texted him to make sure he wasn't a vegetarian and that he didn't have any food allergies. He laughed and responded no. I created a charcuterie board with meats and cheeses and some fruit and vegetables. I also grabbed a couple of Italian cookies from my favorite bakery across town.

As I was leaving to meet him at the marina, I realized how ridiculous my food choice was. The board, which was wrapped in saran wrap, nearly took up my entire front seat. And I'm pretty sure that there wasn't a cooler in America that could comfortably hold the platter and keep it cold. Luckily, it was a fairly mild day or else we'd both likely end the date with listeria.

I threw my bag over my shoulder and made my way to the marina carrying the two foot by three foot sized platter with me. Connor was standing on the dock, beaming up at me. I had never seen him look so casual. He had on a pair of black and gray board shorts with a gray hooded sweatshirt. A pair of slide on shoes were on his sockless feet. High-end sunglasses kept me from seeing exactly where his eyes were focusing.

"Selena! Let me help you!" he said, reaching out to grab the board from me. "Wow! This is some spread!"

"Yea, I guess I didn't really think it all the way through," I said, trying to hide the red that had once again taken over my face. I felt like Baby from Dirty Dancing, uncomfortably showing up with a watermelon at the party...

"What are you talking about? I cannot wait to eat this."

His warm smile made me believe him.

"So, do we need to go to the office?" I said pointing to where the rental office was located at the end of the dock.

"Nope, it's all set. I already put our drinks on board," he said, pointing to a beautiful power boat. It was big, beautiful, probably twenty feet long, but not obnoxious. It was perfect for the two of us.

He got onto the boat first and put the platter down on the seat, quick to turn and put a hand out for me. I nearly bumped into him as I stepped on board while a small wave raised the boat up and then back down. I grabbed onto both of his biceps while I tried to regain my balance.

"Oh! Shoot! So sorry," I said now standing straight and holding onto the seat. Except I wasn't. I hope I have to grab onto him about a hundred more times today.

"Don't be sorry Selena. You are welcome to hold onto me as much as you want today," he said with a quick smile. Shit, had I said that out loud?

Out of another mouth that comment would have completely failed. It would have rubbed me the wrong way and been a complete turn off. However, I loved hearing it from Connor. I smiled back at him flirtatiously.

The boat was designed with a bench in the middle with a console and steering wheel in front of it. There was also a bench at the front as well as the back of the boat. Connor moved the ridiculous platter to the bench in the back and suggested we wait to unwrap it until we were anchored. He opened his cooler and offered me a drink. He had water and sodas and a bottle of champagne.

I grabbed a water and took a seat next to him on the center bench. He pulled out of the marina like a pro and within minutes we were out in the harbor, making our way to the open ocean.

"I take it you do this a lot?"

"Why do you say that?" he asked. "I used to do it a lot when my sister's kids were younger, but to be honest, I haven't done this in years."

I had assumed this was his go-to first date. Hearing that it was usually an activity reserved for family sent a pang of warmth all the way down to my toes.

We did our best to make small talk but it was hard to hear each other over the whipping wind.

"I am heading out to Boater's Island. Figure we can park and eat and talk better there. Does that sound ok?" he asked. He had cut back the throttle so that I could hear him.

It's like this man could read my mind. I nodded, smiling up at him. I could only imagine what my hair looked like at this point. The wind was throwing it in different directions and occasional splashes of water would sprinkle over us. I threw it up on top of my head in a messy bun.

It took about a half hour to get to the island. There were at least twenty boats tied up near the shore. Others were anchored a short distance from the beach. Connor had cut the engine and we floated as he looked out at the beach, clearly making a plan.

"I planned on pulling up to shore. The guy in the boat shop said it's a nice sandy beach so we shouldn't have any problems. But one of us will have to jump off to grab the rope."

"Oh, I'm happy to do that!" I said, suddenly looking down at my very white tee shirt. Connor was clearly thinking the same thing as me. Hopefully he wasn't also thinking that I was a total idiot.

"Here," he said, taking off his sweatshirt and handing it to me. "Throw this on, just in case."

I put it over my head, it was so warm from him, and his smells. It smelled of wood and spice and absolute deliciousness.

Connor idled the boat closer to the shore then cut the engine and lifted the propellers. Without asking any questions I looked over the side of the boat, estimating we were in one to two feet of water, and jumped.

Connor ran over to the side of the boat, unprepared for my dismount.

"Selena! There is a ladder on the other side! Are you ok?"

I had landed like a pro and managed to hold my tee and his sweatshirt up high enough, avoiding getting soaked. I smiled up at him.

"Whoops! Guess I took the hard way! I'm good! Throw me the rope!" I said as I walked towards the beach, slightly embarrassed.

I caught it on the first throw. Pretty impressive if I did say so myself. Connor was in the water and at my side within seconds. He grabbed the rope behind me and we pulled it onto the beach until it was firmly planted.

We used the ladder to climb back onto the boat. He pulled a collapsible table out from one of the storage compartments on the floor and poured us each a glass of champagne while I unwrapped my charcuterie board, which had only slightly jumbled in the ride. I had a few serving spoons and spreading knives in my bag that I put out with plates and silverware.

"You think of everything Selena, don't you?"

"You should talk!" I said, pointing to the plastic but still very trendy champagne flutes we were drinking out of.

He smiled. Conversation came easy. I tried to hide my expression when it came up that his residency in Holly was only temporary. Apparently I did not hide it well.

"I moved here four years ago to help my sister. I only expected to be here a year, and time just kind of got away from me. It's not like I'm moving across the country. I have an apartment in the City, so really not that far away, and who knows when I'll actually get back there," he said, convincing me that it was not a big deal.

"What about you, Selena Rossi?"

"What about me?"

"Are you planning to be a Holly lifer?"

The way he asked it wasn't insulting, but it was certainly a question I had surprisingly never asked myself. I truly didn't have an answer.

"For now it is what makes sense for me. I help my family a lot, but I am definitely not convinced that the Parker Miller School is where I want to start and finish my career. But don't tell your niece that!" I quickly added.

"Your secret is safe with me. How's your mom doing? And your sister? That is a lot of change."

"My mom is actually doing great. I think she's relieved. Sylvie is a little bit lost, but I think it is all for the best. She is actually renting a house with my friend in the Hamptons this summer. It will be good for her to try something new, you know?"

"You didn't want to go?" he asked.

"Where? The Hamptons?"

He nodded.

"It's beautiful there, but I think I've passed the point of being able to have roommates. And living in someone else's house just doesn't sound relaxing to me. I've been helping my mom a lot with my grandmother, and I just set up a little design studio in my apartment, so I have plenty to keep me busy."

"Did you design that shirt?" he asked, pointing to my tee.

"I would hardly call it designing, I literally just cut the back of a shirt and sewed a panel into it."

"Do you always sell yourself short, Selena Rossi?"

He was smiling, eyebrows raised.

I grabbed a handful of pecans and pretended that wasn't the sweetest compliment I had received in a long time.

"I have quite a few events out at the Hamptons this summer. I'm trying to get out of most of them, but that isn't an option for all. Maybe you could come with me? You could visit Sylvie too?"

Was this guy making plans with me for the summer? I smiled, but quickly changed the subject, reminding myself that I was absolutely not about to jump into another relationship. Even if it was with Connor Steer. This was my summer. I was not going to hand it over to another man.

I was going to be free, and a little bit wild. Although last time I tried to be wild I ended up in the hospital.

"Sorry, if that was a bit forward. I didn't mean to get ahead of myself," he said.

I smiled, waving him off. "All good."

I wanted to tell him it was something I would have said. Something I would have normally assumed as well. However, I was no longer my normal self.

"Did you bring a suit?" he asked, pointing his head towards the water.

"Umm, definitely not. It's freezing!" I said, pointing to the towel that was still draped around my legs after my brave jump off the boat, now realizing that I was still wearing his sweatshirt.

"So why is a handsome guy like you single, Connor?" I asked, my turn to be bold.

"Wow! Getting down to business, are we?" he paused, clearly deciding the best way to answer my question. "I kind of put my life on hold when I moved out here to help my sister. Every woman I've dated seriously grew frustrated with the time I was spending with Sarah and her family and was trying to get me to move or spend less time in Holly," he trailed off, "and that really wasn't an option for me at the time. They came first, and most women did not appreciate that," he said, looking out at the water. "But, like I said, I think the whole 'Uncle Connor' thing has run its course. The kids really don't need much from me and my sister is doing really well. I'll always be close to them, but I think they are ready for me to move along with my life, if that makes sense."

I nodded, letting him know that made perfect sense.

The rest of the trip was spent casually sipping champagne and getting to know each other. The more I learned about Connor, the more I liked him. I hated that. My plan to seduce him for a wild night and never see him or call him again felt like an impossible feat. I mean, the second part anyways...

We got back to the marina around three and it took us both a minute to lose our sea legs. We emptied our items off the boat and were met with the awkward decision of what to do next. Despite being covered in a mist of salt, my hair a rat nest of wind blown snarls, I wasn't ready to say goodbye to this man. But I had to play it cool.

"Well Selena, I would understand if you were ready to get home-"

"I'm not." Shit. That came out before I even had time to think about it. Oh my god, does he think I am desperate?

"Good," he said, warmly. I relaxed.

"There's a cafe on the other side of the marina? Want to go grab a cappuccino or something and we can figure out a plan from there?"

I smiled, nodding my head. It sounded perfect.

Chapter Forty-One

SYLVIE

I had two weeks to tie off my life in Holly before heading to the Hamptons, and it went by in an absolute blur.

I spent days training my mom on the accounting software and invoicing system that I set up for her on her home computer. It was exhausting, but I truly sympathized with her as technology had never been her strong suit.

I visited Nonni almost every single day. The guilt I felt for leaving my mom and sister to handle her health was overwhelming but they both assured me that six weeks would go by fast and they would manage just fine without me. I knew they were right, but each time I visited, she felt less and less like the Nonni I so deeply adored.

On my last visit I found her in her room, sitting in her recliner chair reading a book that was upside down. She did not have her usual reading glasses on and the room was so dimly lit that she couldn't have seen the words on the pages if she wanted to. When I walked further into her room so that she could see me, she looked up at me with no reaction.

"Are you here to pick up the slacks and dress?" Nonni had asked, looking around as if we were suddenly in the shop. She looked confused, scared even.

"Nonni, can I take you to the dining room? Would you like some coffee?"

I did my best to redirect her and the dining room had enough entertainment to keep us both occupied for the rest of our visit. While every part of me wanted to give her a big solid hug goodbye as I left, I knew better. It would only agitate her. Instead, I held her hand for an extra minute as I arranged her in front of the television in the multi-purpose room with the rest of the post-dinner crew. The television blared the sounds of a black and white game show.

Selena was taking care of Toffee while I was away and insisted that she would not let her be lonely. She promised to spend extended amounts of time with her when she visited to feed her and empty the litter box. If I was being honest, I wasn't terribly worried. Toffee wasn't much of a people person, and I admittedly wasn't home all that often anyways. I had left little post it notes around the apartment reminding Selena (who I knew needed no reminders) to do little things like sift through my mail and water my plants.

Selena planned to visit multiple times so I knew that my goodbyes, especially to her, were very temporary. However I did give her one last squeeze and felt my eyes fill up unexpectedly. I wasn't sure if it was the nerves or what, but the unfamiliar territory that lay ahead of me was overwhelming.

Before leaving I had to register for a few summer classes and was forced to open up my college inbox. There were eleven emails from Simon. Their subjects ranged from 'I'm so sorry,' to 'please read me,' to 'I miss you terribly.'

I was gutted, just seeing his name, let alone seeing his words. How quickly he had reminded me why I avoided relationships and putting my heart on the line. Before I was tempted to read any of them, I immediately moved them to the deleted folder of my mailbox. I had to move on and leave Simon in the past. I would never be able to trust someone that kept secrets like that. Getting out of town was going to be the best thing for me.

TWO WEEKS LATER

Two weeks 'out of town' and I go to bed most nights wondering about those emails. I have no doubt I could extract them from the dark underbelly of my inbox trash can, but I've held strong and left them untouched.

I've been an official Hamptons Summer Girl for fifteen days and counting. The transition has been shockingly hard. Despite having some friends, well, acquaintances, really, all of which stemmed from Holly, I am a stranger here, and so is everyone else. Also, I'm broke. The money that walked past me in the grocery store and on the street was intimidating and a bit overwhelming. I had never seen so many high end cars and handbags in one trip to the market.

My rental was at least more set in reality. Tanya was an absolute doll, but she sure did like to talk. Maura was cute and shy; an undeniable introvert. Tommy was a bit of a problem. He was flirtatious and annoyingly good looking. He was literally a walking red flag and I was pleased by my growth for recognizing it. Tanya said that until I had arrived, she had barely seen him. But suddenly he was cooking house dinners and inviting us out to join him and his friends. I politely declined most offers but he was persistent and resilient...so it truly felt like only a matter of time.

In the end I decided to take two summer classes because the faster I could get to my degree, the better. The classes were long but I absolutely loved their content. All the quizzes and research I had done panned out. I was enrolled in an Interior Design as well as an Industrial Design class, and had worked with my advisor on the possibility of changing majors. I finally felt like I was on a path towards happiness.

This time around I was taking intensives during the day, leaving my afternoons and evenings free for the beach and to help Tanya work the catering tent of some at the most glamorous summer parties I had ever even imagined.

When she mentioned the catering position over the phone I hesitated. Although I knew that I needed to make money, I also had to limit my earnings in order to continue my unemployment. It was all very confusing. But after the first week it became clear that this would not be a problem. Most of the money came in as cash and the tips were incredible.

I'm not sure what I expected, but I did not think I would see Christie Brinkley and Bethenny Frankel on my very first night of work. The list of celebrity sightings grew with every job and I found myself working in and out of houses that were nicer than anything I'd seen on the Real Housewives.

Imagine the most gorgeous gardens and landscaping, beautiful pools and patios, all hugged by the backdrop of Long Island Sound. There were hydrangeas for days and I had never seen the results of more plastic surgery in my life. We wore white button up shirts with baby blue bow ties and black aprons. These uniforms actually made us invisible to party goers (unless they wanted something of course).

The first few jobs I was tasked with included cleaning up dirty plates and glasses, alerting the kitchen staff (that worked out of everything from trucks to make shift kitchens in driveways) when we were low on crudite platters and if the clients looked happy. Definitely not glamorous. But as my third week on the job started, I moved up to walking around with passed hors d'oeuvres. Suddenly I was much more visible. Sought out even; who doesn't want the attention of the woman carrying a tray of hot food?

While walking with a tray of bacon wrapped water chestnuts and lamb lollipops I found myself on the outskirts of many introductions and conversations. Most or nearly all led to talk of money, career or plans for renovations of their Hamptons or city homes. Some were uptight, egocentric, and privileged, others seemed so down-to-earth, approachable and even kind.

I've always considered myself someone who did not need male attention, but as I stood here in this unattractive uniform going entirely unnoticed by this patio full of beautiful people, I began to realize that maybe I've taken it for granted. I stopped a few times, trying to make eye contact with a good looking man here or there but rarely was the eye contact returned, unless they wanted an appetizer.

Ugh, gross. Who was I right now?
I'm better than this.

My tray was officially empty so I turned to head back into the house to the kitchen. Rarely, but sometimes we were allowed to work out of the host's kitchen, and today I understood why. Did an actual chef live here?! There were three wall ovens, two dishwashers and I was convinced they didn't have a fridge, until I saw the chef open what I thought was a long cabinet. Two side by side refrigerators masked in white wooden cabinets.

The rooms that I could see were dripping with arrangements of pink and yellow flowers. Every piece of furniture was white, even the rugs. Did people actually use these rooms? Impossible to think that kids could live in a house like this.

"You're on champagne duty, Rossi," said Frank, the crabby catering manager that oversaw the kitchen and the waitstaff.

He handed me a bottle of champagne with a white cloth napkin wrapped around the neck.

"The glasses are out there on a table, go help Tanya fill them. Apparently someone wants to say a toast," he said, shaking his head in annoyance.

Was he slurring his words? Was Frank drunk? I had been warned by Tanya that Frank often snuck drinks but had yet to notice it.

I took the bottle from him and made my way to the patio doors before I had time to check him over. I stepped outside and scanned the patio for Tanya.

Her back was to me as she bent over a table covered in champagne flutes.

I lined up next to her and began slowly filling the glasses in the back row.

"I think Frank is drunk," I said, without even looking at her.

"Well that wouldn't be a surprise," said Tanya. "My first week on the job he let a wedding cake sit in the back of the catering truck. It melted so badly that he was using the cake cutter to re-spread the frosting. It was humiliating. By the time we brought it out it looked like a family of mice had found their dinner on it. But these people were drunk enough to think that the mess of a cake was a new-age work of art. I have no idea how he did it, but he convinced them it was beautiful!"

My bottle was now empty, but before I had time to walk back to the

NOT AS IT SEAMS

kitchen another server, Owen, was back and handing Tanya and I each a new bottle.

We were just about done when a beautiful couple walked over in our direction.

"That's Jude," whispered Tanya.

"Who?" I whispered back.

"You know, Jude Law," she said, pulling me backwards, away from the table and out of earshot.

I had a better view of the couple. I recognized him. He was older but intensely handsome, tanned with light brown hair. I wonder if he dyed it to be that color? She was much younger. Blonde, beautiful, all the things you'd expect of a woman at a movie star's side.

He raised a glass and clinked it with a spoon, drawing the attention of the crowd.

"Folks, thanks so much for coming out-"

"Shit, he's doing a toast and he's the only one with a glass of champagne. Quick, help me pass these out!" Tanya whispered, handing me a tray from the stand that sat by the hedges lining the patio. I followed her lead and began filling my tray with the champagne flutes.

Tanya squatted down a bit and next thing I knew she popped up with a tray of about fifteen glasses. I watched as she extended the tray to folks and they grabbed their glasses right off of it.

I slid my hand under the tray, trying to mimic her squat but standing up much slower than she did. I could feel the weight of the tray wasn't level so I did my best to adjust my hand underneath. To avoid drawing undue attention, I was repositioning the tray at the same time that I began walking over to the crowd of party guests who all appeared enthralled with whatever Jude Law was saying.

I bent my arm down a bit as a suggestion to those with empty hands to grab their flutes. The first few people seemed to understand and rather than passing them around, filling the hands of the crowd of people that they stood in, they took only one for themselves and then looked at me as if to say 'you're in the way.'

As I lifted my arm back up higher and moved to the right side of the group I was surprised to feel a dip in the pavers under my feet. Before I had a chance to adjust my footing I could feel my tray lifting in the direction of the older couple now standing in front of me. The man, who had to be about seventy five years old, saw the disaster coming and the fragile looking woman at his side.

As I felt myself losing control of the tray, my natural instincts kicked in and I swatted the tray straight down to avoid spilling champagne on any other party guests. Only problem was - this man's back was directly in line with my 'swat.'

There was no taking back the swat though, and when I opened my eyes I saw the chards of about thirteen champagne glasses sprinkled across the back of his seersucker jacket, trickling down his leg and pooling on the ground at our feet.

The party went absolutely silent, followed by quick gasps of breath.

"Oh my God sir, I am so so sorry. Are you okay?" I said as he turned around, looking to see what the hell just happened. "Are you hurt?"

He went to brush the glass off of his back, before the woman at his side grabbed his hand.

"You're covered in glass Mick, don't touch it." She was shaking her head.

Tanya had rushed over and Jude was no longer speaking. Everyone was just staring. My head was throbbing as heat packed in around my temple.

The man was taking off his jacket. I was relieved to see no signs of blood coming through the back of his white t-shirt. Frank had spawned out of the kitchen with a tray and was beginning to clean up.

"Sir, we will dry clean that jacket for you, we are so terribly sorry for our server's clumsiness."

"That is not necessary, I am fine," he said, turning and looking at me with a shockingly kind face. The noise of the party had picked back up and Jude was back at the microphone talking about saving some endangered mammal or something.

"Better than the red wine I spilled all over a guest when I waited tables," he said, now laughing a bit. The woman he was with shot a nasty look back at him, seemingly disappointed that he wasn't upset with me.

"I've never carried a single glass on a tray. I have no idea why I thought I was ready to carry fifteen," I joked.

"Sorry about that Sylv, you've been picking everything up so quickly that I honestly forgot you are new to this," said Tanya.

Frank had pushed the crowd to the other side of the patio so that we could clean up all the glass safely. As I knelt down, grabbing as many shiny pieces as I could, I waited with quiet dread for Frank to bend over and let me know I was fired.

I looked up to see where he was, only to see him with two open and very full bottles of champagne under his arm as he walked back towards the kitchen. It was then that I knew my job was safe and this was going to be an interesting summer…

Chapter Forty-Two

SELENA

Monday morning came quicker than necessary. Queso was pacing at my bedside, his nails clacking on the hardwood floor with urgency. My summer schedule meant no alarm clocks, but I could alway count on Queso to get me up before eight.

I swung my feet off the side of the bed, noting that it was 7:46 am. My head throbbed with reminders of the champagne, cheese and caffeinated beverages that I had last night. I smiled thinking about it.

Connor and I spent two hours gazing into each other's eyes over cappuccinos at Cafe Wave and finished the night with dinner at Lorenzo's next door. It was the longest first date I had ever been on. And even still, I did not want it to end. Connor was such a fascinating man, super successful but humble, and incredibly handsome but graciously unaware. I could tell he was holding back a bit; there was a slight reservation to him, but for once I think I was doing the same.

He had offered to drive me home, but instead he walked me to my car. When we got there I found myself looking at my feet, navigating the best way to handle the situation. According to my original plans for the night, I would have forcibly pushed him against the car and smashed my body into his with a kiss letting him know it was only the beginning. But I literally couldn't do it. I didn't want this to be one night.

So instead I shyly began my goodbyes, thanking him for a truly great day. The ball was in Connor's court. And he picked it right up...

"Today was really great Selena," he had whispered before gently leaning down and planting a kiss that didn't suggest we do anything but say goodbye. He held my mouth with his and we just stood there, heat bouncing from my body to his. When he stepped back he smiled at me. "I really look forward to seeing you again," he said and then opened my car door for me. I practically fell into my car, feeling drunk with adrenaline and sexual tension.

He texted me about fifteen minutes later to make sure I got home okay.

I couldn't let him consume me.

I needed a clear headspace. A creative palette.

I took Queso out and fed him and then got dressed for a run. I needed to sweat out any toxins that my body was harboring after my day of fun.

I had a meeting with Lea Campbell today and I wanted to impress her. I had no idea what to expect and if her request would be anything I was capable of, but I was excited to hear more. We were meeting at one at a building on the outskirts of town, closer to the city, in an area that I wasn't super familiar with. She only described it as her 'workspace.'

From there I planned to visit Nonni. Albeit a little earlier than usual, but without Sylvie the dinners were just too difficult. Some days it felt like I was sitting at a preschool classroom table, and other days it felt like I was eating in a morgue. We never knew who we were getting when we walked into the memory care unit. The anticipation gave me a stomach ache each time I visited, but I would not turn my back on Nonni. She was in there, deep down but somewhere.

By the time I ran, ate breakfast, showered and got ready it was nearly noon. I had bounced back and was feeling clear headed and excited to meet with Lea. I grabbed a sketch pad and threw it into a canvas tote with some colored pencils and even tossed in my sewing tape just in case

I was going to be taking Lea's measurements. A bit presumptuous, but best to be prepared.

The drive across town was slow. It was lunchtime and a lot of people were out and about. When I pulled up to the address it looked like a desolate warehouse. It was almost creepy. I drove all the way around the building, looking for signs of life. When I got to the rear right corner there was a glass portico with a few logos on it and a lined parking area with multiple cars. I breathed a sigh of relief. This looked legit.

I pulled Lea's text up to remind myself of the instructions to find her space. Once inside I was to go up the stairs to the second floor and enter the third door on the right. As I made it to her door I noticed the names of businesses I had never heard of on the first three doors. I stopped, looking at the logo etched in plastic attached to the wall beside her door. *Behind the Scenes.* Hmm.

I looked at my phone, I was a few minutes early, but not terribly so I opened the heavy aluminum door. Inside was a huge open space filled with beautiful, elaborate and unique items. The room was as big as three of my apartments put together, with high ceilings and just one wall blocked off the restrooms. Movie posters, set designs, costumes and props were everywhere.

A beautiful woman popped out from behind a form that held a flapper-style dress.

"Miss Rossi!" she said, smiling as she made her way to where I was standing.

She extended her right hand.

"I'm Lea Campbell, it is so nice to meet you. Thank you for driving out here!" she said.

Lea Campbell was everything Sylvie had said she was. She was a tall, thin woman with radiant, wavy black hair, enchanting brown eyes and a figure that would compliment any dress created. Her firm handshake let me know that she was more than all those things. She was strong and confident and likely commanded the attention of any room she stood in.

"No problem at all, it's nice to meet you as well."

She pointed to a bistro table set in a corner that had a coffee bar at its side. "Let's take a seat. Would you like a coffee? Or tea?"

"I'm fine, thank you."

"Well, I'm sure you're wondering why I have you here," she paused, looking for my reaction. I smiled and nodded.

"Selena, your costumes were absolutely exquisite. My daughter played the flute in the orchestra for the musical and I was completely taken by your creations. All of which I was told, were created by you - from scratch! You created the patterns? Is that right?"

I could feel myself blushing with pride.

"Yes, yes, that is correct."

"In addition to Maeve, my freshman, I have a six year old daughter, Lexie. Her dance company is looking for custom made costumes and I would like to hire you to make them. We would need six costumes. They want them to be lilac in color and have a whimsical butterfly feel. But you have total creative control," she said smiling at me. As if she had just given me my big break.

You had to be kidding me.

What a giant waste of time.

The six months ago version of me would have accepted this underwhelming opportunity. I would have ruined my summer trying to work with lycra and stressing over creating six of the exact same costume. But this was my summer.

"That is really so kind of you to think of me for this. However, I think your group would be deeply disappointed if I were to work on these. I have no experience with the lycra type fabrics that would be needed for a dance costume but even more than that, I am only comfortable creating one-off custom designs. I have no experience in replicating six of the same design."

"I think you could do it," she responded. You could tell that Lea Campbell was not used to being told no. "Also, we have not yet discussed payment."

"Oh, that is not-"

"I'd pay you five thousand dollars for the six costumes," she said before I had a chance to finish.

I was temporarily stunned. Like I had just been gut punched and was waiting for my breath to return. Five thousand dollars?! Why on Earth?

She must have seen the surprise in my face.

"I am working with a top name director and want her to bring her film to my festival next year. She will be attending this show and I am willing to use every tactic in my arsenal to grab her attention. If it means having the most beautiful, intricate dance costumes. That is what I'm willing to do."

"I've never made a bodysuit, let alone a leotard. And I have never made any items for a child. The sizes and proportions are completely out of my skill set. I just fear I will let you down."

What was I even saying? I was making it sound like I was considering it.

"Trust me, honey. I saw that Cinderella costume. If you can make that. You can literally make anything."

Showering me with compliments, this woman was a genius.

I just looked back at her, still unsure of how to get out of this. But also, did I want to get out of this? Five thousand dollars was a lot of money! Getting into Lea Campbell's inner circle could also be extremely valuable.

"I would need to think about it. When would you need them?"

"That's totally fine. I do not need them until the end of August. The show is actually in the Hamptons. That is where all the girls are for the summer so I would need to get you out there for measurements."

I nodded, doing my best to pretend it was totally normal to talk about a dance class stationed in the Hamptons for the summer.

"Okay, can I get back to you by Friday?"

"Please do," she said, following my lead as I got up from the table.

I looked around at her space.

"I know, it's a lot. I have so much memorabilia from all the events over the years that I lease this space as a bit of an office but mostly it's a storage space. My husband thinks I'm a hoarder. I prefer to say I'm a memory preserver," she said with a wink.

Chapter Forty-Three

SYLVIE

The week went by in a blur and tonight I had my first catering job since the champagne incident on Sunday. I came home and drank a bottle of cheap white wine and found myself pacing outside of Tommy's door looking for the ultimate distraction. The devil on my shoulder suggested I camp out with hopes of 'accidentally' bumping into him in the hall. To my great surprise, my thoughts turned to Simon the second he stepped out of his room.

The old Sylvie begged me to use those feelings as the motivation I needed to rip Tommy's clothes off. Instead I asked if he had a pen I could borrow, like a complete and utter idiot. He looked as confused as I felt. I walked back to my room squeezing the pen, like the lingering thoughts of Simon I wanted to push out of my mind. Refusing to think about what those feelings meant.

I threw myself into my school work for the week and was absolutely killing it in both classes. Tonight we were getting picked up by Lucas, who usually drove the catering truck, as we were not allowed to know the location of the private house event we were working. I thought this was absolutely ridiculous. Why did I care where this party was being thrown?

Tanya told me not to question it, but to instead think about what this could mean. This party was likely being thrown at a huge celebrity's home and it would be filled with equally famous guests, maybe even the President. I've been working on my facial reactions when bumping into celebrities with every job I worked.

Two weeks ago we saw Kelly Ripa and Mark Conseulos at a boutique in town. The second I saw them I molded myself into a clothing rack, trying to hide. Tanya and Maura were both very confused.

"What the hell are you doing?" Maura asked.

"I don't want them to see me!"

"Do you know them?" asked Tanya.

I looked up at her, considering her question. Slowly straightening up and stepping out of the clothing rack, I smoothed out my dress and dropped my sunglasses down so that I could stare at them unabashedly while fake fumbling through the sale rack.

"Would you like a picture?" asked Mark, basically calling me out.

So, yea...I'm smooth around celebrities.

Tanya and Maura both reminded me of this as we piled into the white unmarked box truck Lucas had pulled up on our crushed white stone driveway in.

I did my best to pay attention to all the twists and turns on the way so that if I needed to come back one day, I could. I was lost by the fifth or sixth turn. About thirty-five minutes later we arrived at a metal gate with an attendant.

Lucas pulled out a piece of paper from his pocket and showed it to the attendant. He looked at it and then called someone using a walkie talkie. The two gates separated opening to long white paver lined paths with beautiful landscaping trailing both sides of the windy driveway. When we reached the sprawling estate that sat directly on the water, we parked alongside six or seven similar looking trucks.

There were service workers everywhere. A band was setting up on a stage that looked like it had been built for the event. There was another group putting together what looked like a runway that went across the mammoth-sized pool. There were large, white, pristine tents scattered throughout the property. Men were on ladders hanging intricate floral chandeliers and twinkly lights. Another group was setting tables with more plates and forks than I had ever seen at one seat.

"You ok?" mouthed Tanya.

"Yea, sure," I said, trying to act casual and unimpressed. Like I pulled up to houses like this all the damn time.

"Over here," said Lucas pointing to a simple white tent hidden behind the pool house. Sides were drawn down on three sides so that party guests would not be able to see inside it. This was going to be the headquarters for our makeshift kitchen.

"Wow, this looks like a huge party. And a sit-down dinner? How in the hell are we going to do all of that? Just us?" I asked Tanya, now panicking a bit.

"Calm down, we are only in charge of the appetizers. Some overpriced celebrity chef and his team are handling the dinner." Apparently Frank had overheard me. "And don't worry, you don't even have to handle drinks tonight," he smirked. "They have another company here handling the bar and passing cocktails."

He shook his head laughing as he walked back towards the truck, pulling a vape pen out of his sleeve.

What an asshole.

Chapter Forty-Four

SELENA

I had yet to give Lea Campbell a response. I actually went to the store and picked up some fabrics to see if I was even capable of creating overpriced leotards. I had some fun with it and next thing I knew I had a sample for her. I had researched the average measurements of a six year old, but who knew how this would actually fit on a young girl. I didn't dare put it on my form. I wished so badly that I could talk it through with Nonni.

While at the fabric store I, of course, bought a bunch of new prints. I had three new dresses designed, created and ready for summer outings, hopefully with Connor Steer. We had been in touch throughout the week and even met up for a drink last night. He was buried with work and wasn't getting home until late but did everything short of begging to see me.

After my second visit of the week with Nonni I was feeling down and his text was just what I needed to pull me out of a dark mood. He chose a restaurant close to my apartment and came straight from his train to meet me there.

It was Thursday so the bar was packed but I was able to get us a table tucked away in a quiet corner. I ordered a glass of Sauvignon Blanc and watched for him at the front door. When he arrived I could see him excitedly searching the restaurant for me. When we eventually locked eyes his posture changed, he shot straight up, a huge smile taking over his face as he walked in my direction. He was in office attire but had loosened his tie and rolled up his sleeves. He ran his fingers through his hair as he took his final step towards me. He stopped, leaning down over me and leaned down to kiss me. The feeling of his skin against mine sent pin pokes up and down the back of my legs.

I took a quick swig of my wine as he went to take his seat. Conversation came easy and before we knew it we looked up and saw that the restaurant had cleared out.

"Any chance you're free tomorrow?"

"Like, tomorrow night?" Who was I kidding, I was free all damn day, but I was trying desperately to be evasive.

"Like midday tomorrow and into the night?" He scrunched his brows down and wrinkled up his nose, his glasses pushing up the bridge of his nose. "I realize that this is soon and this is forward, but it would technically be our third date-"

"Oh, I see! Is that why you squeezed in this late date tonight?" I laughed. "Checking the box on date number two?" I asked playfully.

"Maybe! Isabel Ferragamo is one of my clients," he paused, clearly looking to see if I knew who she was. As if I would maybe never have heard of the most talked about up and coming fashion designer.

"Mmmhmmm... go on!"

He smiled.

"Well, she is being honored at a Hamptons Magazine party and launching her new line at an estate in the Hamptons tomorrow and, well don't repeat this, but we are working on a big licensing deal and the potential buyers are going to be there. Her agents want me there in case any outside negotiations are discussed. And I thought it might be fun if you came with me. I mean, absolutely no pressure and-"

"I'd love to!" I said, unexpectedly grabbing onto his arm.

I pulled back and leaned in my chair. What in the actual?... What was I doing? I was not supposed to do this. I was supposed to leave him waiting. I was supposed to have slept with him already! Damnit!

"Do you want to come back to my place?" I asked, a little panic in my voice, pointing to the now completely empty dining room. My tongue trailed across my upper lip as I stared into his eyes, stopping at the corner when I felt something crusty. What was that? Oh my God. Was that bread? Did I have a piece of bread wedged in the corner of my lip?

I stood up before I had a chance to dive further into a pit of embarrassment.

Connor stood up, and pulled the chair out behind me.

"Selena, I would love nothing more than to come back to your place, however I have a ton of things to tie up at work so that I can play hookie with you tomorrow. I booked us on the noon ferry, so-"

"That was very presumptuous of you," grateful to talk about something other than the fact that I just got completely denied.

"A man can hope," he said, smiling at me.

He walked me to my car and as we stood to say our goodbyes he leaned into me, seemingly about to kiss me. This time he stopped, and kept his mouth about an inch away from mine.

"I am really looking forward to spending the day with you tomorrow Selena."

There he was saying my name again. I grabbed his shirt and pulled his mouth back to mine. I could have stayed there kissing this beautiful man until the sun came up.

He gave me one last kiss and then stepped away.

"What do I wear? Bring?"

I was stressed just thinking about it.

"I would be disappointed if you didn't wear a Selena original," he said smiling as he stepped away.

I had so many questions. Were we coming back tomorrow night? I should assume we were just going for the afternoon, right? I had to call Sylvie, she would know.

By the time I got back and settled in at my apartment it was after eleven. I couldn't remember Sylvie's class schedule, but thought twice about calling her so late. I would reach out to her in the morning.

Only problem was, I oddly overslept, and Queso didn't wake me up until after nine! I was shocked and a little bit perturbed. By the time I went through my summer morning routine with him it was nearly ten. I had reached out to my neighbor Vivian who also had a Chihuahua. We helped each other out with our dogs. She was retired and needed much less help than I did, but she never seemed to mind when I asked her to let Queso out a few times or to feed him. I added Toffee to her list too.

It was nearly ten thirty when I called Sylv, but no answer.

I need your advice - call me as soon as you're free! I texted her.

I had to carry on with my day as there was a chance she was locked in an online class and wouldn't get back to me until it was too late.

I picked up my phone and checked the weather app. It was going to be low eighties, sunny but breezy so the ferry ride was sure to be cool. I decided on one of the new dresses I had created this week. It had a beautiful hot pink and black pattern, as if someone with a brush of hot pink paint had painted hieroglyphics signs all over black fabric. The dress flowed down to my ankles but was cinched at my waist and was form fitting across my chest. The faux buttons that led down the bust were a sexy touch I thought, thinking of Connor. The spaghetti straps were just enough to tease him and I hoped he would be pushing them off my shoulders tonight.

I chose a straw woven crossbody bag that I found at a consignment shop in the Village on one of Sylvie's and my adventures. A black platform wedge completed the look and I loaded my neck and chest with layers of simple gold jewelry. I stopped to look at myself in the floor length mirror that hung on the back of my bedroom door. I turned and looked at my profile. *Not too shabby, Selena!* I felt like a million bucks!

I double checked my bag making sure that I had extra hand sanitizer, sunscreen and a full first aid kit, as well as every painkiller sold over the counter. I even threw in some ginger lollipops in case the ferry ride was rough.

Chapter Forty-Five

SYLVIE

It felt like we had been prepping for hours, but guests were finally beginning to arrive. Escalade limos were dropping guests off by the dozens. Each guest looked more glamorous and dazzling than the next. Apparently tonight was the Hamptons Magazine 'Must Watch List' party. The party was to celebrate this year's issue of 'New York's Rising Stars.' Selena would have loved it. They even had a floating catwalk across the pool so that some up and coming designer could launch a new collection.

"Can you make sure that the charcuterie table has all utensils of the and serving spoons and knives out Sylvie? You shouldn't drop anything doing that, right?"

Jesus Christ. How long was I going to have to hear about it?

I did not answer, in fact, I didn't even acknowledge Frank's existence. I grabbed some serving spoons, knives and a tray and walked away without saying a word. I could barely heard Frank's mumble "Someone's sensitive!"

It was my first time out on the party floor since guests had arrived.

There was a tent for the cocktail hour, which is where most of my work would take place, along with a dinner tent that was connected to another tent with a dance floor and stage set up for a band. All of the tents hugged the sides of the pool with the catwalk down the middle. There were eye-catching flower arrangements that alternated from high to low on the dinner tables, and pillars with arrangements on the top in the cocktail tent. The blues and peaches were flanked by lush greens and whites. I would say it all looked straight out of a magazine...but literally, this was all going straight INTO a magazine! The money on display was like nothing I had ever imagined.

"Excuse me miss, do you know if you'll have stuffed mushrooms?" asked an older gentleman.

"I'm honestly not sure but I can ask and get back to you."

He smiled and walked away. I wasn't sure if he truly wanted the mushrooms, or if that was his hint that he was ready to be served hot appetizers. I went back to the kitchen tent after adding the additional utensils to the most intricate charcuterie board ever seen on Pinterest.

"I think they're ready for us," I whispered to Tanya. "The rich people want food, and they want it now!" I giggled.

Tonight Frank insisted we serve with white cloth gloves (I felt ridiculous). We loaded up our silver trays and headed out to an even bigger crowd. I was immediately surrounded by beautiful people in stunning dresses and custom seersucker suits holding fancy cocktails. Their attire alone must have cost more than my summer's rent!

I was a bit surprised but mostly relieved by how kind everyone was. No one turned up their nose or treated me like I was the hired help (well, except for Frank, but Lord knows what his beverage of choice was tonight!). I had recognized a few faces from the morning news programs and I swear I saw New York's Mayor Valentine but otherwise, celebrity guests did not seem to be in attendance. I turned to restock my tray when I saw him from across the tent.

My heart began to thump so loud that I swear it might disrupt the party. I stepped to the side, hiding a bit behind a group of socializers to get a better look. Yup, there was no doubt about it. Simon Carlino was standing across the tent talking to a beautiful woman. They were sipping what looked like white wine and smiling, and likely having the best time ever. Simon was the kind of handsome that caught your eye. Stopped you in your tracks and made you question how you knew him, or how you could possibly get to know him... he was ridiculously hot.

And an asshole.

Simon was an asshole.

And I sure as hell did not want to be caught serving up appetizers to him and his new girlfriend. Hell, maybe she isn't new. Maybe they have been together this entire time.

I ducked behind a large group as Simon and his mystery woman turned and were headed my way. Lifting my empty tray up to the side of my face to shield it from Simon, I beelined for the kitchen tent and found myself begging Frank to let me be the tray loader tonight.

"I need you out there Sylvie, nobody wants to take appetizers from ugly men like Lucas and me!" said Frank.

I looked over at Lucas, who was definitely not ugly and he shrugged.

"Well, do you need someone to do dishes? I can be on the cleanup crew."

"Sylvie, you've been hired to pass around appetizers. I am sorry if I took my jokes too far. I have full confidence that you can handle it; you don't need to worry about dropping your tray!" mumbled Frank as he pulled a hit from his vape pen.

It was clear that this was a fight that I was not going to win.

"Take these salmon crackers out there, fill up your tray," said Frank.

I reached down to start filling my tray only to see that my hands were shaking. My heart rate suggested I was running on a very steep hill and so did the sweat dripping down my lower back. I pulled one of the extra silver trays up and used it as a mirror, quickly checking myself to be sure I didn't have food in my teeth or that my hair wasn't a mess. I felt ridiculous.

I slowly went back out to the tent which was now loaded shoulder to shoulder with guests. There was a chance that I wouldn't even see Simon again. There had to be five hundred people here.

I kept my head down and focused on emptying my tray as fast as humanly possible, and made it through three more rounds of passed hors d'oeuvres without seeing Simon. I was starting to breathe normally again. My heart rate had decelerated and I was having fleeting moments of completely forgetting that Simon was here with a beautiful woman.

"Sylvie!?"

"Sylvie!"

No. Way.

I turned and saw a hand hysterically motioning up and down in the crowd like a rock band fan on meth.

"Selena?" I yelled back, still not seeing her.

I looked down at my tray which was thankfully empty. I dropped it by my side and moved through the crowd in the direction of her voice.

We nearly bumped into each other, forcing me to take a step back and survey my obscenely beautiful twin sister.

"Oh my God Sylvie!!! I tried calling you this morning, but never in a million years did I think you would be working here today!" She leaned in and hugged me.

"I'm with Connor, play it cool," she whispered in my ear as if I was the spastic one.

We unlocked our bodies making room for Connor to push into our small bit of space.

"Hey Sylvie, what a coincidence, huh?!" he said.

"Selena! That dress! Holy shit! Did you make that!? You look stunning!"

She smiled and nodded, running her hands over the beautiful pattern.

"I told her she should walk down that runway!" Connor said, looking at her with pride.

I had so many questions. But I didn't have time to embarrass Selena.

"Where are you guys staying?"

"Oh, we're not, just here for the party and then-"

"Well I did book a room at a bed and breakfast down the street just in case we have too much fun and don't want to deal with the hassle of the ferry," Connor said nervously.

I just smiled, it was kind of fun to watch him squirm like this.

Selena's cheeks reddened and it was clear that she was excited at the potential overnight. She just smiled back at him.

I took that as my cue.

"Well, listen, I need to get back to work, I'm sure we'll bump into each other like five more times." I leaned over to Selena's shoulder and whispered in her ear.

"Not a word, but Simon is here. With a gorgeous woman of course," I added.

Selena frowned. "I'm so sorry Sylv, that is so lousy. What did he say?"

"Oh, I did not talk to him, and I don't plan to. This is a big enough party, he doesn't even need to know that I am here."

Before she had time to ask me any more questions I gave her a kiss on the cheek and turned to head back to the kitchen tent, catching stride with Tanya as she headed back too.

"Selena is here!"

"What?!"

"I know, I had no idea. She is here on a date! And he is hot!" I laughed even as I said it.

"Oh, and Simon is here too," I added.

"Like, Simon Simon?" she turned to look at my reaction. Last weekend we stayed out on the patio drinking way too much wine and told Tanya and Maura all about Simon. It had been weeks. I had no idea why I was still talking about this man.

It was infuriating.

Chapter Forty-Six

Selena

The ferry ride to the Hamptons was easier than I remembered. Connor and I found seats on the middle level next to a window that kept us out of the wind. Connor reacted the way I had hoped he would when he pulled up alongside my apartment building.

"Selena Rossi, please tell me that beautiful dress is an original," he got out of the car to greet me. He kissed my cheek and stopped, keeping his mouth next to my ear. "You are a knockout Selena."

It's like he knew what it did to me when he said my name. His lips so close to my ear, it made my knees tremble.

He had a car lined up and waiting for us at the ferry's port and suggested we stop at his favorite cafe in Southhampton to grab a beverage and freshen up. It was perfect. We ordered iced chai lattes and sat under an adorable yellow and white striped umbrella on the sidewalk. I was able to brush out my hair and touch up my makeup before we hopped back into the livery car.

"Where exactly are we going? Is it someone's home? A hotel?"

"It's a secret."

"What do you mean? How can it be a secret?"

"The invitation only gave directions to a parking lot. From there, limo services will be shuttling guests to the actual party location. All I know is that it is in Southampton and folks in the city are expecting it to be the party of the summer," said Connor.

"Fancy," I said, while offering Connor a squirt of my hand sanitizer.

"It's a thing for you, huh?" he asked, pointing to the bottle. "I don't mean that in a negative way. I just notice the way you're careful. Like I noticed you didn't touch any of the railings on the ferry today. You have great balance." He was smiling.

"Yeah, it's annoying, I know. My family lets me know it's a problem, often...but I think they will thank me one day."

"It's not a problem for me, but something that's good to know. I'm guessing that massage parlors and pedicures are a hard no for you," he said with a laugh.

"Hard no!" I emphasized. "Sylvie loves them. She is always begging me to do sister spa days, but I just can't do it. The germs in those foot tubs..." I shuddered at the thought.

He looked at me, smiling. He put his hand on my thigh. I looked up at the driver to see if he was watching us from the rearview mirror. The sunglasses made it hard to tell.

We both looked out the windows gasping at some of the luxurious homes that lined the streets, but really I was only thinking about the warm hand that was splayed across my upper thigh.

"The lot is right up here, Mr. Steer," the driver said, interrupting my dirty thoughts.

We pulled up beside a stretch Cadillac limousine.

"I'll shoot you a text when we are ready to meet you back here," said Connor as he handed the driver what looked like a very generous tip.

Connor got out first and hustled to meet me on the other side of the car, quickly grabbing my hand as I got out.

He shared with me that my mom had just finished tailoring the tan colored suit that he was wearing. He had purchased it directly from Isabel Ferragamo herself and he paired it with a slim fitting white button up shirt, with the top two buttons' left undone (swoon), an expensive looking belt and a pair of loafers that exposed the tops of his feet and ankles. He looked like he should be walking in this fashion show tonight.

I was relieved when we got in the limousine and were alone. The driver let us know we would only wait five minutes to see if anyone else needed a ride.

"So how do you feel about celebrities, Selena?"

I wasn't sure what he meant.

"What do you mean?" I asked, amused.

"Well, these parties tend to be pretty loaded with them. A real who's who…I didn't know if that would be exciting for you or annoying."

"If you're asking if I'm going to act like a starstruck idiot, then no, I promise I won't embarrass you. But I'm human, I do get a kick out of seeing celebrities!" I laughed, making sure he knew I was having fun with him.

"I think you are going to get a lot of people coming up to you to ask about that dress," he said while leaning his face closer to mine. "You really have no idea how beautiful you are, do you?" he whispered, melting me into the leather seats of the limo.

I made the first move and moved away from the seat, pulling myself closer to his mouth, sliding my tongue across his, hungrily kissing him. If it wasn't for the fear of the limo door opening at any moment, I would imagine our clothes would have been off by now.

Suddenly the partition between us and the driver rolled down.

"Looks like it's just you, we should be there in about ten minutes," he said and immediately began to roll the window back up.

Connor and I looked at each other and laughed.

"I would be perfectly happy never leaving this limo," Connor said, bending over to kiss me one more time.

"Same," I said. "But since we are getting out, I really need to pull myself together!"

We laughed as I fixed my hair, and smoothed out my dress. I was completely frazzled.

"Do my germs stress you out at all Selena?" Connor asked with a smile on his face. But I could tell it was an honest question.

I paused briefly, unsure of how to answer him. He was right, I normally did a bit more relationship history research with a man before shoving my tongue down his throat. But for some reason, with Connor, I was throwing most of my hang ups out the window.

"Not at all," I said and then gave him one final deep kiss before the limo started down a long windy crushed shell driveway.

We pulled up to the most unbelievable waterfront estate that I had ever seen in person. The lush property was lined with high end tents covered in twinkly lights and intricate flower displays. The place was glowing with the blues and pinks and peaches of the summer in the Hamptons. Even from a distance I could see the most exquisite patterns and dresses on thin, beautiful (rich) women walking about the property.

"Ready?"

He put his bent arm out for me.

"As I'll ever be."

As we walked the path to the party there were signs staked into the ground with a picture of each honoree, from high end real estate brokers and gourmet chefs to news reporters and fashion designers. So many names that I recognized. It was truly going to be a Who's who.

We were shuttled in the direction of the bar which was attached to a 'cocktail tent.' There was a charcuterie board that nearly went the length of the space. Guests walked around with picture-worthy cocktails garnished with tropical flowers and skewered fruits. A few people waved and nodded in Connor's direction, but so far we were on our own. I had to admit, I liked being on his arm.

We went to the bar where we bumped into some of Connor's colleagues. He introduced me as his 'special guest.' The man was constantly making me feel exactly that...special.

We turned to walk further into the tent when I noticed a familiar face in the waitstaff's penguin-like ensemble, and I did a double take.

"Sylvie?!"

She couldn't see me but was looking all around trying to figure out where my voice was coming from. I had been trying to reach her all day! Never had it crossed my mind that Sylvie might actually be here too!

We finally connected and I felt whole again. I was so happy to see her.

Except she didn't look as happy. Initially she did...but I could see the truth behind her eyes.

When she leaned in to share that Simon was here, it all made sense. It had been a few months, and she was still devastated by this guy. Before I had a chance to tell her she needed to talk to him...she was gone.

I asked Connor if we could go back to the walkway to look through the honoree photos, but he had a better solution and pulled a magazine insert that was piled on a table beside the bar. It had a list as well as photos of all the nominees, and sure enough, in the Restaurateur section, there was a photo of the mystery man himself, Simon Carlino.

Ok, Simon, you better hope we don't bump into each other tonight, I thought to myself. *You mess with Sylvie, and you mess with me.*

Connor gently nudged me and I looked up to see a beautiful woman headed our way.

"Darling," she said with an accent as she leaned in and kissed both sides of Connor's cheeks.

"Isabel, you look beautiful. I'd like to introduce you to my date, Selena Rossi."

She looked me up and down. Staring intently at my dress.

"Parli Italiano?" she asked, stepping back and admiring me some more.

I was taken aback.

"Un po, I speak it with my family, but I'm not fluent," I responded, smiling back at her.

"Your dress," she said, holding my arm to suggest I turn around. "Who made?"

Connor was beaming at me, he took a step away, just watching with a smile. I could tell he was charmed hearing my Italian. While my family liked to pretend that dating an Italian was the only option in our family, but that had been proven untrue over the years. When I asked Connor about his family's heritage last night, he was timid to answer. I didn't wince when he responded with a combination of Greek and English; just relieved that there was some Mediterranean in there.

"Umm, I did."

"You make?" she asked, clearly not believing me.

"Yes."

"Who taught you this?"

"Mia madre e mia nonna," I said, smiling confident that I said it correctly.

She returned the smile.

"You are very good."

"Isn't she?" added Connor. "Are you ready for your show Isabel?" he asked as she turned and looked at him.

She nodded. "You give me her number," she pointed to me while talking to Connor. "We meet soon," she added.

I nodded, unsure of what else to say. My face remained calm while my insides hosted the center ring of a three ring circus.

"If they are here, tell them we do business on weekdays, not weekends," Isabel said to Connor.

"Of course. I hope it's a great night for you."

She smiled at both of us and then walked away.

"Oh my, I can't breathe."

"Right?! I'm telling you Selena, I knew she was going to freak out over that dress. I mean, I know I'm a lawyer, so what do I know...but your talent is so clear that even I see it."

Before I could even think of who might be watching us or what such a public gesture could mea I was on my tip toes leaning into him for a kiss. He wrapped his arms around my waste and gave me a squeeze. I came back down onto my flat feet but somehow I did not feel the earth below them. Was I floating? Was this real life?

Chapter Forty-Seven

SYLVIE

The cocktail reception lasted two hours. The bar in the dining tent had now opened and we were on cleanup duty in the cocktail tent. It was the least glamorous part of the job. We did our best to clean dishes off site but we were stacking trays in metal wheel carts and wrapping them with commercial saran wrap so that nothing spilled in the truck when I heard a familiar voice outside the tent. Selena.

She was talking to Tanya.

"What are you doing over here Selena? Get back to the party," I said as I stepped away from our makeshift kitchen.

"He's not with a beautiful woman, Sylvie."

"What?! What are you talking about? Simon? How do you even-" I paused. "Are you trying to tell me you think she's ugly?"

"No, I mean he's alone, he is not with a beautiful woman. He's sitting at a table with a guy that looks a lot like him, and his date is beautiful. Maybe that was who he was talking to when you saw him," she said, like a goddamn detective.

I concealed my relief with more questions.

"How do you even know who he is?"

I waited. Of course she figured out who he was ...this was Selena I was dealing with.

"Sylvie, I'm just saying. He's out there, alone, he's one of the honorees tonight! Restaurateur to Watch!"

"Really?"

"Yes! You should talk to him,"

"I can't Selena," my voice had gone flat. "I'm working. Plus I do not want to ruin his big night, I'm sure I'm the last person he would like to speak to."

"You know, sometimes you're stubborn Sylvie," she said curtly, and turned on her heel and walked back towards the dinner tent. The band had picked up and was playing some yacht rock hits.

I was not stubborn, I was practical. Also, I was smart and protective of my own damn self. I refused to ever experience a moment like Selena did that day with Jack in the city. I was not going to let a man make a fool of me. Ever.

"She's got a point you know," said Tanya. "Sounds like he owes you an explanation, but you haven't given him the chance to give you one."

I had only known Tanya for a few weeks, and I had a few weeks left in this living situation, so it was probably untimely to tell her to *go screw*. So instead I did the safest thing and offered her a smile, and then marched back to the cocktail tent for more cleanup.

When I got to the tent, Frank looked like he had steam coming out of his ears. He was very passionately speaking with Lucas, his lips tight, trying his best not to raise his voice but between his red face and his flailing arms, he might as well have been yelling.

I kept my head down, cleaning up the charcuterie tables, trying to look uninterested while surreptitiously eavesdropping.

"You literally have one job."

"I know Frank, like I said, I have no idea how this could have happened. I am so sorry."

Oooh, this did not sound good.

Frank stormed away and went behind what had been the cocktail hour bar. He pulled out an open bottle of hard liquor that I did not recognize and went stomping back to the kitchen tent.

"Fuck," Lucas mumbled.

"What's going on? Are you okay?"

"Well, I'm about to get fired, so I'm not great Sylvie," he said flatly, rubbing his hands up and down his face. "I'm sorry, I didn't mean to snap."

I stood there waiting to see if he wanted to elaborate.

"I lost the keys to the box truck."

Yikes.

"Ooo, I'm sure you've gone over it a million times in your head, but any idea when you had them last?"

"Yes, I swear I set them down on one of the tables in our kitchen tent when we first set up, but I scoured the place and they are nowhere."

"Well, we still have a ton of cleanup to do, so there's plenty of time for them to turn up. Is the truck at least open so that we can load it?"

He nodded. Clearly he needed this job.

"They will turn up Lucas, I'm on the hunt for them."

He smiled and got back to what he was doing before Frank tore him a new one.

We had the truck packed up. We were ready to leave, except we had no way of getting home. Frank was so drunk that he had fallen asleep on a bench on the side of the driveway. It was better that way, he was a lot less angry when he was asleep. Prior to crashing he informed us that we were not allowed to use the party's limousine service, so it did not leave us with a lot of options since the driveway had to have been a mile long and no cars were allowed down it. Lucas had called a friend to come pick him up and he was planning to walk into town and meet his friend there. He very graciously offered Tanya and me a ride, but we decided to pass.

We had both taken off our bow ties and gloves and Tanya was now removing her apron.

"Dinner is over, everyone is either dancing or too drunk to notice us. I say we go and enjoy ourselves a fancy Hamptons party. Selena will get us home!"

"We can't walk up there dressed in this!" I pointed to our black skirts and white button down tops."

Tanya untucked her top and unbuttoned a few buttons at the top and bottom of her shirt then tied the bottom into a knot.

"You've got a tank under there, it's a hot night, just lose the button up," she said forcefully, starting to unbutton it for me.

"You're crazy, no way."

"This is your summer to be free, Sylvie. It's your summer to have some fun. Adulthood is waiting for you on the other side. I promise, you will wish you wore the tank and had the fun..."

She was right.

She was absolutely right.

I took my shirt and threw it into the back of the truck. My white tank dipped as low as the ones I liked to wear to ladies night at Giuseppi's. I should feel comfortable in this. If only I didn't have to worry about bumping into Simon.

"First things first," Tanya said as we began walking over towards the party. "To the bar, Sylvie!"

I smiled at her as she grabbed my hand.

Chapter Forty-Eight

SELENA

We were assigned table number seven for dinner and I was dying to see who would sit with us for the meal. We walked into the most breathtaking tent, though it didn't feel like a tent, it felt like a ballroom with no walls. The ceiling was draped with intricate flower arrangements and lights that pooled into chandeliers and the tablescapes would likely be the featured picture in the next issue of the magazine.

Looking out past the tent all you could see was the coastline and water. I felt so lucky to be there, but horribly out of place. I squeezed Connor's hand for reassurance as we made our way to our table. Most of the guests were already seated at table seven. Connor introduced me to three of the older partners from his firm that were accompanied by their wives as well as Isabel Ferragamo's publicist, Stacey. She looked grateful for my arrival.

"Please tell me who you are wearing," she said before I had even put my napkin on my lap. She was eyeing me up and down. "I saw you across the tent and have been dying to know."

"Well, actually, I made it," I said quietly.

"What?" she responded about ten decibels higher than she started.

She was looking at Connor, impressed.

"What about the pattern? Where'd you get the pattern?"

"Well, I designed it myself, the fabric is from a boutique shop in Connecticut."

"You have to meet Isabel, she is going to go crazy for this," she said, now touching the fabric that drooped down over my legs.

"She already told me to give her Selena's number," added Connor.

We chatted a lot about fashion and design and I found myself having a great time at the table. The food came out in waves from the attached kitchen tent. Although it looked and smelled beautiful, there was just something about food coming out of a tent like that, it gave me pause, and the germaphobe in me insisted I would end the night with food poisoning.

Connor must have noticed my hesitation.

"What's up? Is everything ok? I can ask for something else for you? I noticed you didn't eat anything during the cocktail hour either, everything ok?" he whispered as he squeezed my hand, genuinely concerned.

"Yeah, I just am not sure if I'm interested in food poisoning tonight," I said very matter of factly.

Connor laughed. I wasn't sure why, I was not joking.

"Selena, I promise you that the chef's hosting this dinner are some of the finest in the country, if they poisoned this crowd their careers would be over."

"I promise to never take you anywhere that serves shady food Selena," he again whispered, this time his face was practically touching the side of mine.

"You guys are adorable! How long have you been together?" interrupted Stacey.

"Oh, we're not to-"

"Only a few weeks," Connor cut me off and smiled over at me. "We're new."

I took a deep breath and cut into the filet mignon. It was cooked beautifully and the aroma alone made it impossible to ignore.

We are new... he said 'we.'

I was not going to let my guard down and throw myself into

another relationship, but he was making it really hard to stick to my guns.

When we were finished with dinner the bar area filled with people and the dance floor was hopping. The lead singer came on to announce that the Isabel Ferragamo fashion show would take place in thirty minutes, and pointed to the catwalk at the side of the tent that somehow floated across what looked like an olympic sized swimming pool.

We finished up our meals and went over to the bar area, adjacent to the dance floor. It made for great people watching while Connor socialized with colleagues and peers. I had decided to try one of the prickly pear martinis and could feel the booze starting to hit. I was moving a bit with the band, so when somebody came up from behind me with a hug I nearly screamed. I turned in shock to find Sylvie.

"Surprise!" she yelled.

"Sylvie! What are you doing?" She was still wearing her black cocktail skirt but had lost the tie and the button up and was left with a sexy white tank top.

"Long story, but hoping we can sneak out in your limo and then we will call a car service once we get to the parking lot?"

"Of course!"

Tanya appeared next, dressed similarly. Her outfit reminded me of the scene in Pretty Woman when Richard Gere was bringing Julia in off the street and into the fancy hotel for the first time. She had clearly done her best to make her white button up shirt look sexy and fashionable.

"So we're just going to party and have fun! Where's Connor?"

I pointed to him deep in conversation with someone he had introduced me to, but I had no recollection of their name.

"He's a fox," said Tanya.

I put my finger up to my lips, shushing her.

"Let's go find Simon," I said to Sylvie.

She shook her head.

"Absolutely not."

I grabbed her hand and walked her over to one of the stands that had the magazine insert. I opened up to the page that featured Simon. Sylvie grabbed it from my hands, reading it intently.

She closed it and put it back on the stand. Silence.

"It's a big night for him, huh?" I asked, trying to break the awkward silence, despite the band and crowd seeming to grow louder by the minute.

The song was done and an unfamiliar man stepped out in front of the microphone.

"As a kick off to introduce all of tonight's honorees, we would like all of you to crowd around the catwalk and watch Isabel Ferragamo's 2024 Summer Collection hit the runway! Bravo Isabel!"

The crowd went wild with applause. It was mostly women making their way to the edges of the tent to get a look. Although it was dropping, the sun was still shining bright, illuminating the catwalk. It got a helping hand from the strategically placed spotlights and the colored lights added a bit of mood lighting. A deejay had taken over and EDM music blared.

The show was something I would never forget. The models and clothes were equally beautiful and when Isabel stepped out at the end to walk behind the trail of models and close the show, you could see her happiness even from fifty feet away. It was a moment that I hadn't even allowed myself to dream of, however here I was, imagining being in her shoes. I had never been to an official fashion show (unless you counted the one in front of Jordan Marsh in the mall that Nonni took me to when I was about twelve), let alone a party in the Hamptons. I felt the need to pinch myself.

Suddenly warm hands came in from behind me and wrapped around my waist. Connor! I had pretty much ditched him at the start of the show. I quickly turned.

"I'm so sorry, I just kind of took off on you there," I laughed, knowing that Jack Webber would have been furious with me.

He laughed and looked over at Sylvie.

"I saw that you and Sylvie connected in the tent. Guessed she might be better company for a fashion show than me. It was amazing though, wasn't it? The crowd ate it up!" He was smiling.

I relaxed.

"She is amazing. What a show! Oh, Sylvie and my friend Tanya are hoping to get a ride back to our car with us, they will call a rideshare from there or something. I guess their work truck's keys went MIA."

"Of course, but why don't we drive them home?"

"That would be great. If you don't mind."

There had to be something wrong with this man that had not yet surfaced. Maybe he was afraid of spiders, or clowns. Maybe he had three nipples or something. I laughed to myself at the thought.

"What's so funny, Selena Rossi?"

I closed my eyes and took a deep breath, it's like he knew my name coming from his lips did something to me. When I opened them his mouth was on mine. Just for a second, but it acknowledged that he knew what that breath meant.

"What do you say we get out of here soon?"

I looked over at Sylvie who was now making a kissing face at me.

"There's someone here that I think Sylvie needs to see. Let me see if I can make that happen, sooner than later. Because yes, I am anxious to leave with you."

I squeezed his hand and planted a kiss on his cheek. I was definitely loaded with liquid courage.

Chapter Forty-Nine

SYLVIE

I couldn't help scanning the crowd for him.

I did not want to see him.

I guess I did not want him to see me, but I was actually desperate to see him. I was still so upset with him, but reading the program I was also so genuinely proud of him. It must feel so amazing to be recognized like this.

The fashion show was over and nearly all the party guests were in the area of the dance floor. I stopped after my second martini knowing that I had a long night ahead of me, still not entirely sure where we were or how we were getting home. Tanya on the other hand was finishing up her third mojito and seemed very unconcerned about our return trip.

She was out on the dance floor with Selena looking like they were up to no good. I stood there, casually staring at every face at the party. Hoping I would see Simon before he sees me, and hoping I never had to see his 'non-date' again.

I felt awkward standing and staring without a drink. I went to the bar and ordered a glass of Prosecco because nothing bad ever happened when I sipped Prosecco and turned to make my way back to the edge of the dance floor when I bumped right into Simon, nearly spilling my drink on his linen jacket.

"Sylvie?" he asked, shocked to see me.

He looked genuinely shocked. He did a double take, likely noticing my drab outfit paired with Nike sneakers.

"It's a long story," was all that I could muster up.

"I can't believe it's you, you're here," he was smiling, and looked a bit overwhelmed.

"Yup," was all that I could get out.

"Hey, any chance we could go somewhere a bit more quiet to catch up?" He was gesturing toward the cocktail tables sprinkling the lawn outside of the tent.

"Oh, I don't want to take you away from anyone or anything; have a great night Simon."

I immediately turned, face filling with heat and eyes brimming with tears. What was it with this man? It hurt a million times more seeing him in person.

He gently placed a hand on my shoulder, sending shivers all the way down to my toes.

"Sylvie, wait. You're not keeping me from anyone or anything. Please talk to me," he pleaded.

I nodded and looked all around for the beautiful woman I had seen him with earlier. She was nowhere. I followed him out onto the grass, grateful for the quiet.

"What an awesome honor Simon, you must be so proud."

Stick to the high road Sylvie, stick to the high road...

"Yeah, it's cool I guess. My whole family is here, they are much more excited about it than I am. But it's good for the business I suppose," he was looking down at his beer bottle that he had placed on the table. "Sylvie you have to believe me that I had no idea. My father handles all the real estate, I literally had no idea."

I took a sip of my drink and looked out past him at the water, unsure of what to say.

"Maybe, but eventually you knew Simon."

"You're right, and if you read any of my notes you would know that it is my biggest regret. A week before my dad spoke with your mom I found out. I think I was literally frozen with shock and uncertainty. I had no idea what to do. You must believe me that I would never intentionally do anything to hurt you or your family."

I let out a deep breath and I looked away from the water and back to Simon, his eyes boring into mine pleadingly.

"You're all I think about Sylvie. This night should be so exciting but it isn't, I wanted it to be a night I shared with you. I had to pick out bar fixtures last week and I hated everything, the decisions left me frozen and missing you. I couldn't do it."

The sincerity in his voice was undeniable. I noticed I had been holding my breath while listening to him. I let it go.

"I've missed you too."

He grabbed my hands and turned me to face him so that the table was no longer between us.

"I am so sorry for the business decision that my father made. When I made the connection I begged him to reconsider. Just know that it pained him to do it, but it was what he had to do in order for us to move forward with our plans. It was not personal or done with any ill will."

"I know that."

"You do? Do you believe me Sylvie?"

I nodded.

"I honestly think it was the best thing that could have happened to our family. My mom is at peace, her main concern was me. It forced me to tell my family about my classes and my unhappiness at the store. Turns out my mom was ready to downsize and work from home, anyhow. And well, now I'm free. I'm confused and slightly unemployed, but I'm free."

"Why didn't you return my calls or emails? You blocked me Sylvie!"

"I know, I just...I guess I've never been in a situation like this."

"Like what?"

"Where I cared about someone. And then got hurt," I said, now looking down at our hands.

"You care about me?"

He was smiling now.

"I did," I said now smiling back at him so he knew I was teasing.

"But what about your date?" I said suddenly snapping back to reality and looking over at the tent to see if an angry blond was headed this way.

But all I saw was Selena and Tanya. Arms draped across each other's shoulders watching us as if we were their new favorite romantic comedy.

"My date? What are you talking about?"

"I saw you earlier! Beautiful blond ring a bell?"

He started to laugh. What the hell?

"You mean Katie? I've been told that Dom's wife is a knockout but I only see her as my brother's wife. She's here with us, do you mean her?"

Oh my God, what was I doing? Was this really me? Getting jealous of his sister in law?

"Oh boy, seems I got that a bit wrong."

"ATTENTION LADIES AND GENTLEMEN," a loud voice boomed over the sound system. "We would now like everyone to gather around the dance floor so that we can acknowledge all the recipients of tonight's awards."

"We should get back in there," I said, grabbing my drink.

"No way Sylvie, I am not letting you out of my sight," he grabbed my hand and we walked back towards the tent together.

Chapter Fifty

Selena

Tanya and I stood at the side of the tent intently watching Sylvie and Simon interact. I had truly never seen her behave like this with a man. They both looked so pained. Tanya and I did our best to read their lips but we were coming up short.

A few minutes in, it appeared they had some sort of breakthrough. Their body language had changed, both had inched closer to each other, their shoulders dropped, and their hands naturally folded together.

"Yes!" I said high fiving Tanya.

Connor stood next to us shaking his head and laughing at the whole thing.

When the emcee announced that the award ceremony was beginning, Connor suggested we take a seat back at our table. Tanya seemed perfectly happy where she was and Sylvie would probably appreciate less of an audience. While walking back to our table I heard my name.

"Selena? Selena Rossi?"

Connor and I both turned. Connor must have spotted her first.

He whispered under his breath, "How the heck do you know Lea Campbell?"

I looked up and saw her walking in our direction.

"Oh wow, Connor, how are you?"

"Very well Lea, I would introduce you to Selena, but it appears you already know each other!"

She was looking me up and down. To some people this would be offensive, but it's much different when you're wearing a one of a kind dress designed by yourself.

"Did you make this Selena?"

"Well, I mean I didn't design the print, but yes, I did."

She stretched herself around my side so that she could see the back of the dress.

"It's exquisite."

"Thank you."

"She's amazing," added Connor, while nudging me.

"Did you have a chance to make a decision on my offer?" Lea asked.

I wasn't sure if it was the compliments that bolstered my confidence, or the prickly pear martinis, but I responded without hesitation.

"I have, I was going to call you on Monday. It really isn't in my wheelhouse Lea. I've never made more than one of anything. It just really isn't something I'm comfortable with. I was thinking I could see if-"

"That's a shame. My daughter will be so disappointed."

She was eying my dress again. Her six year old daughter will be disappointed that I am not making her tutu? Was she serious?

"Well, have a great night Lea. Again, I was very honored by the ask."

I was disarmed by my own honesty. I turned my back and tugged at Connor's hand to head back to our table.

"What the hell was that all about?"

After I explained we shared a laugh.

"Imagine having that much money?" I said, before thinking about it. How wealthy is a contract attorney?

We sat and watched as many familiar and unfamiliar faces were recognized on stage one at a time. Sylvie was standing to the side of the dance floor with Simon, she looked so happy. So content. It was a version of her I don't think I'd ever fully seen before.

"She looks happy," Connor said, watching me.

"If he hurts her again I'll kill him."

"Oh wow, should I be worried? Are you a violent person, Selena Rossi?"

"Well, I did dump a very cold glass of water over the last man I dated, so yes, watch yourself."

He laughed.

"Is that what we're doing? Are we dating?" he said, squeezing my leg underneath the table.

Shit. I said I was not going to 'date' anyone. I was going to take some time for myself...no rushing into things...

"Yes, yes, I think that's what we are doing."

His hand was now running up and down my leg, driving me absolutely wild.

My attention snapped back to the emcee as he announced Simon Carlino and made mention of his new, yet-to-be named restaurant in the Village. A group two tables away roared with applause and catcalls. I looked them over, debating whether or not I thought of them worthy of Sylvie.

They looked like they were having so much fun together. Actually high fiving each other as Simon approached the stage to receive his award. Sylvie stood to the side of the dance floor beaming. I watched as Simon made his way off the stage. He lifted his plaque up in the direction of his family and then immediately turned all of his attention to Sylvie. His eyes fixed only on hers.

He walked right into her arms and kissed her. Suddenly the table went crazy. I looked back at them and they all looked shocked and then immediately excited. Were they high fiving each other? Again?! I couldn't help but laugh.

"Looks like they figured it all out," Connor said, now smiling too. "Does this mean I get to take you home soon Selena?" He was whispering in my ear, just close enough that his lips brushed my skin.

"Check please!"

We both laughed.

"Let me go check in with the lovebirds and Tanya and see what the plan is, I'll be right back."

I didn't have to go far to find Tanya. She was sitting at a table with three people that appeared to be her long lost friends.

"Selena!"

"Hey Tanya, we're going to get out of here soon, can we give you a lift?"

"These are actually our neighbors! They offered to drive Sylvie and I home, although I don't think she's leaving with anyone but Simon," she said smiling and pointing to the happy couple as they walked across the room hand in hand. "Ok, I'll check in with her now! Awesome to see you!" I said as I leaned over and gave her a quick hug.

Sylvie and Simon were no longer locking lips or arms, but she was standing beside him at his family's very animated table. She was shaking hands and even welcoming a few hugs. I could tell she was overwhelmed, but she was doing great. I stood off to the side waiting until they were done.

"Selena! I was hoping I would find you!" said a voice from behind me.

It was Lea Campbell. Dear God this woman was relentless.

"I respect you for saying no," she said, gently.

Her demeanor appeared completely different then the last two times we spoke. Her voice was gentle, her body language, approachable. I wasn't sure what to say, so instead I just smiled.

"How long did it take you to make your dress?"

"The better part of a day I would say."

"You would not believe the chatter about it tonight. I mean, that dress was the focus of many dinner chats. I hear Isabel Ferragamo is dying to bring you into her office."

"Wow, that's really kind. Thank you for saying that," I said, still not entirely sure how to receive all these gracious compliments.

"I am going to the opening of the new Joey King movie next Friday. Do you think you could put something together for me? It can be as fancy or as casual as you want it to be, I would let you run with it. Full creative freedom."

"Seriously?"

"Very seriously," she said, now smiling. "We could meet on Monday so you can take my measurements. Would you be able to pull something together that quickly?"

"One hundred percent, Ms. Campbell."

"Lea, call me Lea."

I leaned in to hug her. It went horribly. Apparently Lea was not much of a hugger. It translated into more of a bro tap, but I was not going to let that dampen my mood.

"You have my number, text me your availability sometime tomorrow. I can meet you back at my warehouse or if you prefer, I can come to you. You can let me know what I owe you at the end."

"Umm, okay, your warehouse is great."

As she walked away I stood for a minute, shaking, replaying our conversation in my head. Never in my wildest, okay, maybe in my absolutely craziest, most wildest dreams did something like this happen to me. I took a deep breath flushing the butterflies out and bringing myself back to reality as I looked back up in the direction of Sylvie and Simon.

The introductions appeared to be over. I walked toward Sylvie, but didn't go all the way over. Being her twin, I knew damn well that the last thing Sylvie was ready for was to introduce me to Simon. She would do it when she was ready. I stood there boring my eyes into her knowing she would eventually feel them. You know, 'twin power.' It didn't take long.

Fine, I motioned her over with my finger.

"What's up?"

"Connor and I are heading out in a few. Tanya said your neighbors are here. She's over at that table with them and she said they can bring you home, but we can too if you're more comfortable."

"Umm, I think I'll probably end up leaving with Simon," she said shyly.

"Mmmkay, Sylvie," I said smiling.

"Please don't be weird, Selena."

"I know, I know, I'm leaving you be. We will get to know each other just as soon as you're ready," I said, gesturing to Simon. I leaned in and gave her a hug.

"You deserve to be happy Sylvie, you deserve all of it," I whispered in her ear.

"And you, my dear, do too. There's a very distinguished-looking, hot man standing about two tables away staring directly at your ass."

We both laughed and looked at Connor who stood from a distance watching us. We waved and he just smiled, his eyes locked on mine.

"Looks like it's just you and me," I said smiling as I made my way over to him.

Chapter Fifty-One

SYLVIE

Joseph Carlino and the rest of Simon's table of supporters were everything he had described them to be. His dad walked straight over to me as we approached their table.

"Sylvie Rossi, as beautiful as her mother," he said while extending his hand.

"Nice to meet you."

"Meet me?! Sylvie I held you and Selena in your grandmother's shop when you were babies!" he laughed. "Your mom has forgiven me for my difficult business decisions, I hope you can too. I need you to know that it was a very difficult-"

"I forgive you," I said, interrupting him so that he didn't have to get into it. "It was all probably for the best, my mom is very happy working out of her home."

"And what about you Sylvie? Simon was most worried about you."

I looked over at Simon, everything about him so gentle and sweet, I can't believe I didn't give this man a chance.

"I'm figuring it out, but it was honestly what I needed to get me started on a new path," I said smiling. "But enough about me! How about that award Simon just got!"

"Your designs are what got the magazine's attention Sylvie," Simon said, stepping towards us.

"I highly doubt that! I'm pretty sure beautiful plates do not get you awards like this!" I laughed.

"Very humble woman you are Sylvie. Well you two should go spend some time together," said his father, clearly very aware of our situation. "And then convince her to come back to help you with the rest of it!"

We said our goodbyes and took the car service to Simon's car that was parked in a top secret lot. We had yet to discuss our plans from here, only that I was subletting in Northampton for a few more weeks.

When we both got into the Jeep, he looked over at me, as if to assess the situation.

"So, I'm trying really hard not to be presumptuous Sylvie. I know it's late, but I'm not ready to say goodbye to you. I have a room booked just down the street."

I looked at my watch, it was only ten.

"What if you brought me back to my place, it's only like five minutes from here, I could take a two second shower and change out of this? I'm actually starving, are you? We could maybe go get a late bite and a nightcap?"

He was smiling.

"That sounds perfect."

And it was.

While I showered Simon grabbed a pizza from the shop down the street, I grabbed a blanket and packed a bag with wine and glasses. We walked down to the private beach that we had access to from our rental. We talked and laughed and stole kisses every chance we got. When I looked at my phone it was almost one in the morning. The pizza was barely touched but the wine was nearly gone.

We were now laying side by side on the blanket, the edges pulled up over us to warm us from the cool night breeze. My head fit perfectly in the nape of his neck and his warm arms glided up and down mine pulling me closer and keeping me toasty. Simon and I had a lot of catching up to do. He winced the first few times I mentioned the process of shutting down the shop, but I think we both felt peace when I spoke of my mother's new-found happiness. We talked about the classes we were taking and the job searching process. He was unquestionably jealous of the fact that I was sharing a house with a guy named Tommy, but relieved to hear that I'd be home in a few weeks.

We lay there, side by side for hours, both asking questions and telling stories.

When I woke up the sun was peeking up from the base of the horizon. I could not believe we slept on the beach. That was definitely a first for me. I was careful not to move and disturb Simon, I could tell by the steady breath that breezed quietly passed my ear that he was still asleep. At some point I must have rolled over onto my side and Simon had followed me. His left leg was draped across my right leg, both of us laying like fancy flamingos. His right arm was tucked under my neck and head and his left arm lay heavily across my waist. He had managed to tuck his fingers up underneath my sweatshirt and had a firm hold on my rib cage.

I felt calm. I felt at peace. My life has been plagued with so much uncertainty, so much doubt the last month that I think those few hours of sleep beside Simon provided the most rest I'd had in weeks.

He stirred, pressing his body into the back of mine. He might not have been awake yet, but I would argue that parts of him were. He went to move his arm but quickly realized it was tangled up underneath my shirt. His hand felt around, trying to recognize his surroundings, and then he moaned into my ear.

"Sylvie," he whispered. I looked back at him. His eyes were still closed.

"I cannot believe we slept on the beach."

"Is the sun up? Did we lose our privacy?" he asked, eyes still shut. But the smile was growing on his face.

"Oh, it's making its way up. No privacy here."

"Dammit," he said and with little effort flipped me over to face him.

He was struggling to open his eyes, fighting against what was now a very bright sky. He was squinting but looking right at me.

NOT AS IT SEAMS

"How far is your bedroom from here?"
I jokingly punched him in the shoulder.
"Not close enough."

Chapter Fifty-Two

SELENA

I could hear my phone ringing but waking up in an unfamiliar bed had me completely out of sorts. I looked all around, searching for where it was coming from. Connor began to stir too. I grabbed the sheet and pulled it up over my chest as I leaned across Connor to grab the phone that I had finally found on the nightstand next to him. Before I could grab it he pulled me down on top of him and kissed me.

I smiled and pulled away, reaching for my phone.

I grabbed it and rolled over to my side of the bed, Connor swiftly rolling with me and tucking me into his side, molding his legs behind mine.

I looked down at my phone, two missed calls from my mother and one from Sylvie. I looked at the time, it was eight thirty. Wow, we had slept in!

"I'm so sorry, my family is trying to get in touch with me."

I pulled myself away from Connor and looked all around for my clothes. Instead I grabbed Connor's button up shirt and threw it on.

"That looks much better on you," he said.

I smiled and pulled the bathroom door behind me, unsure of who to call back first.

I hit send over Sylvie's name. What was going on? Why were they calling so early?

"Have you talked to mom?"

Not even a hello first.

"No, why? What's going on?"

"Where are you?"

"I'm at a bed and breakfast in Southampton with Connor, why?"

"Send me the name, I'm on my way."

"Sylvie what is going on?"

"Where are you?"

"Umm, it's called..." I looked all around the bathroom for a clue. I popped my head out the door and asked Connor.

"The Point."

"Holy shit, that's like the nicest-"

"Sylvie, tell me what's going on."

"It's Nonni, she's in the ICU."

I breathed out a deep, long sigh. Deep down I knew this was about Nonni the second I heard my phone ring.

"Mom is with her. They found her unresponsive last night and were able to revive her. Dad has called from mom's phone a few times with updates. Selena, she's not breathing on her own. Dad said we should get there as fast as we can. Simon and I are going to come pick you guys up."

"Oh my God." I hung up the phone with Sylvie and threw my hand up over my mouth to catch the sob that had escaped me.

"Is everything okay?" Connor asked from the other side of the door.

"Umm, no, not really. It's my Nonni," I mumbled out between breathless tears.

"Let me in, Selena." He opened the door and I fell into his arms.

Within ten minutes we were all squeezed into Simon's Jeep. This is not the way any of us wanted to meet.

Chapter Fifty-Three

SELENA

We got there in time to say goodbye. Our parents had already made the decision after the physician's consultation that they would take Nonni off the respirator once we arrived and all had time with her. She went peacefully and that was all any of us could have asked for.

We walked down to the hospital chapel with my mom and dad before we left for the night, each of us lighting a candle.

My mom had been stoic, and brave, she hadn't even shed a tear.

"You don't need to be so strong mom," Sylvie said on the elevator down to the parking garage. "It's okay to let it out."

"She's been gone a long time bella. I'm relieved that she's back with Papa. I bet she's already busy cooking and sewing and singing," my mom said smiling with tears brimming her eyes. My dad squeezed both her shoulders and hugged her from the side as we walked.

Although they had offered to stay, Simon and Connor had dropped us off at the hospital directly from the ferry and then both went home. Connor had sent multiple texts checking in, I could tell he felt so helpless not being here.

I looked at my phone, it was four in the morning. My dad was going to drive Selena and I back to our Holly apartment building. I felt like I could sleep for a week. We planned to meet at my parents at noon to help make the funeral arrangements. Nonni had insisted that she wanted to leave this world quietly, riding off into the sunset to meet Papa. She did not want a wake or a banquet. She simply wanted her immediate family to go to church and then say goodbye to her at her final resting place, followed by a homemade Italian dinner. Who would we be not to honor her request?

I showered and crawled into bed at five. I sent Connor a text so that he would understand why my phone was on silent for the better part of the morning. I was shocked when he responded.

Thanks for letting me know. I hope you get some rest. I am so sorry for your loss. I'd like to bring your family dinner tomorrow night. Give me a call when you wake up. Sweet dreams Selena.

Despite being drained of all emotions, physically and mentally exhausted, I still felt a chill run down my spine reading his text. I closed my eyes and drifted off to sleep thinking of the amazing night we had spent together the previous evening.

Our family meeting went as expected. We laughed, we cried and we made some phone calls to friends and family we thought should know of her passing. We planned a private church service for the following evening that would end with Nonni's burial next to Papa. Mom seemed satisfied. Sylvie and I took separate cars as I was headed to Lea Campbell's warehouse for our meeting at three.

I considered canceling but knew that Nonni wouldn't have wanted that. Despite dressing her in my mind I hadn't had time to sketch anything. I felt unprepared and very nervous. When I got there I was even more surprised because we weren't alone.

"Selena Rossi, meet Elaine Summer and Sam Dumais. Elaine is my publicist, and Sam is my stylist."

I looked at both of them. My heart began beating out of my chest.

"Oh, wow, so nice to meet you both."

"Don't worry, we are not here to pressure you in any way, just excited to meet you as Lea told us great things."

I could barely hear what any of them were saying; my heart was pounding so loudly in my ears that it felt like we might be experiencing the ripple effects of an earthquake. Why did I know the name Elaine Summer and why did I know it was not a name I wanted to hear again. I took a deep breath and brought myself back to the room.

"Wow, that's very generous of her. I'm sorry that I do not have sketches or fabric samples or anything yet. I'm dealing with a bit of a family emergency. But I can assure you that it will not stop me from creating something beautiful for you."

Lea laughed. "We did not expect those from you. In fact, leaving it up to you and the surprise of all of it makes it much more exciting."

I looked over at Elaine, sizing her up and down hoping that I would recall how I knew that name. Maybe it's a popular name, I'm sure there are many Elaine Summer's in Greater New York City...but still...

"Agreed," added Sam nervously. "Except I feel like we should just have a quick chat about what photographs well and the areas that Miss Campbell likes to accentuate and-"

"None of that Sam, I trust Miss Rossi does not need the lecture. In fact," she was now looking me up and down. "We have similar figures, don't put me in anything you wouldn't want to wear yourself. That is my only rule."

I smiled. Despite being a bit older than me, I would take that compliment all day long.

I took her measurements and was relieved that no one asked about the family emergency. I didn't need to cry in front of these strangers.

We said goodbye with our double cheek kisses that still made me horribly uncomfortable. I was grateful that none of their lips actually touched my cheeks, but to be sure I would stop at the nearest clean restroom to wash my face.

As I fastened my seatbelt I looked up and the lightbulb went off, I realized how I knew Elaine Summer. Elaine fucking Summer was the reason my summer started two months early. Elaine fucking Summer was the mother of the entitled Parker Miller junior, Cullen Summer. The one who spent most days in the art room rolling up small balls of clay and flicking them at other students. The Cullen Summer who did not turn in a single assignment all year long. To a class where he could literally draw a stick figure on a piece of paper and turn it in. But his obnoxious, presumptuous self felt that the rules did not apply to him.

Did she put the two and two together? Did Lea tell Elaine how we met? She was the owner of the public relations agency that represented Lea, but her opinion of me should have no jurisdiction over Lea's relationship with me? Right?

I imagined working day and night all week long only for Elaine Summer to reject my work as payback for failing her son in art class. She didn't say a word to me today, only nodded and smiled. Was that part of her strategy to destroy me? There was nothing I could do about any of it, nothing I could say. I had to leave this up to her and fate, hoping that it all works out.

I had texted Connor a note earlier to let him know that although I appreciated his offer, I had to get a jumpstart on my designing for Lea. I was desperate to see him again, but between my high-flying emotions and this deadline looming over me, I knew that this wasn't the week to fall in love.

He appeared to understand but that didn't stop him from sending flowers to me, my mom and Sylvie. Who the hell was this guy? There had to be something wrong with him...how much longer would I have to wait to figure out what it is?

This is a reminder to myself to cyberstalk him in my downtime tonight, see what dirt I could uncover. He's probably the mastermind behind some horrible legal pyramid scheme. Or worse, he is probably the kingpin smuggling drugs out of the city and into Holly. I suddenly wanted to see where he lived. Who was I kidding...I wanted to see where this man slept.

Chapter Fifty-Four

SYLVIE

Nonni's services were simple, thoughtful and small, pretty much a direct reflection of the woman that she was. It all felt a bit mechanical and robotic for me. I wasn't sure who I was mourning, the Nonni that I last saw or the Nonni of all my memories. I did my best to remember her the way she would have wanted. But I knew the grief would come in waves; possibly forever.

We celebrated her life as she would have wanted. Selena and I joined our mom to empty her belongings from the Springs at Holly Valley. We wanted to do something thoughtful for the administration there in Nonni's name and decided to donate a pasta machine as well as a sewing machine for the Activities Director to use for the cooking and crafting clubs. I knew it would have made Nonni proud and very happy.

By Thursday, life was mostly back to normal, which felt really rotten to admit. How could we lose the matriarch of our family and already be back to our everyday lives? I was beginning to feel like I really had no reason to stay in Holly. My mom was back to being busy with her business and Selena was consumed by a top secret design project plus she was a smitten kitten for Connor. I had seen Simon twice since he drove me home from Long Island. We had yet to spend the night together with the exception of our night on the beach. I would be lying if I didn't say I was anxious.

He asked me to the restaurant for a pre-ladies night dinner and said to be prepared for him to present a business proposal to me. I had no idea what that could possibly mean. I was able to borrow Selena's computer and attend most of my classes, so with the exception of letting Frank down for one event, I didn't feel too stressed about my quick departure from my summer getaway. Frank said I had a week to grieve and then he expected me back. Seemed fair enough to me.

When I arrived at Giuseppi's I noticed multiple members of the staff taking a second to stop and check me out. I would be lying if I didn't admit to liking it.

Simon snuck up behind me. "There she is," he said, kissing my cheek and grabbing me by the hand and leading me towards the kitchen.

"Do you have a table back here?" I laughed.

"Business first, dinner second."

We took a turn at the far back of the restaurant and traveled down a hallway to what I assumed was the office.

"Take a seat," he said pointing towards a chair as he stepped behind and sat down at a large mahogany desk.

"This is formal," I said, looking around at the framed pictures that covered the walls.

"My dad's," he said pointing to the pictures, many of which featured Joseph Carlino.

"So, this is strictly a business conversation Sylvie Rossi. Several weeks ago we hosted an exclusive media day at the new restaurant, inviting writers and industry leaders to come in to see the progress of the restaurant as well as sample an initial tasting menu from Chef Gianni."

I nodded, unsure of what any of this had to do with me.

"Long story short, they all seemed to really loved Gianni's food, but the restaurant design was what they all wanted to write about. Many of them asked for your contact information, including other restaurant owners. You've really got something here Sylvie."

The heat that was so quickly filling my face was not enough to stop me from smiling.

"Really? I mean, let's be serious here Simon, you made a ton of those decisions. You are selling yourself short if you give me credit like this!"

"Nope, they got specific, everything that made them react was directly correlated to one of your choices."

I didn't say anything. I just sat there actually accepting and appreciating his compliment.

"There are still a lot of decisions left to be made and I would like to hire you as a design consultant. Your name will then be attached to this project and with professional photos and such you will be able to begin your portfolio."

Ideas began flooding my now very excited brain.

"Why are you doing this Simon? You don't owe me anything? I would do it all for free, and you know that."

"That would be taking advantage of a beautiful woman that I am hoping will agree to be my girlfriend."

This time it was his face that reddened. He looked shy, nervous even. He ran his hands across the part of his dark hair and then began fidgeting with a pen on his desk.

"What happened to strictly business Mr. Carlino?" I asked, trying to lighten the mood.

"I would be honored, on all fronts," I added.

A smile brushed across his face and he immediately stood.

"Do some research, decide if you want to propose an hourly or a project rate. I was hoping you would say yes, especially since I've already planned to take you to the restaurant tomorrow to show you the scope of work."

Simon made his way over to me and pulled me to my feet and then into him for a very nonprofessional kiss, his lips trailing down my neck and pushing my sleeve off my shoulder.

"What is it with you and offices?" I said as his lips and hands continued making their way down my body.

"Sorry," he said, laughing but also a little embarrassed.

"Trust me, I wasn't suggesting you stop. However, there is a restaurant full of people on the other side of this door. What if we eat and plan to continue this conversation at my place tonight?"

"It's going to be really hard to concentrate at dinner with an invitation like that," he kissed me again. "You have no idea how much I missed you, Sylvie Rossi."

"Oh, that is where you're very, very wrong."

Chapter Fifty-Five

SELENA

I left Lea's warehouse and looked at my phone, it was not even four. If I hopped on the train now I could be in the garment district before five. I knew I needed to get there for not only materials to get started, but mostly for inspiration.

The fabric stores all closed at seven. My plan was to walk the stores for fabric sample ideas and then find a place to sketch. Lea had left the parameters of the project so wide open that I was both overwhelmed and uninspired.

When I finally got to street level, the sidewalks were jam packed with the city's nine to fivers leaving for the day. The fashion on the street ranged from casual to business to some looking like they were straight off a runway. It was like nothing I would ever see in Holly, or anywhere else for that matter. I took some time just sitting on a bench, watching all of it.

With it being summer, and Lea's long lean body I quickly decided it would be two pieces. I bought two yards of three very different fabrics, some liners and the paper board for the patterns. I would use the time on the train to sketch.

It was nearly nine when I got home and I was equal parts famished and exhausted. So when I saw the note on my entryway table from Sylvie, I wanted to cry.

You are a very busy girl with a very secret project. A very handsome man named Connor reached out to me and asked if I would put some food in your refrigerator as well as a bottle of wine. He also left a card in a sealed envelope that I desperately wanted to open (I didn't).

He's got it for you, BAD! Don't forget to eat, Sleen! Take care of you! XOXO

Another perk of sharing keys with your sister I suppose.

I walked into the kitchen and saw a bag filled with rolls, cookies and a bag of potato chips. On top of all of it was a yellow sealed envelope. Before I opened it I opened the door to my fridge to see what he had dropped off. Oh my God, it all looked so good. There was a Greek salad, a bottle of white wine, some dressings and in the foil lined container was a salmon dinner with risotto and asparagus. Yumm. He even wrote out instructions to heat it all up.

I preheat my oven, popped the aluminum container inside and grabbed the envelope anxiously.

It was your typical Hallmark sympathy card, but the left side of the card held a long, hand-written personal note from Connor.

Selena,

Extending my deepest sympathy for the loss of your grandmother. I vaguely remember her from the shop but I can see how truly important she was to your entire family. I look forward to hearing all about her. I hope your meeting with Lea went well and she didn't offer you more money to make her kids' tutus. You're better than that Selena. Like, way better. Also, you're a great kisser. Did I tell you that yet? I think about the next time I can kiss you pretty much all day long. I'll give you space this week as I know you're busy but please let me know when I can see you again. I've got it bad for you.

XOXO

Connor

I giggled at the coincidence, pressing the card into my chest and leaning against my cabinets all googly eyed. I had it bad for him too. I wanted to see him soon, hell, I wanted to see him right now. But I was exhausted, and had a full day of work tomorrow. I settled on a text.

You have no idea how much I appreciate your delivery. I just got home and I am starving. I cannot wait til the weekend to see you. I'll need a break by tomorrow night. Catch up then?

I hit send.

I immediately saw the three dots appear.

Cleanest restaurant in the city. They even bagged it wearing gloves (he added a wink emoji), eat it without anxiety Selena. Can I cook you dinner at my place tomorrow?

Sounds perfect. Send address.

PS - Should I pack a bag?

I sent it before I even had time to think about it. It was like an extraterrestrial being stepped into my body and grabbed my phone right out of my hands. I don't remember ever being so forward. I mean, we did spend an amazing night together in the Hamptons, so it wasn't like it was completely out of left field.

It's like you're reading my mind. I would love that.

And there it was. Done. I was now forcing myself onto men. I was basically suggesting that I show up to his house naked and take advantage of him. Where was the old Selena that would have offered to bake a dessert? Was she still here? Did she even exist?

Chapter Fifty-Six

SYLVIE

I rode with Simon into the city on Friday morning just after rush hour. He told me nothing about what he had planned, only that our commute was purely social, no business. We spent most of it talking about my grandmother. He was so genuinely interested and we found so many similarities between her and Papa and his own Italian grandparents. It felt so good to talk about her. Not the version of her in a locked unit, but the healthy, robust woman that she was as for ninety-nine percent of her life.

Neither of us made any mention of the looming question regarding my return to the Hamptons. Selena didn't even seem interested in the question. She asked if I would meet her in the city tonight at six. It left me in a bit of a predicament, but when she suggested I also bring Simon I knew I could make it work. I had thrown a cute cocktail dress in the backseat of Simon's Jeep on top of a suit that he had in a garment bag. We were going to play the day by ear but he was convinced we would have plenty to keep us busy.

The moment we stepped inside his yet to be named restaurant. I did my best to pivot to a pretend design expert. I threw a pencil into the side of my bun just to really send the message out to the space. A group of contractors were applying plaster to the walls of the main dining room and a group of technicians were servicing the walk-in cooler. Everyone seemed to work a little harder and stand a little taller when Simon entered the room.

I walked behind him slowly, looking around at all the improvements that had been completed. My jaw dropped when I saw the wall paper.

"Oh, I have to check out the bathrooms! Do you mind?" I asked as I pushed the swinging door to the women's room open.

Simon laughed and nodded at me.

"Look at the men's too, sugar scrub should be in next week."

"I love them!" I said, squeezing his hand as I followed him towards his office.

"So what is left to decide on?"

We were both sitting in his office, he swung the monitor of his computer over for me to see what looked like a checklist. He printed it out and handed it to me, warm off of his printer. My eyes ran up and down the list, excitement spreading through my chest and into my belly. The hostess stand, menus, signage, and name (wow, I'm guessing that one is not meant for me), advertising, art to be hung in the restaurant, final menu design, dining chairs, and a few other things that would need explaining.

"Oh, lots of fun stuff, where do you want my help?"

"With all of it Sylvie. I'll point you in the direction of vendors and you can take it from there. We are on a tight timeline so that will have to be taken into account with each decision..."

He rambled on as I smiled and nodded my head to give the illusion that I was digesting all that he was throwing at me. But really I was fixated on the opportunity rather than the mission. How could he be so comfortable leaving these big, fun and mostly exciting decisions in my incapable hands? I didn't get it.

"You can do this Sylvie," he said, reaching across the desk for my hands. Clearly I wasn't great at hiding my emotions.

"I don't get it. You're taking such a gamble on me Simon. Don't you think you should work with someone more qualified?"

"Nope."

He handed me a folder filled with contacts, catalogs, budgets and deadline information.

"Go through all of this, map it out, figure out the hours of time this will take. Come back to me with an hourly rate or a project rate by Monday. Also, I don't mean to be so bossy or to be forcing this on you Sylvie. I know you're trying to figure out what you want to do, so if this is not it, don't be afraid to tell me no! Well not me, the project! Please don't say no to me!"

He was smiling and squirming. He was adorable and thoughtful. But was this a ploy to keep me from going back to the Hamptons? Did he always come up with jobs to keep the women that he dates close by?

"We hired a public relations agency to help with the opening, your name will be attached to everything Sylvie. We will have professional photos taken for the website and social media that I can share with you and you can use them for your future portfolio or even a website," he sounded so excited when he spoke about it.

Was I just letting this unquestionably handsome man decide my future line of work? I mean, he was doing everything short of naming my own design business! But this was nothing like working for my mom and Nonni. This spawned from something that I was actually interested in. Something that I slightly proved to be good at, right? I truly felt happy... and excited...and nervous and scared...and a little bit turned on by his faith in me.

Just go with it. Don't overthink.

"Ok, I'll go through everything this weekend for sure," was all I said in return.

"Thank you," he said, holding my gaze.

"What are you thinking?"

"It's a lot to process. If I do it, I want to do a good job. I don't want to let you or your family down."

"Which is exactly why I think you're the perfect person to do it!"

He was standing now and pulled me up to my feet and immediately brought me into his chest. He held me there for what could have been minutes or maybe even hours. I didn't know, nor care.

"And now, for inspiration, we eat," he said, pulling me out of his office by hand.

Chapter Fifty-Seven

SELENA

I've never worked harder on one thing in my entire life. I also don't think I'd ever wanted someone's approval as badly as I wanted Lea Campbell's. I was so anxious about her fitting on Thursday afternoon. After multiple trips to the local fabric stores and a pattern that underwent about five major changes, the final dress was stunning, or at least I thought it was!

I stood in the mirror turning side to side to see how everything sat on me (Lea was right, we had the same measurements within millimeters). Her legs ran much longer than mine which would only accentuate this silhouette. I chose a beautiful bright fuschia that I knew would absolutely pop off of Lea's tanned skin. The detailwork along the gaping v-shaped neckline consisted of fuschia lattice work with a nude liner and it gave the impression of showing much more skin than I actually was. The bottom piece was a flowy skirt with a sexy slit up the front of the right leg that made the ensemble come alive. The fringe that ran from the waist up and over the shoulders created a slim, sexy silhouette.

I couldn't help but shake my hips and laugh at the fringe's response.

I was beyond proud. Sam, Lea's stylist, was meeting us at the fitting today so that he could plan her shoes and accessories, but I felt confident that a sexy black heel was all she would need to stun on the red carpet. Lea hadn't mentioned the name Elaine Summer again so I carried a golf ball sized hole in my gut wondering if she would also be in attendance.

I pulled up to the warehouse and was relieved to only see two cars by the entrance to the back offices. Hopefully this meant that it was only Lea and Sam. I was a big bag of nerves. What if I missed the mark? What if Lea hated it?

I took a deep breath, remembering Connor's words as he snuck out of his bed early yesterday morning. "You are good enough to be doing this Selena. Go to that office with confidence tomorrow." I had pulled him back into bed to be sure he remembered me at work all day long. The cleanliness and style of his apartment made me fall for him even harder. Turns out he wasn't much of a cook, but he did his best to hide the foil trays that the restaurant must have provided for our dinner. However it gave us both a good laugh and I didn't even fret about the kitchen that cooked it.

When I knocked on Lea's office door it was Sam that greeted me. He looked me up and down trying to peek into the garment bag slung over my shoulder.

"Eeeek," Lea squealed from across the room. "We are so excited to see what you came up with Selena."

I smiled and hung the bag on the garment rack next to the floor length mirror behind where Lea was standing.

"Oh, I hope you like it," I said, taking a step back as it was clear they wanted to take things from here.

"If there are any issues with the fit I actually brought a machine with me so that I could do some alterations on the spot here, and-"

Before I could finish my sentence Lea was unzipping the bag. I brought my shaky hands up to my mouth with nervous anticipation.

She pulled the dress out of the bag and it stood there on its hanger. Exposed to someone other than me for the very first time. Maybe I should have gotten a second opinion? Like sending a selfie or two out to friends and family. What if it was too short? Too low cut? Underwhelming?

The room was completely silent. Sam held a pen near his mouth, in deep thought. Like he was Tim Gunn looking for kind words to offer a failed design. Lea picked it up and turned it around, clearly noticing the movement to the dress with the fringe.

I watched it move too, except I was looking for imperfections, loose hems and other design flaws.

The room was still silent.

"Holy shit," Sam whispered under his breath.

"Right?" added Lea.

I couldn't read them; their comments were not exactly context clues to their feelings.

"You made this in three days?" asked Sam.

I nodded, still not sure if that was a compliment or an insult.

Lea was suddenly disrobing. Her shirt was off and next went her bra and pants. She stood there in a pair of super unnecessary spanks as Sam unzipped the top and carefully placed it over her head. He did the same with the skirt and she stepped into it gently. Sam zipped up the skirt as Lea stretched to pull the zipper down that ran along on the side of her rib cage.

It fit her like a freaking glove.

She looked unbelievable. My jaw dropped.

She looked at herself in the mirror, eyes wide, and lasering back and forth between the dress and Sam.

She shimmied her hips, watching as the fringe playfully bounced from side to side.

Sam was smiling.

Right? That was a smile? It was a smile of happiness, right? Not a laughing at the preposterousness of the dress smile? Right? Oh my word, someone say something for the love of God!

Lea was smiling back at Sam, and suddenly she turned away from the mirror and looked at me. Sam turned as well.

She grabbed my hands with hers.

"You really have no idea how talented you are, do you Selena?"

The relief sent tears to the corners of my eyes.

"You like it?"

"Like it?" erupted Sam. "It's iconic! She is going to shut down that red carpet Selena!"

"Well, does it fit okay?" my eyes darting to her hips and then her bust and then the hemline that sat in the middle of her thighs.

Lea walked across the room and used her toes to snag a pair of black stiletto heels. She walked back to us like she was Bella Hadid hitting the red carpet. She was stunning.

"Oh dear," said Sam. "I'm going to Winston's to borrow some outrageously expensive earrings for you to add to the 'fit,' and then honey, you are done. That dress does not need any accessories. I wouldn't want to do anything to steal the spotlight away from that number. And I never turn down accessories!"

Lea and Sam laughed together as if it was some sort of inside joke.

Before taking off my creation, Lea walked over to her desk and grabbed something out of her purse. She was pulling out a checkbook and a pen.

"What do I owe you Selena?"

I hadn't even thought about it! I had spent a couple of hundred dollars on materials and probably spent about thirty hours making it. But it didn't feel like work, so does that even count? I mean, I loved making it.

As if she could see the blank expression on my face.

"Would five thousand be fair?" she asked, straightfaced.

I tried not to show her how shocked I was.

"Oh, wow, I don't think you need to pay me that much Ms. Campbell."

"You call me Lea. And if I can give you any advice as you begin to launch your label, do not sell yourself short Selena."

She was very serious. And what was she even talking about? 'My label'?

"Thank you very much," I said as I accepted her check. "For everything, thank you for the opportunity."

"I am emailing you four tickets to the premiere. I recommend you attend the carpet, there will be seats where you can watch. There may be some people that want to talk to you there Selena," she winked at me.

"I think your life is about to change," said Sam as he began to unzip Lea from the skirt.

"Let me have Elaine reach out to you, she can help you with talking points and just prepare you for any media attention that might come your way."

The mention of her name brought me back to Earth. Reality was suddenly slapped across my face like the tortilla Tik Tok challenge that we had to ban from the lunchroom.

"Oh, thank you so much, but that will not be necessary. You've done plenty to help me and I really appreciate it."

I was suddenly ravenous for the exit sign.

"Well at least let us send you some professional carpet shots when we are done. Watch for it on the socials too, this is going to photograph so well," said Sam.

I had nothing left to say and simply smiled, clutching a check that was more than my monthly paycheck as a teacher. I stood at the door trying to process everything one last time.

"What should I wear?" I asked, now looking at Sam. "Tomorrow night?"

"Anything! You can be super casual or as fancy as Lea, but whatever you do, be sure it's an original," he winked at me.

Chapter Fifty-Eight

Sylvie

I followed Simon out of his office and turned to a room I had not yet seen. The back wall was a huge blank canvas of stucco; capped off wires hung down in the middle of the room over what had to be the biggest dining table I had ever seen. Two folding chairs sat across from each other in the middle of it. The room was dimly lit by the candles that trickled from one end of the table's center to the other.

Two servers came in and poured us glasses of bottled water and then asked for our drink orders.

I looked at him, lifting one eyebrow, trying to figure out what exactly was going on.

"I thought this would give you some inspiration and some confidence in your decision to work with us. I have big dreams for this private dining room and even bigger dreams for our menu, so I thought I could let you experience both," he was smiling.

The food was absolutely incredible. Nonni would have loved it, although she would have commented on the smaller portion sizes and fancy platings.

I looked around the room and through the glass into the restaurant. The thought of having a hand in this design was giving me butterflies and the smile on my face was becoming impossible to hide. I felt so uncomfortable putting a price tag on my unqualified help but also I had upcoming bills to worry about.

"What are you thinking about?"

"I really want to do this. I am excited at the thought, but scared of disappointing you, or letting you down."

He reached across the table and grabbed both of my hands.

"I have complete faith in you Sylvie."

"I feel weird asking for any kind of payment," I said shyly.

"Ok, what if I made it easier on you and showed you a quote I was given by a professional design company. You can think of them as your competition. And you can price yourself accordingly?"

"If you don't mind, that would be great."

He popped out of his seat and headed towards his office. He was back within minutes carrying a manila envelope. He dropped it on the table in front of me. I flipped through it seeing catalog cutouts of lights and chairs circled and highlighted and quickly flipped through until I saw the last page with a breakdown of the agency's pricing.

My jaw dropped.

I looked up at Simon to see if he agreed with me that this was ludicrous. His facial expression remained unchanged.

I looked closer at the quote to see if it included the actual purchase of the chairs and lights. It didn't.

"Twenty five thousand dollars? Are they out of their minds?"

He laughed.

"Time is a valuable commodity, Sylvie. You can take that with you for your research," he said gesturing towards the folder.

I passed it across the table to him.

"No way, I want to have a completely fresh take, no outside influences," I smiled at him.

"Smart woman."

"I'll do it for ten."

"Deal."

He reached out and shook my hand and then hoisted himself up over the table so that his lips would reach mine.

"I would have done it for five," I whispered quietly as my lips pulled away from his.

He leaned back into me and whispered, "I would have paid twenty. I'd really like to take you home now Sylvie. Like, to my home. To my bed."

"Oh no, my company has a strict policy. No dating clients."

I was teasing, but also bringing it up as it was a valid concern. We were both back to being seated.

"I think your company should get all the rules together after you complete this project," he said and winked at me.

"You're probably right. Well, I would love to go home to your bed, but we have one last stop before we can go there," I trailed off.

"Right, we are meeting your sister. Should we get ready?" he asked.

I looked for my phone to check the time and realized it was in my bag in Simon's office.

By the time we got back to his office and I checked it, it was nearly four in the afternoon. I had two missed calls and two missed texts from Selena.

Call me.
I'm panicking, I can't keep the secret.
MISSED CALL.
Forget it, it's off. Don't meet me, I'll tell you about it tomorrow.
MISSED CALL.
No need to call me back, I'm good.
I fucking hate people.

What in the heck was happening? Was she okay?

Chapter Fifty-Nine

SELENA

Connor was working in the city and suggested we meet for a drink before heading to the premiere at the AMC Theater on 42nd Street. A drink was undoubtedly what I needed. I was an absolute wreck. I had spent the last twenty four hours frantic over what I was going to wear. I really did not have time to create something from scratch but decided to take a simple black cocktail dress that I had created years ago and give it a bit of a facelift. I even added a few scraps of the fuschia fabric to the neckline.

I wanted to be understated and simple, and I think that I had accomplished that, but traveling into the city on the train was going to be the end of me. I didn't want to sit for fear of wrinkling the dress, or worse, accidentally sitting in something disgusting on the train. But standing in my heels for forty five minutes grasping germ infested metal railings was not exactly relaxing my nerves.

I got to the bar a bit earlier than anticipated as I couldn't spend another minute staring at the walls of my apartment.

Lea said the red carpet began at seven but suggested that I be there no later than six thirty in case anyone wanted to meet or speak with me. Why would anyone want to meet or speak with me? I wasn't sure.

I took a seat at the bar and pretended to agonize over the cocktail menu while I waited for Connor and then sent Sylvie a few panicked texts.

"Selena? Is that you?" asked a familiar voice.

I turned and looked to both sides of me but saw no one looking back in my direction.

"Over here," I looked across the bar to a familiar face now waving at me.

Jack Webber.

You had to be kidding me.

He left the blonde woman who was seated beside him and was now walking towards me.

He might be the last human being on planet Earth that I wanted to exchange words with right now. I refused to even get out of my seat.

As he approached he opened his arms ready to pull me in for a hug. Before he got so much as a step closer I lifted up my right hand and did a close body wave.

"Hi Jack," I said flatly.

He awkwardly fell a step back realizing that hugs were not welcome here. His hugs anyways.

"What are you doing at a bar in Times Square all alone?" he asked patronizingly.

How did I spend nine months with this man?

I stared back at him, tilting my head with a *what the fuck l*ook in my eyes and said nothing.

"Well, it's great to see you."

He paused, waiting for me to say something, and finally I did, for no reason other than the hope that it might make him go away.

"Have a good night, Jack," and then I forcefully spun my legs around to face the bar and the rest of my body quickly followed. What was worse was I now had to face him and his blond companion across the bar. I looked more closely at her now that she was turning to laugh (likely about me) with Jack. Was she the same woman that I caught him with at brunch? It was like that entire exchange had been blocked from my memory. I honestly had no idea. She was very attractive, likely younger than me, and clearly dumber.

"Hey Selena."

A warm hand was on my shoulder, it made me jump.

I turned to see the most handsome man in the city. An electric current gently raked down the back of my neck, my spine, twinkling all the way down to my toes. I noticed the female bartenders agreed as they raised their eyebrows, heads nodding in his direction.

I turned towards him and pulled him in for the most 'extra' kiss I could handle in public.

"Wow," was all he could say as he put his blazer on the back of his chair and sat down beside me. "Does being nervous turn you on or something?"

We both laughed.

I was terrible at secrets. Worse at keeping things to myself.

I sighed.

"What is it? Is everything ok?" he looked concerned, his hand on my lap. "You look amazing, the dress came out great!"

He noticed.

He always seemed to notice.

"I'm sorry. My idiot ex is across the bar with a bigger blonde idiot and I really just guess I wanted to be sure they saw the super hot guy I was meeting."

I was ashamed.

"Oh, I'm always down for making an ex jealous," he leaned down and kissed me again. He pulled away, discreetly scrolling the room. I could tell he knew exactly who Jack Webber was.

"Ok, let's move on, forget him. I need a drink, you?" I laughed.

I could hear my phone ringing from my purse.

"I'm so sorry," I said as I pulled it from my bag. It was Lea Campbell.

"Hi Lea."

"Selena, I'm so sorry. After careful consideration, and with direction from my public relations team we decided to pass on your dress. My team just didn't think now was a great night to arrive wearing something from an unknown designer. My deepest apologies."

She paused, waiting for my response.

"Ok, well you're still welcome to use the tickets to come to the premiere."

And before words could even form, she had hung up.

I sat there, stunned - pained, really. Like a ruthless killer had just found me and stabbed his knife into my stomach again and again. As if it was my turn to present in my middle school English class and my mom's underwear was attached to the side of my leggings. Like I had worked my ass off on something for days after the death of my Nonni, only for some vicious bitch to swoop in and steal the spotlight away from me. My hands began to shake, mostly with anger.

Our drinks had arrived and Connor was now looking at me in concern.

I put the phone down and took a deep breath.

I hadn't even considered this possibility. Elaine Summer. What a-

"What's going on Selena? You look like you just saw a ghost! Is everything okay?"

"She's not wearing it," was all I could get out. I said it so quietly that I wasn't sure he even heard me.

"What? What do you mean? Why?"

Connor turned my chair to face him, shielding me from the possibility of so much as even a glance from Jack Webber.

"Her PR team told her not to wear it."

I had told Connor about Elaine and shared my fears of her finding out who I was and ruining all of it. And sure enough…

He muttered something under his breath.

"I have to tell Sylvie." I grabbed my phone and sent her a note. "Actually, I'll be right back," I stepped off of the bar stool and made my way to the bathroom.

I put the cover down over the toilet and took a seat, proceeding to leave multiple voicemails and texts for Sylvie. I was so angry. I couldn't even cry if I wanted to. These people did not deserve my tears this week, those were all reserved for Nonni.

I stepped out of the stall and went to the mirror, grabbing both sides of the pedestal sink, and taking deep breaths while I waited for the water to warm up. I focused on my breath, in through the nose and out through the mouth. I looked up at my reflection. Red blotches creeped up my neck. They looked worse than I had ever seen them. I should probably get to a doctor, stat.

The door suddenly opened and in walked Jack's date. We made accidental eye contact and I was left with the decision of whether or not to acknowledge her. I offered her a safe, closed mouth smile.

"I'm sorry, I would hate me too," she said and then turned and walked to the bathroom.

"Nope, I don't hate you, only Jack," I said to her from the other side of the stall door and then marched my way out of the bathroom.

Connor was standing outside the bathroom door when I stepped out.

"You ok?" he asked.

"Yup, let's go get drunk Connor," I said and smiled at him, immediately forgetting the life threatening rash on my neck at the sight of this glorious man. He grabbed my hand and we found ourselves on one of the busiest blocks in the city on the most beautiful night.

Chapter Sixty

SYLVIE

I put on my big girl pants and took the ferry back to the Hamptons for the weekend. Despite not wanting to leave Simon's bed Saturday morning, I had a lot of personal business to attend to and I truly just needed to get my shit together.

I packed up my room and let Tanya and Maura know that my room would be available to their guests for the last two weeks of my sublet. No one seemed terribly upset. I didn't see Tommy the entire time I was there. I brought a bottle of wine back to my room and stayed up half the night on Sunday researching high end Italian restaurants all over the world. Checking out their names, their branding and decor and even their menus. Simon's spot had the potential to be on this list of beautiful and delicious eateries.

I went on to research showrooms and design studios that I planned to visit all week in the city. Simon said I had full authority to make decisions. We went over my budget for every item and delivery deadlines and I was on my own. It was so exciting.

I hadn't told Selena about it yet. She was so down after that bitch

Lea Campbell had completely screwed her over that I did not have the heart to tell her my news. I was just glad that she had Connor to cheer her up. Based on the hangover she texted me about on Saturday I was confident he knew the perfect way to handle the situation.

By the time I got off the ferry with all my belongings on Monday it was supper time. Simon had offered to pick me up but my dad had offered too, and I wanted to check in and see how mom was really doing. She was putting on a very brave front for Selena and I...

"Let's get dinner Sylvie," he said after we stuffed all of my bags into the back seat of his truck.

My dad and I never got dinner, just the two of us. I was worried.

"Sure Dad, whatever you want."

He smiled and took me to Cavaleri's, a small Italian restaurant tucked between a smoke shop and a hair salon across from the harbor. It was the rare Italian restaurant that my family would actually eat at. We talked and ate for over an hour and still I wasn't sure what his motive was, or if he had one, until he nervously put his napkin down and looked up at me.

"Sylvie, honey. If you need to borrow some money, I want you to know that we can help you. I have some money saved and I am happy to-"

Oh my God. He was so worried, he actually looked like he might cry.

"Dad, dad," I reached across the table and grabbed his hand. "I'm good, I promise."

"I don't want you to stop taking classes because you can't afford them, *Angioletto*."

"I know, I promise, I've got everything under control. In fact, I just landed myself a consulting job."

He beamed hearing about the opportunity Simon had given me. I was grateful that he did not ask me how I knew Simon or the origin of our relationship. I was not quite ready for those introductions and I didn't want my dad to think I was given it because of our relationship, even though I worried about it sometimes myself. Like, maybe Simon was so into me that he thought I was great, but really, I'm not? Don't they say that when they get older, when a man truly loves his wife he doesn't notice how her body changes and the lines form on her face?... I mean, I'm not suggesting that he's in love with me, or that I am his wife...it's just, maybe he is a bit caught up in our relationship and that's why he liked my ideas?

I shook my head trying to knock away the self doubt.

My dad was staring at me with a smile, he loved knowing something that my mom didn't; it was written all over his tanned face. His salt and pepper hair was hidden by his 'Sons of Italy' hat and the gold chains that circled his neck peeked out the top of his shirt. The lines around his eyes and mouth suggested a life of hard, physical work but also one of many, many smiles. For the first time in my adult life, I could see that I had made my father proud.

Chapter Sixty-One

SELENA

I hadn't been home since Friday afternoon. I had spent most of the weekend in Connor's bed, sometimes with Connor and sometimes not. He was a real trooper on Saturday when I was too hung over to lift my head from the pillow. I think I laid there until dinner time. I came alive long enough to eat a double cheeseburger meal and watch a movie before heading back to bed with him.

Sunday was a bit more ambitious. We rented another boat, this time I left the charcuterie board home but wore a bathing suit I picked up at the nearby Target. We both got in and out of the water a lot and were one of the last boats to leave the beach.

"I want you to meet my sister," he said.

He was so serious when he said it. We were chest to chest bobbing in the ocean, my legs wrapped around his waist and my arms on top of his shoulders. He could touch the ocean floor and I could have too, but we would never really know, because I avoided it at all costs, always.

"Oh, wow."

"C'mon, I met Sylvie."

"Well yea, but that was kind of like an emergency situation. We didn't have much of a choice."

"True, but I did, and it went really well. I'd really like to get dinner with her and Simon-"

"Okay."

"Okay?" he repeated and smiled. He leaned in to kiss me. "And the kids too, of course. You already know Brooklyn, but..."

"Yup, and the kids." I smiled, unsure of why I even hesitated. Likely because of that promise that I made to myself that I was going to be single, play the field, be spontaneous and less cautious. Avoid relationships and love. Avoid the possibility of another broken heart...but here I was. Head over heels for the most handsome, most kind man I had ever met. And now I was meeting his family.

He may not be Italian, or even a generational Italian American, but I was certain that my mom already loved him. It wasn't approvals that I had to worry about.

"Would tomorrow night work?"

"Geez, I figured you meant in a few weeks!" We laughed.

We had been the right amount of busy that I hadn't had time to truly process the week. My feelings about Nonni's passing would sneak out of me unexpectedly and uncontrollably here and there and now, thanks to my job, I had just a touch of rage simmering in my lower belly.

"Can we aim for later in the week? I have some ideas that I want to work on and sometimes once I start it's hard for me to stop."

"Of course," he said, understanding.

It was Monday morning and Connor had dropped me at home on his way to the train. My living room was a warzone of fabric and thread scraps. Just seeing the fuschia color made me angrier. I sent Connor a text knowing he was still on the train.

I want my dress back. Do you think it's unreasonable to offer to refund her if she returns the dress to me?

Not at all. I don't blame you. PS - I have a meeting with Isabel Ferragamo today for the licensing deal. Anything special you want me to say to her? I'm sure she will bring you up!

No, but thank you!

I wasn't quite sure what Isabel's interest in me would even mean.

I looked in my contacts, staring at Lea Campbell's name. Instead, I decided to pull up my computer and see what I could find out about Elaine Summer.

The name of her agency was The Communications Boutique. How original. I rolled my eyes and scrolled over to the 'About' section and dug further into the 'Meet our Team.' Immediately a five by seven headshot of Elaine Summer filled my screen: "Founder."

She described herself as the 'city's best,' with a client roster that included movie production companies, restaurants, nightclubs and a few non profits (to save face, I'm sure). How generous. At the bottom of her profile she wrote: "While my clients are treated like family, no one is more important to me than my immediate family. My precious boys, Cullen and Charlie are the joys and prides of my life." I rolled my eyes again. I probably should stop doing that. I read once that rolling your eyes really strains the muscles around your lids and could lead to sagging of the under eyes.

No mention of the fact that her son was an absolute menace at school and that she was clearly an absent parent that did not read emails.

I grabbed my phone again and pulled up the messages app.

I mean, what would I do with the dress? When did I actually ever go anywhere that required that fancy of a dress?

I slumped back into my couch, holding a piece of the fabric.

But why should something I worked so hard, that I so beautifully stitched, sit in some rich woman's closet only to collect dust?

Would you take me somewhere that I could wear that dress one day?

I was really getting bolder and bolder with Connor.

Challenge accepted. I absolutely will, it is my promise.

Chapter Sixty-Two

SYLVIE

By Friday I had a portfolio of options that I wanted to present to Simon before ordering. He suggested that I just move forward and order them without his approval and I told him I thought that was a really bad business decision. He had worked too hard on the project to just turn it over to someone, even if it was me.

I used my newfound college skills and created a PowerPoint presentation filled with pricing breakdowns, virtual images of the restaurant staged with all of my suggestions as well as a timeline for when everything should be expected for delivery. I was really proud of myself and couldn't wait to show him. I asked that he bring in a few others so that we could hear multiple opinions and feedback.

"I don't want to share you Sylvie," was all that he said.

I rolled my eyes and told him that I would invite his father and brother if he didn't, so when I got to the restaurant on Friday I was grateful to see many familiar and unfamiliar faces surrounding the table in the private dining room. There were family style dishes down the center of the table that made my mouth water. Simon had hung a large white table cloth over the blank wall and set up a smart projector for my presentation.

I was nervous, but too excited to share all my recommendations to let the nerves be a factor. They were anything but a quiet audience. They clapped and cheered for some of my choices and at one point they high-fived. They made me feel qualified and capable and they truly made me want to make this the best looking restaurant New York had ever seen.

The final slide addressed the elephant in the room.

"So, what do we name this beautiful restaurant?"

I paused and looked at their faces before hitting the button on the computer that would bring up my suggestions. Something stopped me.

The men and women in the room were almost all related to Simon. They were all very proud Italians and after looking into their eyes I wasn't confident that any of my suggestions were special enough for what this place deserved.

I pushed the top of my laptop down, closing it. They all looked at me surprised, waiting for what I would say next.

"Now that I'm here, and with all of you, none of my ideas seem special enough. I think we need to all talk it through together."

"No, no, no, we asked you for your recommendation Sylvie," Simon said, challenging me.

My eyes widened, my mouth lifting to smile at him. His confidence in me was really sexy.

"Well, I need to start over, none of my ideas were good enough."

The room was suddenly quiet.

"Il Tavolo Especiale," came out of my mouth before I had time to think.

"The Special Table," said Simon's father for the folks in the room that couldn't do the translation. Lots of smiles and heads nodding.

"*Buon Appetito*," said Dom.

Again, many head nods and smiles.

It was suddenly so obvious to me, how had this not been one of my original suggestions.

"Carlino's. I think it has to be Carlino's," I said matter of factly.

The faces at the table began to tilt and turn, all looking for each other's reaction.

Simon's father broke the silence.

"*Ben fatto* Sylvie! Well done! Yes! It should be Carlino's!"

The room filled with claps and cheers. I looked across the room and my eyes met Simon's. He mouthed 'thank you' to me and the smile on his face made me realize everything went as well as I could have hoped. He walked around the table towards where I was standing.

"Well Miss Sylvie, looks like you have a lot to get ordering," he leaned over and kissed me on the cheek.

"Let's keep it professional, Mr. Carlino," I whispered in his ear.

"Meet you at my place later?" he whispered smugly.

"You know what? I would like to celebrate! Let's see if Selena and Connor want to meet us for dinner? And then I would like you to come back to my place!"

His eyes popped a bit.

"You're going to let me spend time with your family? And see your apartment? Are you feeling ok Sylvie?"

"Don't make me change my mind! I'll make reservations and let you know when to pick me up! I have to get to work!" I said and then leaned over to kiss him quickly.

I went around the room to shake everyone's hands and thank them for their time and opinions. It was the greatest feeling in the world. I think I floated out of the restaurant and onto the street. The thought that only months ago I was wasting away bagging dry cleaning orders for my mother astounded me. I knew that Nonni would be so proud of what I just did and that smile stayed with me all the way back to Holly.

Chapter Sixty-Three

SELENA

Connor had texted me immediately after his meeting with Isabel Ferragamo to let me know that he had given her my contact information and she was going to reach out. Tuesday morning her assistant Bradley called and asked if we could meet on Thursday for a drink at six in the city.

I was meeting Isabel inside the lounge of the Moxy Hotel on West Thirty Sixth Street and was shocked to see her already there and sitting at a table alone, when I arrived. I had imagined her arriving late with an entourage.

We double cheek kissed and then I profusely apologized for not being early enough.

"No need, I was early. I like to have a drink alone after a busy week Selena."

Did that mean I was interrupting her alone time? I was very confused and flustered.

"Let's get right to it," she said ignoring my awkward exchange with the waitress who took my drink order.

She had my attention. My mouth was not working correctly so I decided it was best to just shut up and listen.

"I'd like to bring you in. I'd like to make you a designer on my team."

She paused, waiting for my reaction.

"Wow, thank you so much. I guess I am not super familiar with the business. I thought you were the designer?"

Here we go with the red face. I could feel the blotches forming on my chest as the redness made its way to my cheeks.

"Oh, that's adorable. Yes, of course I design. But I have a whole team. I oversee everyone's designs and give direction to all of my staff, but I am only one person, Selena."

I nodded, taking in what she just said and pleading with my mouth to think through whatever was to come out next.

"Can you tell me a little bit more about the position? What would it look like to be a designer for you?"

She smiled. "My designers all work in my fashion house around the corner," she pointed to the left of us. "We work long grueling hours, but your designs are sketched and we use technology to create mockups. We create our own textiles in-house. We would meet so that I could either approve or scrap your ideas, and then you would have a team of pattern makers, tailors and dressmakers at your disposal."

She paused to make sure I heard everything. I took a large gulp of the glass of Sauvignon Blanc that the waitress had just delivered. This was a lot to process. I loved to make patterns. I loved to search for unique fabrics and work with them in my machines. I loved to drape. I loved to make changes and take chances…

"I would pay you two hundred thousand dollars."

I almost spit out my wine.

I had no words. Last year I earned eighty-four thousand dollars, which is an amazing salary for a young art teacher. One of the perks of working at a private school. More than tripling my salary? This sounded like a no-brainer.

Except it didn't feel right.

Could I even design for someone else's vision? Would I like it that someone else was taking my ideas? That someone else was creating my ideas?

"That is a very generous offer Isabel," I finally got out. "I will need some time to think about it."

She looked shocked.

"But you're an art teacher, right?" She asked, clearly not expecting anything but a quick yes out of me.

I nodded.

"I'll need to know by Monday," her tone had changed a bit. She motioned for the waitress to come over and bring the bill. "Bradley will email you a detailed offer so that you can see the benefits and expectations. These offers do not come around often, Miss Rossi."

"I understand and I am truly honored and flattered. Thank you so much for your time," I was nearly running for the door.

I should be skipping for the door. I should be out on the street excited to share the news with the world. But I wasn't.

I walked to Bryant Park and took a seat at one of the benches. I pulled the Toms flats out of my oversized bag, replacing my heels. I looked over at my phone. It was only six thirty. Crowds of people were out for the night with friends or coworkers and I could sense their delight for the upcoming weekend on so many of them.

Well? How'd it go?

I hadn't told anyone other than Connor about the meeting. I wasn't sure what was going to come of it and I didn't want to get anyone's hopes up, including mine.

She offered me a job.

That's amazing!!!! We need to celebrate!

I don't think I want it.

My phone immediately began to ring.

"Hey."

"You ok?" he asked. "Where are you? I can meet you! I'm still in the city."

"On a bench in Bryant Park," I laughed at how pathetic I sounded.

"I can be there in fifteen?" He asked, waiting to see if I would wait.

"Ok."

We hung up and I continued to people watch and look around the city that seemed to swallow this park right up. Imagining myself being a daily part of all of this. Imagining myself getting to do this every single day if I wanted to.

But did I want to? It was a dream that I don't think I ever really had for myself. To say I was confused and overwhelmed was an understatement.

I saw Connor from across the park. He stood out. He was the kind of handsome that must catch every woman's eyes. When he finally spotted me he stopped. He smiled and almost nodded. I could imagine him saying to himself *'there she is.'*

I went to stand when he reached me and he motioned for me not to get up. When he sat down he pulled me over to his side, my head falling onto his chest.

"You look beautiful Selena."

I wish he could have seen how a simple compliment from him made me smile.

"You look awfully handsome yourself."

He kissed the top of my head.

Summers in the city could be brutal. But there was a cool breeze passing through the park and I could have stayed on the bench folded into Connor for hours. Days maybe.

"Tell me about it," he offered.

I pulled myself off of his chest so that I could look at him and see his expressions while I explained to him the opportunity that Isabel had presented.

"And what are your concerns?" he asked when I was finished.

"Well, I don't know how I would do designing for someone else. I really like making my own patterns and making the pieces myself. I love going into a fabric store without any direction and being inspired." Not to mention someone else's name on my design.

He continued to listen.

"I love visiting the city. But I have never had the dream to work or live here."

Connor nodded.

"That all makes a lot of sense to me, Selena," his eyes were so kind, so patient and sincere.

"She offered me two hundred thousand dollars, Connor. That wouldn't just change my life, but it would allow me to help my family more."

"Does your family need your help?"

I wasn't expecting that as a follow up question.

"What do you mean?"

"Do your parents need your help? Are they struggling?"

"Well, I mean they live comfortably but I am sure they would like to travel, maybe go back to Italy and stuff."

He was thinking.

"Lea Campbell paid you five thousand dollars to make a dress. What makes you think you can't find five Lea Campbell's? Ten Lea Campbells? You could use that money to pay for a trip for your parents, but Selena, it doesn't sound like anyone is asking you to make more money."

"I don't love being an art teacher like I thought I would," I added.

"Okay, noted. But why should you go from one job that doesn't fulfill you to another?"

He was right. But something about the money just didn't sit well. How could I pass that up? Connor could see my mind in overdrive.

"If you took the job, you would hate commuting from Holly. Trust me, it's rough. You would want to get a place down here which would probably be triple the rent you're paying now. Everything in the city is more expensive, groceries, dinners, drinks. And who would help you take care of Queso? You would miss that crazy neighbor next door, wouldn't you?"

We both laughed. It was clear that he was trying to lighten my mood, and I had to admit, it was working.

"I need to think about it. All of it. Let's go home," I grabbed his hand and pulled him up from the bench, grateful that we could ride the train home together.

Chapter Sixty-Four

SYLVIE

Yo, do you and Connor want to grab dinner with us tonight?
Yo? Who are you? Who do you think I am?
Yes or no Selena?
Duh! YES!
Let me just confirm with Connor, but still, YES! Please don't change your mind.
Ok, he's excited too! Want me to make a reservation?

What can of worms did I just open up with Selena? She continued to send me about fourteen additional messages. I made reservations at Lola's and hoped the finality of a time and place would encourage her to leave me alone.

It didn't.

Simon picked me up at seven and suggested that he also grab Selena, but I told him it wasn't necessary (Selena had already suggested we all ride together and I let her know that she was really testing my limits). Selena and Connor were, of course, already there when we arrived. Selena was drinking a glass of white wine at the bar, Connor's arm draped across the back of her chair. They looked so happy, so comfortable together. It made me so happy for her.

She had texted me just as I got into Simon's car. *Promise I'll play it cool tonight...* We were about to see if that was even humanly possible for her.

"I have a feeling Selena's going to be a lot tonight, just warning you," I had said to Simon in the car ride over here.

"Don't worry, I can handle it. But why do you say that?"

"She's never met anyone I've dated."

He jumped a bit in his seat dramatically.

"Anyone?!"

"Not since my junior prom."

Now he was laughing, like really laughing.

"Sylvie Rossi, you are such a mysterious woman. I feel so honored to be the first."

"Well I've never really dated anyone," I added nervously. I had alluded to this many times with Simon but never stated it quite so honestly.

"What do you mean? Like never for more than a month? A year? I need more information Sylvie."

I sighed at the pain of this conversation.

"I don't want to get into it, and I'm sure you don't want me to either. But to put it to you bluntly, there were, of course, men that I would see regularly after nights out at the bars, but I have never been on more than three dates with the same person."

His mouth opened to say something.

"That's enough. We're not talking about it further."

We both laughed and he grabbed my hand.

"Well I'm honored to break this streak," he pulled my hand up to his mouth and kissed it.

I said nothing, but leaned back, smiling thinking about the amazing day that I just had and hoping it would continue with dinner.

Chapter Sixty-Five

SELENA

Sylvie was glowing. Her happiness was contagious, infectious, palpable even. Her and Simon weaved in and out of conversation with the ease of a decade long marriage. She caught me staring at her and shook her head, begging me to stop.

Although we had met before, it was mid crisis. I hadn't taken the time to truly meet Simon, to inspect him and break down his worthiness of being with my sister. He was a big man, probably six foot three and his frame suggested he was strong and athletic. His thick, dark hair and olive skin were all the Mediterranean qualities that Nonni had sought for us in a man. She would have loved everything about him. She would have squeezed his cheeks and tested his Italian. She would have cooked multi course meals for him and when he finished she would have pushed for him to eat more.

"Tell them about today," Simon playfully nudged Sylvie's arm, cajoling her to spill the beans.

"Tell us what?" I asked.

She looked back at Simon, smiling.

"Well, I'm trying something out. Something I really like, and am testing to see if I'm good at it."

"I promise you - she's not just good at it! She's amazing!"

"We really don't need to hear about your sex life," I said quietly and turned to see Connor laughing.

"Funny. No, really, I have been helping Simon with some of the design decisions for his family's new restaurant and today I got to present some ideas," she said casually.

"I knew you were going to undersell yourself," added Simon.

"Months ago Sylvie helped me with some decisions and challenged me to try some things I wouldn't have considered. People have been freaking out over them and our company has hired Sylvie to complete the design process for us."

"What?! That's amazing Sylvie! Why didn't you tell me this?" I asked while I leaning over to hug her.

"I don't know, you were so busy with the dress and stuff," she said, checking me out to make sure I was okay at the mention of it. "I wasn't sure if they would even like any of my ideas. But the meeting was today and I think it went really well."

"It went amazing. My family loved all of it!"

We spent most of the meal hearing about Carlino's and checking out some of the photos that Sylvie had on her phone. It all made so much sense. I could create the clothes, but Sylvie was always the one that could style them. Of course she would make an amazing designer!

"I'm pushing her to go out on her own, use this project as a start to her portfolio. I know other hospitality groups are going to be fighting for her after this!"

Simon spoke of her with such pride and affection.

Connor reached under the table and grabbed my hand, squeezing it. This didn't exactly feel like the right time to bring up the decision that remained on my plate. This was clearly Sylvie's night and I was not about to take that away from her.

Chapter Sixty-Six

SYLVIE

I rolled over to face my bedside table, anxious to see how late I had slept. It was nearly ten. Wow! I rolled back over and saw the bedding pulled back on the other side remembering the night with Simon. Did he leave?

I lifted myself up to get out of bed, and that's when the smells hit me. Was that bacon? Did I even have bacon in my fridge? I grabbed my robe from the chair in the corner and opened the bedroom door.

"Good morning Sylvie."

Simon stood there with a spatula in his hand wearing nothing but his boxer shorts and my cupcake and unicorn apron. Was this real life?

He met me in the doorway and pulled me in for a kiss. He pressed against me, hard enough to remind me of the night we had spent together. Suddenly, sleeping until ten made more sense.

"I would love to bring you back to bed but I don't want your omelet to get cold."

"Omelet? Am I dreaming?"

We both laughed as he pulled out a chair at my table and went to pour us both a cup of coffee.

"I'm pretty sure my fridge only had condiments and cheese in it. I don't understand how you did all this?"

"I'm an early riser. I ran to the grocery store. Let's just say I bought enough so that we can do this as many mornings as you let me," he was smiling. "I even got the paper. The Design section on Saturday is where you need to be Sylvie."

"Oh, I love the Design section. Selena and I used to fight over it in high school." The Saturday edition of the New York Telegraph included a glossy insert with Real Estate, Design and Fashion articles and photos. I know Selena still reads it, always trying to stay on top of new trends in fashion.

"Simon, this omelet is amazing," I said, moaning with every bite.

Our meal was interrupted by three quick knocks at my apartment door.

Simon looked at me confused.

There was only one person that knocked like that. I walked over to the door and looked through the peephole, and sure enough…

I opened the door enough so that my head could stick through the crack of it.

"What's up Selena?" I asked, shielding her from anything and everything happening inside my apartment.

"Can I come in?" she asked, Connor popped up behind her, holding Queso. He waved with an uncomfortable smile

"Umm, I'm kind of in the middle of something, Selena."

What in the hell was she doing? We don't do this to each other when we are single, so we certainly don't pop into each other's apartments when she knows damn well there's a handsome man likely in bed with me.

"I promise, it's an emergency," she looked back at Connor for reassurance. He shrugged and then nodded.

I tied my robe a bit tighter and looked for Simon. He was walking out of my room, jeans now on and he was pulling a shirt over his head. I loved that he had packed a bag for the night. I tried to apologize to him with my eyes and he mouthed 'It's okay.'

I opened the door wide, reluctantly inviting Selena and Connor in. What kind of an emergency could this possibly be?

Selena looked at my table, realizing she was interrupting breakfast, but she nearly ran when she saw the unopened Telegraph on the counter.

"Did you see it?" she motioned towards the paper.

"See what Selena?"

Sometimes her drama exhausted me.

"That bitch! She did this!"

Simon and I both turned to Connor, hoping he could tell us what in the hell was going on.

He opened the paper and pulled out the glossy Design insert, flipping through the pages until he stopped. He left it open on the dining table in front of us.

Simon and I stood side by side, reading the article headlined TEACHERS SHOULD FOCUS ON STUDENTS, NOT DESIGN DREAMS.

As soon as I saw the title my hands went up, covering my mouth. Selena stood beside us with her arms crossed over her chest. Connor had a gentle arm wrapped around her waist and kept bending down, kissing her on the top of her head.

The article was a gross opinion editorial written by none other than Elaine fucking Summer. While she never named Selena, she made it very easy for an interested reader to do the tiniest bit of detective work to figure out it was her. She accused her of devoting her time to her hobby, not her students. She also went on to say her designs were 'mediocre at best' and from what she had heard 'a low level art teacher that has clearly forgotten the importance of elective classes providing a boost to high performing student's GPAs.'

"What a bitch. I am so sorry Selena."

She was just shaking her head and began pacing back and forth in my very small living room. She looked to be having a bit of a psychotic meltdown. I braced knowing that this would likely end with a visit to the emergency room. I wondered if Connor was prepared for what was sure to come.

"They didn't name you," Simon offered.

"I said the same thing," added Connor, clearly unsure of how to help Selena.

"She named the school, it doesn't take Sherlock Holmes to figure out it's about me," said Selena. "Can I sue her for defamation?"

For once, her dramatic reaction felt warranted.

"Anyone want a drink?" asked Simon. He pulled out two bottles of champagne from the fridge. Did he seriously buy those while I slept too? Next he grabbed a bottle of orange juice. "Mimosas?"

I gave him a closed mouth smile, to let him know I appreciated what he was doing. He really just needed a cape and maybe a pair of tights or something. He was my superhero.

Connor raised a hand requesting one.

Selena was still pacing.

"I already sent my principal an email. I'm sure he will respond by letting me know I'm fired."

Connor handed her a mimosa, and squeezed her shoulder.

"I think Elaine Summer looks and sounds like a lunatic. I think very few people will take the time to read it, and those that do will not be concerned enough to do any further research."

"I agree," I added, nodding towards Connor, hopeful that together we could thwart her Category five meltdown.

"I knew she was behind Lea Campbell's last minute change of heart. But this! This is next level! Her asshole son got a D in my class. He deserved an F!"

Selena crashed onto my couch and took a swig out of her drink.

"Ahh, this is delicious Simon, thank you," she sounded exhausted.

Selena looked around the room and surveyed the now cold food on the table.

"That looks really good, I'm so sorry to crash on you guys like this. I swear we don't usually do this to each other," she said, looking from Simon to Connor.

Chapter Sixty-Seven

SELENA

It was nearly dinnertime when I looked around the room, all of us drunk and in our pajamas and realized we had overstayed at Sylvie's. Simon had eventually made a hot brunch for all of us but soon the champagne ran out, the vodka bottle was empty and I felt a lot less angry but much more tired.

When we got back to my apartment I leaned into Connor, forgetting the horrible morning that we had turned into the most fun I've had since my senior year of college. There's just something magical about day drinking.

"I know it was terrible for you and I'm so sorry, but I had so much fun today Selena," he said, playfully kissing my neck as I pulled away from him.

I could tell he was as tipsy as I was.

"I know what you mean," I smiled back at him.

"Should we give Lea Campbell a call and tell her how much her publicist sucks?" I asked, pulling up the Contacts tab on my phone.

He gently grabbed my phone out of my hand and put it on the ironing board next to my sewing machine.

"Let's deal with them tomorrow. I say we order takeout and bring it to bed with us."

"I can't believe it's only six. I think that sounds perfect."

By six thirty we were in my bed passing containers of egg rolls and boneless spare ribs while the fourth season of Suits blared on the television.

"Is this what your office is like?" I pointed to the television and we both laughed. A twinge of jealousy crept over me imagining beautiful women in sexy suits parading around

Connor all day at work.

"I know it's the last thing you want to think about right now, but something to keep in mind. I have another summer party in the Hamptons next weekend. I'd love to whisk you away for the night if you are up for it. Think about it."

"Will Elaine fucking Summer be there?"

We both laughed.

"Honestly, I fucking hope so."

We put the food on the side table and pulled up the covers, and that is exactly where we stayed until the sun peeked through the curtains on Sunday.

"What time is it?" Connor asked, noticing that I had stirred.

"Five."

"Oh boy, I was guessing you were gonna say nine or something!"

"Well I think we were both asleep before eight, so I guess we had it coming," I grabbed his hand, pulling him out of bed and into the shower with me.

By seven I was fully dressed and famished. I was too hungry to even remember that my entire professional life was in shambles. Connor had gone home because he couldn't bear the thought of wearing his same outfit for a third day in a row. He offered to come back and spend the day with me but I knew I had to face my problems and told him I needed some time to think.

I couldn't make any moves on an empty stomach so after making a subpar frittata I pulled out my laptop to see just how bad the damage was.

I started with my email, curious to see if my principal had responded or if anyone had reached out after reading the article.

Hi Selena,

Yes, I did see the OpEd article, but I wouldn't have if a friend hadn't forwarded it to me. The fact that she included the name of our school is really disappointing to me and I would assume that this is all very upsetting to you. Sadly none of this surprises me and I was waiting to see if there were any repercussions from the article. I do believe and hope that we can move past this now.

In moments like this I generally turn to the school's Public Relations Advisor to see if we should publish a statement, but sadly, Elaine Summer is the person in that role. I am working on some talking points if anyone from the media reaches out to me and I planned on sending those points to you as well, so please be on the lookout.

I plan to let folks know that you were disciplined with a two month leave. There have been instances where the school's board or committee catches wind of the situation and demands that a faculty member be terminated. I will do my best to avoid that situation. But again, be prepared for anything.

Also, I saw your costumes at the play, you're a very talented designer Selena, I truly hope that you can see this article for what it is.

Best,
Dan DiMatino
Principal, Parker Miller School

I grabbed a magazine off the table and began fanning myself with it. This was humiliating. It was degrading and most of all, it was unfair.

What I would do to get Elaine Summer alone in a room.

My thoughts immediately go to a very pregnant Charlotte York on the city corner bumping into Mr. Big in the first *Sex and the City* movie.

"I curse the day you were born."

She had said it with such authority, such conviction. I would give up my parking spot for an opportunity like that.

Chapter Sixty-Eight

SYLVIE

The following week was a flurry of showroom visits, measurements, orders and prayers. Despite having no official idea what I was doing, I was desperately trying. I downloaded a project management app and had a line item for every decision being made, followed by status updates, pending arrivals and notes. I also ate into my savings and purchased some design software so that I could create more detailed virtual layouts of the restaurant.

I had been up every night past midnight teaching myself through the help of YouTube and some design forums. I couldn't believe how confident I was feeling by the end of the week.

Aside from an amazing six foot long raindrop glass solitaire chandelier, I had not made any big decisions for the private dining space but knew that it needed to be extra special. I wanted to recreate the feeling of sitting around the table with Simon's close knit family sharing a meal for all of Carlino's patrons. And that is when the idea hit.

I made some phone calls to friends that I knew were like family to Simon and his father, and the wheels for my special project were in motion. Simon had pretty much stayed out of my hair, occasionally asking in the mornings what my plan for the day was, or if any big deliveries could be expected.

We were spending nearly every night at his place or mine. I didn't even recognize myself. I would occasionally pull back and question what I was doing, but could not bring myself to stop. I wanted Simon. I wanted him for breakfast, lunch and dinner and I liked being with him just as much when we were fully clothed. I liked being with him when we were sober, and I of course liked him when we were overserved. This was untouched, uncharted, virgin, if you will, territory for me.

The grand opening for Carlino's was in three weeks and we were meeting on Friday morning with the public relations agency that Simon had hired to review publicity packages, photography schedules and a chef's table-testing for media only. There were so many soft, hard, kinda soft openings on the schedule that I couldn't help but giggle at the sexual innuendos that were passed around by email on the daily.

When I got to the restaurant Friday morning I was relieved to see that the chairs had arrived, the tables were dressed exactly as instructed by the virtual models I had provided for Simon and his staff. Some additional lights were in and there was a crew working on a terracotta tile wall design that would be flanked by pops of live ivy.

I stood in the doorway and just smiled with pride and excitement. I hoped that guests would walk in and feel the warmth that I did every time I stepped inside.

"Whatcha doing?" Simon was standing on the other side of the restaurant, staring at me. Despite waking up together, I insisted we commute separately. Simon did not protest but definitely thought I was being a bit over the top.

I walked his way, both of us turning towards the private dining room where we would wait for the public relations team to arrive. I had been back and forth with our account manager Kendra Roffo all week for scheduling and sharing of information, but I was very curious to hear the official launch plan she would present to Simon today.

Simon brought in a carafe of coffee and placed it by a tray of warm croissants in the center of the table. He truly knew how to host and entertain.

"The sign is going up tomorrow," I said.

His eyes perked up. I had worked with his graphic designer day and night until we got it right. It was a nod to the Italian restaurants of our parent's heyday, and featured a very simple cursive font in red neon lights that would sit on top of a bed of ivy over the main entrance door. I had one made to hang over the bar as well as a smaller one for the back entrance, because we wanted 'Carlino's,' wherever we could, front and center, not to be forgotten..

I could hear chatter coming from the front of the restaurant.

Simon got up and stood outside of the door, waving them in.

"Welcome," he said.

"This is even better in person, it is stunning," said a female voice. I'm guessing it was Kendra.

A few other women chimed in with kind comments and questions. I saw them approach the room through one of the glass walls.

"Should we go around the table and introduce ourselves?" said the oldest of the four women. She was a visibly assertive woman, an alpha who was clearly the boss of the other three.

"Kendra, why don't you go first," she said, looking at a pretty young blond, maybe twenty two years old, tops, who sat to her right.

As we went around the room with introductions, butterflies filled my stomach as we neared my turn. I felt ridiculous referring to myself as a designer, but Simon had reminded me multiple times both last night and this morning that it was time to own it.

"Umm, hi, I am Selena Rossi, I am working with Simon on a lot of the design decisions for the space," I said, smiling at Simon for reassurance.

The boss lady's eyebrows lifted. She had not yet introduced herself.

"Is your company based in the City?" she asked me.

I looked at Simon who nodded his head. We had discussed the importance of my company, (assuming I was on the brink of creating one) having a mailing address in the city. Simon feared that I wouldn't be taken as seriously with a Holly address, and I was quickly realizing that he was right.

I nodded and she smiled at me, pleased with my response.

"You do beautiful work. I am Elaine Summer," said the inquisitive alpha to my left. "I am the owner of the agency and will be overseeing Kendra and her team on this project. I assure you that you are in the best possible hands and whenever I am needed, I will pitch in to help ensure that your opening is the talk of the town." She was looking directly at Simon, smiling.

My mouth dropped. How had I not thought of this? How hadn't Simon? We have been doing business with this diabolical bitch for two weeks! I looked across the table at him, his jaw tight and his eyes searching mine for our next move.

I widened my eyes so big that they began to burn, but I could not stop them. Elaine rattled on and on about her agency and pride in her work...and more bullshit.

"Excuse me Elaine, can I see you for one second, Sylvie?" Simon gestured out to the hallway and apologized again to the rest of Elaine's very young team of publicists.

He gently grabbed my arm and pulled me into his office, closing the door behind him.

"Holy shit Sylvie, I had no idea. I swear to God, I had no idea. Kevin at Lantana's gave me the company name and I am embarrassed to say that I did absolutely zero research before calling them. The receptionist put me directly in touch with Kendra, I had never heard Elaine's name until today."

Simon was pacing back and forth in his small office. I had never seen him like this. His hand continuously running through the back of his hair.

I didn't even know what to say.

He paused, and looked up at me, sadness in his eyes.

"She could ruin me Sylvie."

"What?"

"If this goes sideways, all she needs to do is tip off one food reporter, one critic, and we're done, over, *fatto*."

"No way," I pleaded with him, but as I stepped back, again watching him pace, I realized that he was right. Elaine Summer held all the power. I have never hated anyone more. I wanted to go out there and Charlotte York her. What was that line?

I regret the day you were born? Something like that. God I hated her.

"We say nothing," I said calmly. "Kendra is our point of contact, we do not have to work with Elaine again. Just for this meeting, that is it."

He pulled me into his chest.

"I am so sorry, Sylvie."

"I know."

Chapter Sixty-Nine

SELENA

It took the Board a whopping three days to catch wind of Elaine Summer's scathing article. I was emailed an official notice of my termination by five on Thursday. After phone calls from both the president of the board and our principal I was grossly sick of hearing things like 'our hands are tied,' 'she put us between a rock and hard place,' 'this is not someone that our school would like to go to war with.' Know what I wanted to tell all of them? That they were absolute pussies. I hated using that word, in fact, I never used it, but if ever there was an occasion, here it was!

I sent Connor a quick text to lie and let him know I was feeling sick and heading to bed. When really I powered off my phone and laptop, poured an oversized glass of the strongest Titos and tonic that my stomach could handle, blasted an angsty playlist and pulled out my sketch book.

By three in the morning I was very drunk, but had used a variety of black fabric scraps and created the most sexy, edgy, truly emotional cocktail dress that I had ever attempted. It was not something that I would ever dare wear myself, but I knew the asymmetrical cut up the right thigh paired with the daring neckline would have sexy twenty somethings craving a night out in it. Sylvie would slay this dress.

I had powered on my phone before going to bed early in the morning but refused to check messages or emails before crashing face first into my pillow. I woke up to my phone ringing.

I looked up at my nightstand, it was only nine. Who was calling me? I specifically had told Connor that I planned to sleep in, desperate to help him avoid the dumpster fire that was currently my life.

I didn't recognize the number.

"Hello?" Despite clearing my throat before answering, I sounded like a groggy, unemployed, and slightly drunk woman.

"Selena?" the woman on the other end sounded poised, fancy even. The crispness of her accented voice suggested she had been up for hours.

I sat up in bed, grabbed a sip of water from my nightstand, hoping it would clear the frogs out of my throat.

"Yes?"

"Please hold for Isabel Ferragamo." A loud beep followed by soothing elevator music.

Holy shit, I was not in any state for this. My temples pounded and the room was still wobbly. I wiped at my eyes and took another big swig of water.

"Selena?" A woman interrupted the music.

"Hi Isabel."

"Selena, it's been nearly a week-"

"I know, I'm so sorry, I've had quite a bit going on in my personal life and-"

"Selena. You do realize that an offer like this to an untrained designer does not come around very often?" she asked in her beautiful accent.

"I do, I do. I'm truly so appreciative. Honored, really," I was fumbling with my words. "Can you give me one more day?"

"What is the issue Selena? What's holding you back?"

"Umm, well, it's just not a job I have considered. I didn't even know it was a possibility for me, and-"

"You have until first thing Monday morning," she said abruptly and then hung up.

I looked down at my phone, still a bit shocked that she just called.

I opened up my messages and emails and was slightly hurt and disappointed to see that the fifteen hours of having my phone off had resulted in my missing absolutely nothing. Unbelievable!

Good Morning. I sent Connor a text.

My phone immediately began to ring.

Connor was worried and ready to have soup delivered to my apartment. I assured him that I was miraculously healed, however just tired.

"Think you'll be up for the Hamptons tomorrow?"

Shit, I had totally forgotten about the party.

"Oh, definitely," I lied.

"Great. Can I see you tonight, or-"

"Give me one more night to sleep off whatever this virus is, I'll be ready for you tomorrow."

"Are you sure you're okay, Selena?"

"Yup, I'm great." I lied again.

I had twenty four hours to decide if I was going to change careers, figure out how to tell my boyfriend and the slew of people he was likely to introduce me to that I had been fired by my lame art teaching position, oh, and add in slandered by a public relations tycoon in the Sunday paper.

Yup, I was okay. In fact I was great. Like Britney Spears circa 2007, great. Like, J Lo's fourth divorce, great. Like Reese Witherspoon out for a run and getting hit by a car, great. Like Steve Harvey crowning the wrong Miss Universe great. I was just fucking great.

Chapter Seventy

SYLVIE

Simon and I had muscled our way through the rest of the meeting. I was unable to meet Elaine's eye and instead focused all of my energy on Kendra, Simon did the same. It completely unhinged and disempowered Elaine, and I absolutely loved it.

I still wasn't sure how to handle things with Selena, I don't know if she could be rational enough to understand why Simon couldn't fire or confront her. I hated keeping things from her and tossed and turned about it all night.

Around four in the morning Simon whispered into my ear.

"I think you should tell her."

I flipped over to face him. "I can't, she won't understand and it will only make her upset with us."

"Maybe, but I think she will come around and understand. She will probably be mad for a few days. But clearly keeping this from her is going to tear you apart." He pulled me closer to him, beginning to kiss me. As if he knew I needed it, his kisses turned into something that took my mind off of all of my problems.

NOT AS IT SEAMS

In the morning I shot Selena a nervous text.
Call when free.
Everything ok? Just boarding the ferry with Connor.
Yes.
Ok, I'll call you tomorrow night when we're back.

I gave her text a thumbs up, so far feeling absolutely no relief by reaching out. My stomach rumbled knowing the weight it was to carry for another thirty-six hours. So when Connor called a few hours later I was convinced that they had found out.

"Is everything ok?" I skipped the cordial greetings and went straight to worst case scenario.

"Yes, everything is fine. More than fine actually." His voice was smooth and calm. "Listen, I have to be quick as she is just using the ladies room, but I think tonight is going to be a big night for Selena. I think there will be a lot of eyes on her, and she might like it if you are here. Simon too."

"What are you talking about?" I asked, he was being so mysterious.

"We're attending a client party tonight in Sag Harbor, should be a Who's Who in the fashion industry, and if my gut is correct, Selena is going to get a lot of attention. I would like to invite you and Simon to come as our guests. No pressure, and I know it's short notice, but..."

Relief washed over me. I looked at the clock. It was just after noon.

"We will be there. Text me the address," I said and hung up.

Simon looked at me quizzically wondering what I had just agreed to.

"Fashion party in the Hamptons, sounds like Connor is working overtime to cheer Selena up. You game?"

The ferry was completely booked and we didn't want to risk it so I drove. We were on the Long Island Expressway by three, with plans to stop for a bite once we got to town.

Chapter Seventy-One

SELENA

Connor's car was full considering we were only going for one night. He had multiple garment bags strewn across the back seat and the trunk contained bags that had no real explanation. As we pulled off the ferry I still hadn't bothered to ask him about any of it.

"Let's get settled in our rental and then I have our whole day planned out, if that's ok," said Connor. He had insisted we take the first ferry over and I did not understand what hotel or bed and breakfast would possibly allow us to check in at ten in the morning.

As we pulled down a windy sandy road a few miles off the Montauk Highway the ocean suddenly popped into view as well as a string of small beach cottages perfectly aligned along the sandy shore. Connor slowed, checking each one out until we pulled up to a cedar shingled bungalow that couldn't have been more than a hundred feet from the water. A small sandy hill covered in majestic beach grass protecting the home stood between it and the sea.

"This is it," he said, pulling up beside it.

"What do you mean?" I asked, confused.

"I rented it for the weekend," he smiled, knowing he had pulled one over on me. "Why don't you check it out while I unpack the car," he leaned down, unlocked the door and pulled me by my waist into the house as he unlocked the door, kissing my neck.

The house was so unassuming from the outside. The location was obviously amazing but when you stepped in, the entire back of the house was glass with views that most people dream (me, I'm most people) about. Everything was white with accents of salmon and blues. The kitchen was sleek but also so simple. The bedroom also punctuated by a glass wall and views had a balcony with chaise loungers that looked good enough to sleep on. The bathroom had more shower heads than my high school locker room. It looked like a human car wash that I could not wait to step into.

Connor was at the bathroom door, smiling as he noticed my amazement looking at the details throughout the home.

"I thought you could use a weekend to clear your mind, Selena. I think the party tonight will be good for you, but if you want to skip it, we can," he took a step towards me and pulled me in. "I know you're overwhelmed. I know you're scared and you're afraid of doing the wrong thing, but the beauty about jobs is, you can quit them. You can start over. You can pursue dreams, or you can do what makes you comfortable."

The way he said it made it sound so easy. So cut and dry. I still hadn't told him that I was down a choice since I had been fired from my job.

"I bought stuff for a brunch picnic on the beach, what do you say? After that I'm taking you into town and showing you some of the shops. I want to show you off Selena. I have spent way too many summers not enjoying this beautiful place. It has always felt like work when I'm here, but I want to walk down the streets and hold your hand. I want to buy you treats and kiss you on the beach."

Tears unexpectedly rushed to my eyes.

"Are you okay, I'm so sorry, I didn't mean to-"

He was like a dream. He was literally the version of a man that I wished every man before him to be.

"I'm better than okay Connor; your plans sound great."

We eventually pulled ourselves together after testing out the sleeping accommodations and made it to the beach for an amazing picnic (one where I didn't even question the germs involved with eating on the ground or out of containers with no explanation of their origin). Then we went into town for some shopping. Connor insisted on buying nearly everything I touched. By the third store I touched nothing for fear of taking advantage of him. I did not like the feeling of pity, I convinced myself that Connor's behavior was separate from my personal crisis but when he pointed out a puppy and waved me over to pet it I had had enough.

"Can we go back to the house?" I said abruptly.

"Yea, of course. Is everything okay?"

I nodded and we rode back to the rental in silence.

When we got back to the house I went and sat on the back porch overlooking the ocean. Connor stayed inside, giving me the space I so clearly craved.

About thirty minutes later he stepped through the sliding door holding two iced coffees and a brown paper bag.

"Ran out and grabbed some caffeine."

He was so sweet, so kind. He had treated me to such an amazing day and I was being an ungrateful bitch. I looked straight out at the horizon.

"I'm so sorry for my behavior. I just don't want your sympathy, Connor. I know I've complained a lot to you, and my life is a bit of a shit show at the moment, but I really don't want you to feel like you need to cheer me up."

I still couldn't look at him, for fear of seeing hurt feelings.

"I had this planned long before Elaine Summer and the Parker Miller School blew up your professional life Selena. I told you when we first started dating that I would have these parties to attend throughout the summer," he paused, looking over at me. "But I understand what you mean, I was over the top today."

I forced myself to turn and look at him, angry with myself for making him feel bad for spoiling me all day.

"I promise you weren't. I guess I'm just having a pity party today. I was let go yesterday."

He swooped down by my side, wrapping his arms around me.

"Selena, why didn't you tell me?"

He looked angry. I had never seen this look on him.

"Screw them Selena, this is absolutely their loss and your opportunity for change, that is all this is."

"I just feel like a loser, that's all," my voice cracking as I spoke.

It felt so good to have it out there and off my shoulders.

"But I would love nothing more than to snap out of it and enjoy this beautiful rental," I said, shaking it off, standing up and pointing out at the water. "I never even asked you about the party! Who is the client?"

He pulled me into his chest and we both looked out over the water.

"Well, I guess I should have mentioned it before, but tonight is Vogue's summer party. I will have half my client roster there," he said, quietly, eying me up and down for a reaction.

"Holy shit, Connor. This is major."

"Well then I think you'll agree it calls for a major moment."

He left the sliding door open as he walked into the bedroom. He came back holding one of the garment bags from the back seat.

He had only unzipped it about six inches when I saw the familiar fuschia fabric pop through.

My jaw physically dropped. My hands went up over my mouth to hide what had to be a really ugly reaction, but the words didn't come. I was literally speechless. I didn't even know it was possible, or real...

He finished unzipping the dress and stood there, clearly trying to gauge my reaction.

"How did you-?"

"I reached out to her the night of the premiere. I picked it up at her office that same weekend."

A cat literally had my tongue, again. Imagining the logistics of all of it was mind bending.

"We were together that entire weekend! How did you-"

"Except for that hour that I went home to get a change of clothes," he said, smiling deviously. "Are you crying? Are you okay?"

He threw the dress and bag back onto the bed so that his hands were free to grab me.

"I'm happy, they are happy tears!" I said, throwing my arms around his neck. "Thank you so much Connor!" I was covering his face and neck with short smacking kisses.

"There isn't a better event for you to wear it to, than tonight's!"

"You don't think it will be too much?"

"Too much?! It's Vogue, and the Hamptons! The two invented 'too much!"

We laughed.

And before I had time to argue or overthink it, I stood there in the kitchen relieved that the espadrilles I had packed looked as beautiful with the dress as the pumps once did.

Chapter Seventy-Two

SYLVIE

The Long Island traffic was an insufferable reminder of why I always took the ferry. We were in Sag Harbor by five and realized as we sat down for a very late lunch at a swanky bistro in town that we still didn't have any details about the party. I had texted Connor about an hour ago, but he had gone completely dark. If I wasn't sitting across the table from the sexiest man on the island I would have been so frustrated by Connor's lousy communication.

The restaurant was surprisingly busy for such an early hour and the people watching was exceptional. Some of the most beautiful, most fancy, most filthy rich people surrounded us at nearby tables. I noticed a couple of Bravo television stars and one of my favorite news anchors seated at tables across the way. Selena would have loved all the celebrity sightings.

So sorry for the delay. Party begins at six. It's 'Hamptons casual,' whatever that means. Guessing we will get there around six thirty. Thank you so much for making the trip out for this. I know Selena will be so happy to see you. Address to follow.

Connor's text came in just as we were paying the bill and deciding our next move. I had reached out to Tanya and was relieved when she said that they had never filled my room, and I was absolutely welcome to it for the night.

We went back to the house and were equally relieved that Tanya and Maura were working and Tommy was nowhere in sight.

After christening my Hamptons bed we both showered and changed into our party clothes.

"Did you see Kendra's email?" Simon asked when I stepped out of the very steamy bathroom.

I shook my head, unsure of what would make Kendra send an email on a Saturday night.

"She is pushing for a media day on Friday. She wants to do a chef's table lunch, followed by a private Grand Opening," he said nervously.

"Well, you're ready, don't you think?" I asked, my stomach tying itself in knots at the sound of her name. If I didn't tell Selena soon I might actually physically combust, strewing body parts and blood across the room and down the white walls.

"Are we?" he asked.

Nearly all of my orders were in and installed. I was still waiting for the custom wall art that I had ordered for the private dining room, but the main dining room, the bar and the bathrooms were completely finished.

I nodded my head and squeezed his hand.

"I'll be done by Thursday. How about the kitchen staff?" I asked him.

He simply nodded and smiled at me.

"It's been a bit of our love story," he paused and looked at me. "..the restaurant. I don't know if I'm ready to share it with anyone else just yet," he said, casually pulling my towel down to the floor and pulling me into him.

"And no matter what anyone else thinks, we have that," I said, kissing him.

He pulled away slowly, staring into my eyes, one of his eyebrows lifting a bit.

"What?" I asked, confused.

"You didn't even react to what I just said. You would have winced at the mention of a 'love story' a month ago, Sylvie," he said teasingly.

He was right. Simon hadn't just pulled back the curtain on how relationships were supposed to be, he had blown the damn door down. I smiled at him.

"So if I told you I loved you, you wouldn't run?" he asked, his face still so kind but very serious.

I paused before responding, not quite sure what to do at this moment. No one had ever said that to me before. I'm pretty sure my love for him began that night at Starbucks when he showed up with a hot calzone. I probably should keep that to myself. I could feel my cheeks burning and I suddenly felt shy.

"It's okay Sylv, I told you because I wanted to, not because I expect to hear it in return."

"Except I do love you," I said quietly.

"You, Sylvie Rossi, are full of surprises."

Chapter Seventy-Three

SELENA

Unlike the last party, this design and layout didn't have any elaborate tents or fancy catwalks; it felt a lot more intimate and therefore a bit scarier. We left Connor's car with the valet and walked the crushed shell path arm and arm. This party just felt different, or maybe it was me who was different? I was more confident, more relaxed and more sure of myself. When we rounded the back side of what had to be the most expensive house in Sag Harbor we were transported into a whimsical, elaborate party.

There were towers cascading with flowers strewn across the lawn and in the middle was the longest dining table I had ever seen. There had to be a hundred seats around it. The tablescape would surely be featured in the magazine next month. Lights draped from tree to tree and candles and lanterns were strategically scattered. A three-piece band sat in the corner strumming bluegrass music. But the home and the grounds were the real showstopper. I was pretty sure a yacht from *Below Deck* was parked at their dock.

We hadn't even officially left the walkway when we were greeted by a cute young woman that took our drink orders. She let us know there was no limit to what the bar staff could create. I asked for a glass of white wine and Connor asked for a light beer, I guessed we would be her easiest order of the night.

I could feel eyes yes on us as we walked across the lawn to where a group was gathered and appetizers were being handed out. Waitstaff was lined up shucking oysters and serving raw bar delicacies.

The cute waitress from earlier found us in the mix of guests and had a tray with our requested drinks. I hoped the wine would quell my nerves.

Before I had a chance to ask any questions, a man was in front of Connor and had reached up to kiss Connor's cheeks. He went on to stare at me, waiting anxiously for Connor to introduce me.

"Who are you wearing?" he asked in a thick spanish accent.

I guess we were skipping introductions.

I could feel my eyes widen and face lift as I went to answer him.

"Well, me, actually."

He looked back at me quizzically.

"She designed and made it," said Connor proudly, squeezing my side.

The man was dressed with a lot of, let's call it, pizzazz. Clearly he was not afraid to play with prints and patterns. He had on glasses that couldn't possibly have a prescription in them as their shape was like nothing I had ever seen.

"Darling," he said while reaching out his hand to take mine. "That might be the prettiest thing I've ever seen."

"Thank you," I said, suddenly feeling relaxed and maybe even a bit excited.

"Great to see you, Oscar," Connor said as he led us away from him and towards the oyster bar.

"Who was that?" I whispered.

"Honestly, I can't remember who he works for, but he is a designer for one of my clients," he laughed. "What you need to know is that a compliment from anyone in attendance tonight is the equivalent of a James Beard award for a chef. The best of the best will be here. I mean, they might all be douchebags, I'm not entirely sure, but

I know they are the supposed *visionaries* and stuff," he said, making air quotes.

"Selena," said a beautiful accented voice behind us. We turned and saw Isabel Ferragamo standing there. I had prepared myself for this encounter, but had truthfully hoped she wouldn't be in attendance.

After speaking with Connor a bit about business dealings, she turned and looked me up and down.

"You make?" she asked, spinning her finger to suggest I turn around so that she could see the back.

I obliged, and then nodded.

She slowly nodded her head up and down, expressionless. Before I had a chance to overthink it, she was being called over to another group.

I watched her walk away and as I went to turn back to Connor, another familiar face caught my eye. Lea Campbell and I locked eyes. My heart rate picked up as I carefully scanned the crowd around Lea searching for Elaine Summer. No sign of her. My eyes went back to where Lea was standing and she was gone.

"Wow Selena, I've never felt like a bigger idiot," said a voice as she appeared at my side.

"Hi Lea," said Connor.

"You look amazing," she said to me after kissing Connor's cheek hello.

I just smiled, not sure of what to say. Although I knew it was a possibility, I had really hoped that I wouldn't have to see Lea again this summer. Or ever, for that matter.

She leaned in to me and lowered her voice.

"Listen Selena, I'm so sorry for how everything went down," she reached for my free hand and squeezed it. "Really, I'm so sorry."

She was no doubt referring to Elaine's atrocious article.

I couldn't bring myself to speak. Or to smile or gesture or to do anything to make her feel comfortable with what she said. I wanted to leave her hanging here suffering through the discomfort of the conversation.

"I tried to-" she started before Connor had decided that was enough.

"Well Lea, have a great night," he said and then hooked his arm around the back of me and guided me away.

As we turned I now heard my name coming from a familiar voice. I looked up at Connor, confused.

"Selena!"

I scanned the crowd and saw no one familiar, despite the incessant calls.

We turned towards the entrance and saw Sylvie and Simon walking up the crushed shell path. Sylvie was waving in my direction like a lunatic.

"What is going on?" I looked up at Connor, confused.

"I thought you would like some company," he said, smiling at me and letting go of my waist so that I was free to greet Sylvie.

And greet her I did. I flung my arms around her like she had just come off a wartime plane, fresh off the battlefield and out of danger.

"Thank God," I whispered into her ear. Simon shook Connor's hand.

"Holy shit. That dress is everything Selena," she said, standing back, eying me up and down. "Well, what are we waiting for? Are we going to party or what?" Sylvie asked us, as if she was the biggest party animal to ever hit the island.

Chapter Seventy-Four

SYLVIE

Connor had alluded to the fact that this was going to be 'Selena's night,' so I knew better than to bring my bullshit baggage to this soiree but to say that the secret I was keeping from her was killing me was an understatement. Her genuine surprise and relief when she saw me made the travel day completely worth it. Despite looking completely beautiful, she looked nervous, scared even.

"We just finished speaking with Lea Campbell," she said, giving me a pained look after we broke apart from a hug.

"Oh no, how'd that go?" I asked as a nervous knot sunk to the base of my stomach and seemingly like it pulled all of my insides down with it.

"Fine," she said dismissively. "Forget them. I'm so glad you're here Sylvie! What are you doing here?"

"Connor was kind enough to invite us. Give us a first hand look at how the fashion world receives this beautiful number," I said, twirling her around. We had only been here a few minutes and already I had seen wide eyes and whispers targeted at Selena's dress.

"Isabel Ferragamo is here too," she said.

I was sure that Isabel, as well as lots of other famous designers would be here tonight, but I wasn't sure why that one was so important to Selena.

"I'm sure she is," I said, waiting to see if Selena was going to explain.

"I wouldn't worry about it Selena, she knows that you don't plan to make a decision until Monday," started Connor. "Just enjoy the night and don't think about it."

I was confused.

"What am I missing?"

I watched Selena's eyes go from Connor to me and then he dropped his head as if to apologize.

"It's really not a big deal. She offered me a job," Selena rattled off quickly. Like saying it faster might make me miss it...

"What?"

How is this the first I've heard of it? Selena tells me everything! In fact, Selena usually tells me too much! Sometimes I roll my eyes at how much she overshares. Have I been so self involved that I missed a major moment in my twin sister's life?

"I know, I should have told you," she said. "But I just wanted to make a decision before I shared it and got influenced by what other people think I should do. Does that make sense?"

I nodded my head and smiled. I was proud of her.

"That makes total sense. I like this new Selena. But I would have kept my thoughts to myself if you had simply asked!"

"Well, I don't really want to talk about it tonight, let's go have fun," she said, pulling me towards what looked like a margarita station.

Chapter Seventy-Five

SELENA

We hadn't had more than two sips of our fancy hibiscus margaritas when I realized I had lost Connor. I scanned the crowd and saw him speaking with an older, shorter, and very well-dressed man. My Nonni would have wanted to speak to him about the perfect cut of his pants. They both were looking at me as they spoke. I smiled and turned away, slightly embarrassed.

"Selena, I would like to introduce you to someone," Connor said as he was suddenly standing directly in front of me. "This is John Paul Falducci."

I couldn't hide my surprise.

"*The* John Paul Falducci?" I asked before I had a chance to think better of it. "I was so inspired by last Spring's collection," I recovered, earnestly.

He took my hand and kissed the top of it.

"The pleasure is all mine. Connor told me that you are the genius behind that beautiful dress," he said admiringly. His eyes went up and down and side to side. "The fringe is perfection. Connor, please give this beautiful woman my number. Don't worry, she's not my type," he laughed.

"I know John Paul. How is Henrique?"

"Home with our dog, he's not much for these events anymore," he chuckled.

Our evening continued a lot like that. We shared miniature moments of fun and laughter with Sylvie and Simon only to be interrupted by or introduced to everyone from stylists, designers, shop owners and even a few models. It was overwhelmingly satisfying.

The best part was that everyone was here for it. Sylvie, Simon and Connor all enjoyed playing the background role for introductions and shared laughs, but for the most part, they let me have shiny moments.

Connor was now holding nearly ten business cards for me in his pocket and I had saved multiple new contacts in my phone. I was exhausted and ready to call it a night when I came face to face with Isabel.

She stopped in front of me, lifting her left eye brow.

"Well, well, well. Looks like I'm not the only one that can see your talent Selena."

I smiled and nodded, unsure of what to say.

"Should we meet on Monday, or do you think you have an answer to share with me tonight?"

I think she enjoyed watching me squirm. Connor stood about ten feet away with Sylvie and Simon where they all pretended to be in the throes of deep conversation, each of them taking turns to casually glance in our direction.

The band had picked up and most of the remaining guests were dancing. Golden Hour had set down on the coast and the ocean and sky mixed together in the most beautiful painting come-to-life. For a second I was mesmerized by my surroundings.

"Selena?" Isabel asked briskly, jolting me back to reality.

"See the thing is. I didn't go to design school, and I am not a trained student of design. It is something inherent to me. Something gifted to me by my Nonni. It has always been my passion, but I think my enjoyment comes purely from the lack of limits," I rambled, thanks to the liquid courage. "I don't know if that makes any sense. But I don't know that I would still love it, or still be good at it if I was doing it to support someone else's vision."

She was looking at me so intensely, nodding with my words, kindness in her eyes.

"I don't think I would want my designs to have anyone's label on them, except for mine," I finally had gotten to the point.

Isabel stood there, dressed in a colorful, flowy dress that was now moving with the evening breeze. Her hair was down but carefully styled and her hands were covered in high-fashion jewels. Her expression was unreadable. Despite the blaring music, the silence was deafening.

"*Brava ragazza.*"

I was so confused. Why was she calling me a good girl?

"You don't design for anyone but yourself and that is not because you didn't go to fashion school, Selena. It is because you are an artist," she said, gently and quietly.

A warm trickle of pride and untapped emotion coursed down my body, sending warm tears to the corners of my eyes.

"My mentor saw this in me, twenty four years ago. She invested in me and helped me get started. I'd like to do that for you Selena."

"Wait, so not designing for your label? You would help me design my own?"

"We can talk details on Monday, come to my office at noon. We will chat and then have lunch. Throw away all of those cards in Connor's pocket, and bring him with you on Monday. I am happy to share my attorney with you," she said and winked as she walked away. Like a fashionable fairy godmother.

I think I finally blinked and felt the hot tears stream down my cheeks. I stood there for a moment by myself, my back now to Connor and Sylvie. When I turned they were nearly running in my direction with a look of fear in their eyes.

I put my hands up.

"They are happy tears. I am okay. I am great!"

Chapter Seventy-Six

SYLVIE

On Thursday I met the photographer at the restaurant before anyone else got there and for the first time I realized I had completely pulled it off. I had nailed the assignment. The restaurant was stunning. It was art. Nonni would have loved to sit by a window and drink a glass of red wine.

I mean, it would be crazy to take all the credit, but I was so proud and excited to get the digital files from the photographer. She was gone by the time Simon and his family arrived. They were meeting me at ten for the unveiling of the private dining room which until early this morning had been strategically hidden with painting paper so that I could show them all at the same time.

I had stopped at our favorite Italian bakery in Holly before I got on the train and had arranged the table with pastries, bottles of distilled Italian water and a carafe of coffee. I made Simon, his father, Dom and Katie, his mother and a gaggle of extended family members that I literally just met for the first time as they shuffled down the hall, cover their eyes as we rounded the corner.

"Okay, before you look I just want to say what a privilege it has been to work for all of you and I hope that this room will express to you just how special of a family I believe you to be," I said, surprising myself with the emotion in my voice. "On the count of three, ONE, TWO, THREE!"

I watched as their hands moved away from their eyes and they looked into the glass encased room. I had propped the glass door open so that they could step inside but no one seemed to be moving.

I turned to look, trying to experience it with them.

I had taken all of the photos down from the Mr. Carlino's office walls and worked with family members to gather additional images and one by one scanned digital copies without him ever knowing. I worked with a custom company to turn the photo collage I had created into life-size black and white wallpaper that covered the three sheetrocked walls. The glass teardrop chandelier hung down over the beautiful table that they had already selected, which was now surrounded by fourteen very different but equally beautiful and special chairs. The back wall had a custom buffet created from aged wine barrels with a glass shelf which held a guest book so that patrons could share the memory created by their experience here. The far right wall held the only pop of color in the room where a deep red, wooden sign carved in cursive sat over the wallpaper that said '*Famiglia.*'

It gave me the chills.

I turned back towards them as I sensed some movement between them. When I turned I saw Simon and his father pulling away from each other's embrace, his father now wiping his eyes. Dom held onto his mom with one arm and was holding his wife's hand with the other. The silence made the sniffling contagious. And before I had a chance to say anything, Simon's father, Robert Carlino himself, threw his arms around me while thanking me profusely.

"*Bellissimo!*" he finally spoke quietly.

When his father had let go, Simon was waiting for his turn.

"I can never repay you for this moment," he whispered into my ear. The tears were now falling down my cheeks.

"I love you," I whispered.

"You, Sylvie Rossi, were worth the wait!" yelled his brother, Dom. "Now everyone get in here! *Mangiare!*"

Chapter Seventy-Seven

SELENA

I stepped out of the elevator onto the twenty sixth floor and immediately stepped into the inner workings of Isabel's company. She had some sort of company crisis on Monday and our meeting got pushed out to Thursday. I spent the entire week pacing, unsure of what she would present and so confused on what my future looked like.

From where I stood I could see everything from print design software on a row of computers, fabric printers, pattern cutting tables, forms covered in beautiful drapings, rows of sewing machines of all kinds, ironing tables, and even a corner set up with illuminated vanities. This is where Isabel and her team made their magic.

To my far right there was a conference room and then a row of very simple offices.

"Can I help you?" asked a young woman with a measuring tape draped around her neck and a pin cushion attached to her wrist. Clearly there was no receptionist or waiting area. I was a privileged guest of Isabel Ferragamo, and I knew it.

"Yes, my name is Selena Rossi, I'm here-"

"Come on in Selena," yelled Isabel from an office down the hall. The designer that greeted me motioned for me to follow her voice down the hall.

I peeked into the empty conference room that had drawings and photos plastered all over the walls and then two empty offices until I found Isabel and another woman sitting in an office cluttered with fabric swatches, magazine clippings and paperwork.

"Take a seat Selena, Deanna was just leaving," she smiled and motioned for the woman in the chair to leave.

I smiled and nodded my head as we shimmied past each other.

She looked me up and down. Deciding what to wear today had been agonizing. I had settled on a pair of trousers that I had created out of muted green military-style material that had black piping running down the side of both legs. I had been pushing myself to get a better handle on pants construction. On top I kept it simple with a black body suit and a casual black blazer that I elevated by adding a stripe of the green pant materials as well as a stripe of the hot pink dress material from over the weekend to the chest pocket. I could tell she approved.

"Is Connor coming?"

"No, I want to do this on my own. He will review anything before I sign it, but I wanted to be able to talk it through with you, just the two of us first. I am still trying to understand all of it to be honest."

"Sorry for the delay, I had to leave town unexpectedly to help Antonio Gladwell with his London show."

She said it so casually, as if she hopped the D train to help with a friend's sweet sixteen party. Like she wasn't just needed for one of the most up and coming international designers. I closed my mouth for fear my face was saying too much.

"Well it's all quite simple Selena," she said as she handed me a document that had to be about fifteen pages long. "You will have access to this space, you can work here and use my equipment whenever you want. My staff obviously has priority and you are not to use my fabrics. But you can use the software, and even some of my tailors to help with some of the more mundane jobs. If you prefer the privacy and secrecy of working out of your own space, you can come and go as you please. I am willing to build out an oversized office for you here that you can use as a private workspace."

"Why? What is in it for you?"

"Thirty percent," she said matter of factly. "I would like to invest one million dollars into your business, you can use it to hire a team, rent your own space, hire publicists, market to stylists, however you see fit. But I am here to help you and hopefully save you from some of the mistakes that I made as well as the mistakes of others."

Her eyes were kind, genuine, but very serious.

A million dollars? She honestly thinks that I am worth risking a million dollars on? Was she crazy? I expected her to give me five grand!

"I guess I'm still wondering why? That seems like an awfully big leap of faith you'd be taking on me."

"Aren't those the only risks worth taking Selena?" the way her accent rolled the elle in my name, I felt so elevated just being in her company. What would this feel like, if it was all the time?

"I could help you get into fashion week, introduce you to reporters and stylists. I think we could both win from this Selena."

She hadn't necessarily answered my question. But I was content. I looked out the window. She had a marvelous view of the city. Did I want this view? Did I want to be down here? Could I do this? I thought about my life. The last six months had birthed more ups and downs than a game of Chutes and Ladders.

"There's something you should know before we get further into the discussion," I said, nervously. I had spent most of the train ride deciding if and how I would share this with Isabel. "I have a very high powered enemy that could destroy all of this before I even start. I am telling you this because I wouldn't want to hurt your reputation by being associated-"

Was she laughing?

"I must know who this enemy is, Selena. I cannot imagine anyone has a problem with you," she was so clearly stifling a laugh.

"Elaine Summer."

She smiled and turned to look out the window.

"Ah, yes, the formidable Ms. Summer who thought you should be more focused on giving her kids A pluses in your art class," she said sheepishly, monitoring me for a reaction.

"Wait, how did you know that?"

"That bloody halfwit, Lea Campbell had her assistant reach out to me a couple of months back asking for a last minute dress for a movie premiere. She told my assistant the whole story."

"Oh, so that was your dress?"

"Absolutely not. I will never fulfill a second choice request Selena. And when I'm done with you, neither will you."

"But-"

"If it comes down to it, my PR team will eat her for lunch. Forget her, Selena. This is a non-issue. What else are you afraid of?"

"What if I can't come up with any designs? Collections?"

"Do you feel creatively stunted? Do you feel that way now?"

"No."

"Okay then, you have no reason to worry. Your business will likely start from creating one-off pieces per stylist's requests. Women will be begging to get onto your calendar, this I can basically promise you. In your downtime you will dabble in complimentary pieces, and before you know it you'll be showing me your collection. Your point of view is so evident to me, Selena. It is strong, and beautiful. Like you," she said, confidently but with the gentleness of a friend.

I had no questions. I really just wanted to be alone. To think about all of it.

"Review it with Connor, his colleague drew up the offer so he hasn't seen it yet, think about it, but not too long Selena. It expires tomorrow at noon."

My mouth dropped.

"What? Well I'm not Santa Claus, Selena."

And we both shared a laugh.

Chapter Seventy-Eight

SYLVIE

According to Simon the kitchen and wait staff had pulled together an amazing luncheon for over thirty credentialed reporters. Many brought photographers and took pamphlets that I had created for the event with my design company's information. In other words, my cell phone number and my newly created email account. It looked professional and marketable and I just prayed that no one went searching for a website or previous work as they would find nothing.

The new semester started in two weeks and I was registered for two night classes and was suddenly feeling so close to a diploma. I had declared my major and was now focused on design, and entrepreneurship classes. Last week I signed up for a four night website design class on YouTube and was in the beginning stages of creating a business website. The ball was rolling, but I still wasn't sure where or how I wanted it to bounce.

But tonight was not about me. I mean, technically it was a little bit about me, but this was really about the Carlinos. I couldn't wait to see how their family, friends and business contacts reacted to their beautiful new space and menu. Tonight's Grand Opening party had over a hundred and fifty confirmed guests who would be testing the restaurant's staff, food and capacity. It was going to be a Who's Who and I was honored that he thought to invite my entire family. My parents even reserved a room at a boutique hotel around the corner.

Kendra had assured Simon after the luncheon that she would be back for the party as she had invited a few key social media influencers to attend. I tried so hard not to think about the possibility of her arriving with Elaine.

My phone was ringing. I pulled it out and saw Selena's picture on my screen.

People always talk about twins having mental telepathy and other superhuman powers, but Selena and I have both admitted that we sadly did not share them. Maybe it was because we weren't identical? But in this moment I feared that she knew. She somehow found out that Simon and I were in cahoots with Elaine Summer.

"Hey."

"Sylv, I know this is such a crazy day for you and I hate to ask a favor but I think that this would benefit you and Simon as well," she started. Oh my God, she definitely knows.

"Do you have a second?" she asked.

I took a seat, shaking a bit. I looked at the clock, it was nearly three thirty, I had plenty of time to have a complete nervous breakdown and pull myself together before the party started at seven.

"Yes, want to come over?" I asked, shakily.

There was a knock at the door the second I put my phone down.

I opened the door to the biggest smile I had maybe ever seen on Selena. She was dressed in a beautiful yellow shift dress with her hair draped across her left shoulder.

"What in the world?"

"I did something crazy today Sylvie."

Ok, so clearly this had nothing to do with me or Elaine Summer. Crisis averted, for now.

"Tell me more," I said, pulling out two champagne flutes from my cabinet.

"I just left a meeting with Isabel," she started. I squeezed her hand knowing that she was promised big things by her at the end of the party on Saturday night. "Well, we met yesterday and she gave me exactly seventeen hours to look over her offer and make a decision."

"A decision about what? What was her offer?" I was so excited for her I could feel my heart rate pick up.

"Ok, this stays between us. But she offered me a million dollars to start up my own brand, with her owning a thirty percent stake in the company. And she said I could use her workshop and have access to her factory contacts and stuff if I got to that level."

"Wait, a million dollars?"

"Thank God for Connor and Shark Tank," she laughed. "Connor went back with me today and we negotiated to get her to twenty five percent. She accepted Sylvie! We made the deal! I am going to start my own brand!"

We were both on our feet jumping up and down, we found each other and pulled in for a hug while continuing to jump.

"I wish Nonni was here for this," I said, tears hiding in the corners of my eyes. "She would be so proud of you Selena! This is the best news I've ever heard!"

"What did mom say?"

I pretended there was a chance she already told her, but I knew damn well I would be the first person she would come to, as she would be mine.

"Her and dad made a day out of going into the city for Simon's party. They are going to stroll around Little Italy and have lunch. So, I haven't told her yet..."

I knew that but had completely forgotten.

"Sounds like we all have so much to celebrate tonight!"

"Speaking of tonight," said Selena.

Was she going to bail?

"Would it be okay if I invited Isabel to the party?"

"Umm, yes! Would she actually come?"

"Oh yes, she's meeting me there at seven thirty!"

We both laughed.

"I'll let Simon know, he will be psyched."

That was a minor fib, I would have to let Kendra know as she held the guest list. Good Lord I was really playing with fire.

Chapter Seventy-Nine

SELENA

Connor had stayed in the city after our meeting with Isabel. He offered to take me to a celebratory lunch but I could tell he was so busy at work that we agreed to celebrate over the weekend.

I offered to ride in with my parents but they shocked all of us when they went in early, and even more so when they booked themselves a hotel to make a night out of it. I think my mom had been so nervous to be far from Nonni for the last few years, she had forgotten what it was like to get away, or to be spontaneous and adventurous! I was so happy for both of them.

I also suggested that I go in with Sylvie, but she wanted to go in early to help Simon and his family prep for the big night. So here I was, sitting on the train alone looking all hot and fancy.

I spent most of the ride daydreaming about how I would even begin to use the money that Isabel was investing in me. Connor suggested I start by opening a business account on Monday and spend some time in Isabel's studios next week for inspiration and for a birds eye view of business. Her publicist was working on a statement to announce our partnership, but she suggested that I get a bit more established before they release it.

Six months ago the idea of owning my own business would have sent me into a tailspin for fear of shoddy health insurance that would not support my overall well being. But today, and for the last several months actually, I feel healthy. I feel strong and kinda powerful. Connor assured me that there were some good options for small businesses, but that I would have to be a bit more mindful of all of my out of pocket appointments. And for once, I agreed. I have only used hand sanitizer once this entire train ride, and I had waited an extra two weeks to get my flu shot because I had simply forgotten about it. Was this growing up? Changing? I wasn't sure. But I could tell that my focus had shifted.

I wanted to get to the party before Isabel, so I was pleased when the Uber from the train station said it was only a nine minute drive to Carlino's. We pulled up at 7:05 and I smiled the second I saw Connor waiting for me on the sidewalk.

"I didn't want to see it without you," he smiled after he kissed my cheek.

I looked up and down the street, getting a feel for our location and back up at the beautiful windows that lined the first floor of the brick eatery. The simple fluorescent sign was a throwback in all the best ways. By the number of people that passed us and walked in the door, I could tell that this party was going to be a hit.

When we stepped inside, my jaw dropped and my eyes couldn't decide what to look at first. The ivy that crawled down the walls or the beautiful light fixtures that elegantly hung over the bar. The tables and chairs were exactly as they should be. Simple and classy. The rooms were filled with people mingling and laughing over drinks and small plates of cheeses and olives.

"Selena!" yelled a familiar voice.

I looked over and saw my mom and dad. My mother looked beautiful. She wore a black knee length dress that had a metallic cutout on the bottom right hem. My dad kept it simple in khakis and a white button up shirt. They looked adorable.

"You look beautiful Mrs. Rossi," said Connor as he shook my dad's hand.

"A Selena Rossi original," she smiled.

We followed them to a table in a quieter corner of the restaurant and the corner nearly shook as I shared my news with the two of them. My mother couldn't hold back her tears.

"Nonni would love this so much," she said. "This is amazing!"

"You told them?"

Sylvie had snuck around the table. I jumped up to my feet.

"Sylvie, this restaurant is beautiful! Can you give us the tour?"

We spent about twenty minutes both touring the restaurant, and meeting the staff as well as Simon's family. They were everything she had described. I remembered seeing them at the party earlier this summer in the Hamptons and knew that they would just love Sylvie the way we do. It all made me so happy to see.

Mom made it clear that there was no beef between her and Mr. Carlino. I could see the relief on both Simon and Sylvie's faces.

When we got to the front of the restaurant my eyes immediately went to the back of an impeccably dressed woman. She was wearing a very fitted pair of black trousers with a pair of stiletto heels and a perfectly fitted silk top. And she was speaking with-

Holy shit.

Elaine Summer.

I turned to look for Sylvie and Connor and truly anyone that might be able to protect me at this moment. Sylvie turned to look at me, seeing exactly what I saw. Connor was nowhere in sight.

"Selena, I can explain," she said, taking my arm to lead me away. She was shocked when I didn't move. My feet firmly planted.

I pulled my arm out of Sylvie's grip and without giving it a single thought I began walking in the direction of Elaine. She didn't see me coming, she was in a very intense conversation with the beautifully dressed woman.

I didn't care, I was going to interrupt anyone this insolent fool was speaking to.

I didn't even turn to see who it was but took a step into Elaine's personal space so that she was forced to stop her conversation and see me.

We stared, eye to eye.

"I curse the day you were born."

It came out before I had a second to consider. Maybe an alien of some kind had taken over my body and just pushed my thoughts directly out of my mouth.

Elaine looked at me, stunned.

"Selena?" said a gentle, accented voice to my left. I turned and saw that the beautifully dressed woman was the person who had just agreed to invest one million dollars of her money in me. Me. The same person that just told a very powerful woman that I cursed the day she was born. As if I had replaced Kim Cattrall in *Sex and the City* 4.

I gave her a very forced and pained smile.

"Selena, I was just talking to Ms. Summers. I was just telling her how damaging an article such as the one she wrote could be for someone who was trying so hard to follow the rules as a private school teacher."

I turned to look at Elaine. Her expression was unreadable.

"I told her how far from personal your grading system was and that you were in fact unaware that Elaine was your student's mother. And I applaud you for treating each student the same."

She was talking so calmly, so slowly. She had both of our complete attention despite the chaos going on around us.

"Additionally, I let her know that we were in fact going into business together, and my colleagues and I really enjoy dressing so many of Elaine's clients, and it would be a shame if her treatment of you continued."

"I agree to leave the past in the past," said Elaine. "The school had several meetings and votes and in addition to firing you, decided to go back and amend Cullen's grade. So I consider all forgiven, despite the pain your grading put my family through," she said, her hand on her chest as if warning that it nearly caused her a heart attack.

You've got to be kidding me.

My tongue throbbed as I bit it. I refused to acknowledge her comment and kept my entire attention focused on Isabel.

"I think there is room for all of us to be successful in this city. Wouldn't you agree, Elaine?" asked Isabel.

"Yes, I certainly do," she answered, her voice now softened.

"Superb."

"Thank you," I said quietly, to Isabel as Elaine turned and walked right out the front door. I resisted reaching out for a hug, I could tell that Isabel was not the type. "Do you really think she will?"

"Oh darling, unless Elaine wants me to tell every designer in this city that her clients are not worthy of our clothes, she is gonna be your number one fan. This, I promise you," she said, with a devious smile forming on her face. "Now go, enjoy this party. This restaurant is brilliant, thank you for inviting me. We will talk on Monday."

She gave me a quick kiss on both cheeks and said goodbye to a few people before I saw her leave. I was so happy I could scream.

I turned to head back to the table where my parents were sitting and immediately saw Sylvie standing across the way. Simon was next to her, his arm around her, consoling her. Was she crying?

I walked in their direction, worried.

"You have to believe us, we had no idea when we hired this firm," started Sylvie.

"Wait? What are you talking about?"

"Elaine Summer. I hired her agency without doing much research. We were multiple meetings deep with our account manager before Elaine showed up for a meeting. We were so nervous that she was going to smear our name if we fired her," Simon trailed on.

"I should have told you, I know I should have, but I just didn't want to hurt you Selena," said Sylvie.

I did the only thing I knew to do which was reach out and hug Sylvie, while giving Simon's shoulder a squeeze at the same time.

"Wait, you're not mad?" Sylvie asked, still wrapped in my arms.

"Nope, if she wasn't here I wouldn't have had the chance to say what I just did. And honestly, nothing could have felt better than that."

"Oh my God, Sleen, what did you say?"

"I told her I cursed-"

"The day she was born?" Sylvie shouted, cutting me off and finishing my sentence.

We laughed so hard I'm pretty sure we cried. Maybe we did share a twin telepathy!

Epilogue

~Twelve Months Later~

Our shared offices were small so it did not come as a surprise when Emily called to let me know that my two o'clock appointment had arrived. I left my office and stepped into the back room where I did all of my fittings. Her dress was on the form ready for her and I looked to make sure I had my measuring tape and pins for any additional alterations needed.

I could hear Emily offering them coffee or tea as they rounded the corner. I looked up and saw a face I was becoming more used to seeing outside of the movies.

"Hi Belinda," I greeted her with a kiss on each cheek.

"Oh, Selena, it looks beautiful," she said, looking the dress up and down.

"What time is the premiere tonight? I blocked off my afternoon in case it needs any last minute alterations."

I really needed to hire someone for this part of the job but that would require time and also a lot of trust. Isabel assured me that there are loads of capable hands in the city and in her company that would love to work with me. I just couldn't imagine letting anyone else touch my creations. According to Isabel, everytime I did an alteration, my brand, *Sorelle*, was actually losing money.

Luckily the dress fit her like a glove and I got my afternoon back. I was hoping to bump into Isabel at her studio down the street where I was housing and constructing all my looks for Fashion Week. I couldn't believe it was only three weeks away.

I walked Belinda to the door, helping her assistant and stylist carefully handle the garment bag I had sent her off with.

"I cannot wait to see pictures. Have the best night!" I said as I stepped out onto Hudson Street with them and straight into the bustle of a Friday afternoon in Midtown.

I looked back into our office from the street and got that giddy feeling that I still had every time I saw our beautiful awning and sign. Sylvie had worked so hard with her vendors to organically create a space and signage that reflected both of our businesses and was engaging to the hundreds of people that walked by it every single day.

We took a risk in renting a first floor store front, but knew we both needed to get our names out there. The way the shop was split into two with a floor to ceiling window flanking each side of the entry door was perfect, providing Sylvie and I each our own window to spotlight our companies. Although we both used the name Sorelle, we were two separate but very compatible entities.

I looked at the mannequin wearing the infamous pink party dress I had worn the night that Isabel knew she wanted to invest in me. I planned to change it seasonally, but nothing felt more like summer to me than that dress. Sylvie had helped me add to the window's space to create a real Hollywood moment.

Sylvie's side was equally alluring. She had taken the risk and pulled multiple small business loans and showed no signs of looking back. She was a genius for carving out her niche as a commercial designer. The budgets and freedom she worked with made the occasionally late deadline or passionate client seem like a walk in the park.

My thoughts were interrupted as my phone rang.

Conner.

"Hey, what's up?"

"I was thinking, do you want to stay in the city tonight? How early do we have to leave tomorrow?"

We had done a great job bouncing from the city to Holly, rarely sleeping apart. Even Queso had become a bit of a city boy and loved spending time in our office. Connor had taken back his apartment and given up his space in Holly knowing that he could stay with me anytime. Neither of us were totally ready to give up an address and so far, it was working just fine.

"Their graduation is at three. I think we are fine to stay in the city. Just need to get an early jump."

"Okay, I made reservations at a steakhouse close to the campus. I confirmed with Mr. Carlino and between their family and your parents there will be twelve of us."

"Thank you so much! God, do you know of anyone that graduates from college as successful as Sylvie and Simon?" I laughed.

We made a plan to meet after I finished at Isabel's studio and as I packed up for the weekend I couldn't help but stop and look around.

Sorelle Designs was a nod to my Nonni, but truly everything I did was with her in mind. The delight she would feel seeing the work that Sylvie and I were doing was a driving force in everything we did. I had to believe that she had a quiet, front seat to all of it. She would whisper to herself, *la bella vita*, and smile. I knew it.

Italian Glossary

Figarido - daughter
Nipotina - granddaughter
bambina mia - my child
Caro - dear
Figlia - daughter
Molto Bene - very good
Ti Amo Tantissimo - I love you so much
Parli Italiano - do you speak Italian?
Un po - A little
Angioletto - Little angel
Ben fatto - well done
Brava ragazza - Good girl
Sorelle - Sisters
Mangiare - eat
Bellissimo - beautiful
La bella vita - The good life

Note from the Author

Just a quick note to thank my amazing preview crew of readers - Karen and Brenda, your insights were beyond helpful and I'm so grateful for you! Deanna, thank you for elevating this story, I promise to never make fun of your grammar policing again! *Grazie*! I'm a self published author, so despite the many, many reads - there will be mistakes! Forgive me.

Thank you as always to my family, friends, and YOU for taking the time to read this!

If you enjoyed this, please check out my debut novel, *At First*.

About the Author

Nikki Roadman grew up in Upstate New York but has spent the last twenty-five years in the Greater Boston area. She now resides in a small town in Central Massachusetts where she lives with her husband, three teenage children and three poorly behaved dogs. Nikki has spent a lifetime turning her anxiety into humor and hopes that readers can see that sprinkled throughout her writing.

- facebook.com/authornikkiroadman
- instagram.com/authornikkiroadman
- amazon.com/stores/Nikki-Roadman/author/B0CZDZXWSM

Also by Nikki Roadman

At First

Made in the USA
Middletown, DE
16 December 2024